DEATH
IN A LONELY
PLACE

Stig Abell believes that discovering a crime fiction series to enjoy is one of the great pleasures in life. His first novel, *Death Under a Little Sky*, introduced Jake Jackson and his attempt to get away from his former life, in the beautiful area around Little Sky. This book is the second in the series, and Stig is absolutely delighted that there are more on the way.

Away from books, he co-presents the breakfast show on Times Radio, a station he helped to launch in 2020. Before that he was a regular presenter on Radio 4's *Front Row* and was the editor and publisher of the *Times Literary Supplement*. He lives in London with his wife, three children and two independent-minded cats called Boo and Ninja (his children named them, obviously).

𝕏 @StigAbell
📷 @TheStigAbell

Also by Stig Abell

Death Under a Little Sky

DEATH
IN A LONELY
PLACE

STIG ABELL

HEMLOCK
PRESS

Hemlock Press
an imprint of HarperCollins*Publishers* Ltd
1 London Bridge Street,
London SE1 9GF

www.harpercollins.co.uk

HarperCollins*Publishers*
Macken House,
39/40 Mayor Street Upper,
Dublin 1
D01 C9W8
Ireland

First published by HarperCollins*Publishers* Ltd 2024
1

A catalogue record for this book is available from the British Library

ISBN: 978-0-00-851706-9 (HB)
ISBN: 978-0-00-851707-6 (TPB)

Typeset in Sabon LT Std by Palimpsest Book Production Ltd,
Falkirk, Stirlingshire

Printed and bound in the UK using 100% renewable electricity
at CPI Group (UK) Ltd

For Nadine, who is always cold and yet extremely hot at the same time

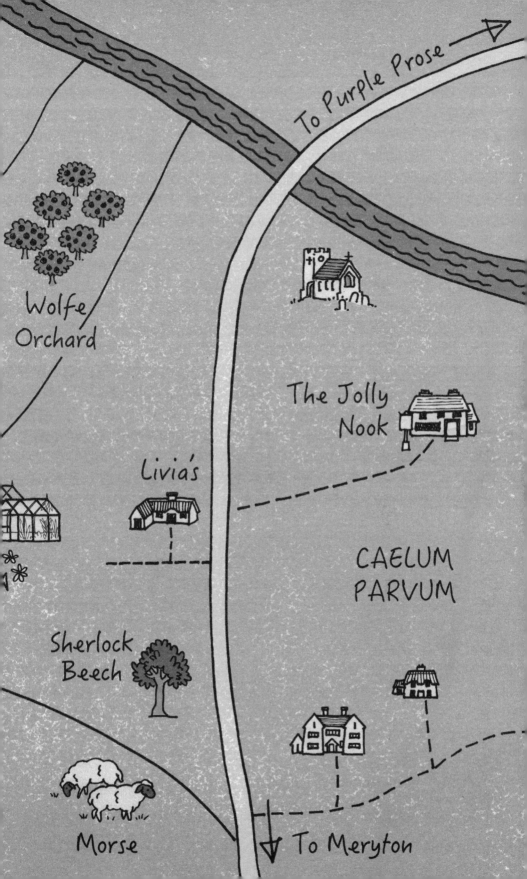

There's a certain Slant of light,
Winter Afternoons—
That oppresses, like the Heft
Of Cathedral Tunes—

Heavenly Hurt, it gives us—
We can find no scar,
But internal difference,
Where the Meanings, are—

None may teach it—Any—
'Tis the seal Despair—
An imperial affliction
Sent us of the Air—

When it comes, the Landscape listens—
Shadows—hold their breath—
When it goes, 'tis like the Distance
On the look of Death—

Emily Dickinson

PROLOGUE

You can see it, if you like, as a thick sheaf of papers, a breeze flicking curiously through them, each page another account of a crime committed, a life ruined, someone's thoughtless desires satisfied without challenge or recourse to justice. Or maybe – this being the twenty-first century after all – it's just a screen endlessly scrolling, a narrative without apparent end, information heaped upon information, case running seamlessly into its own sequel.

And, if you are a quick enough reader, you'll learn of all sorts of examples of human misery connecting back to one group of people, too shapeless to appear visible as an organization, too consistent in their application of power to be dismissed as the product of coincidence.

Their range of activities, their productivity, is as much of a defence against scrutiny as a sign of their continued success. All of these examples of crime, of hurt and grief, are so numerous as to make them hard to link together, to join up into a picture. Until now they have never been connected.

1

To the family missing their youngest child, snatched from their negligent care, there is no glimpse of a pattern, no chance to see how their own devastation had its origins somewhere else. It is part of a figure so intricate that it cannot be perceived in close-up, particularly by those blinded by despair.

We're talking of the husband and wife, who wake up that morning with normal grumbles and gripes about life, but confident – without even thinking about it – that their world would be intact by evening's close. Then their son disappears, and their world is ended. If you were to catch their eye, weeks and months after the snatch, when hope had burned down to nothing more than an ember, you would always be able to see something – an emptiness, an absence – that they could never conceal. Part of them, maybe a light, maybe their soul (if you believe in that sort of thing), gone forever.

You don't want to imagine the feelings, or the fate, of their son himself. No sane or humane person would. Someone too young to understand the adult world in normal circumstances, now grabbed from outside their home, hustled into a van, drugged and baffled, and then who knows what follows? You don't want to read what happens next, the thought is too awful, you think immediately of those closest to you, already replacing the true victim with an imaginary version from your own family. His plight now a bit diminished, the inherent selfishness of empathy. You turn the page to another story, hopeful its horror will be less.

And maybe it will be. Children always make tales of cruelty worse. Take instead the two business rivals, scrapping over some mining territory in China. It is not edifying, it is morally wrong, it is catastrophic in its own way. But you can read on at least. One man decides – the actors in these appalling dramas are often, but not always, men – that he cannot defeat his opponent through conventional means. So he pays for someone to arrange his ruin: drugs planted, allegations of inappropriate behaviour, hitherto exemplary accounts discovered to be tainted by fraud. The framing is brilliantly done, drum-tight, no possible means of wriggling free. His family deserts him, his losses mount incalculable, and he ends it all with an antique shotgun blast through the mouth one day in the office that is about to be taken from him.

The page might turn again. Two cyclists lying crumpled at the side of the road, limbs cast at impossible angles, blood smeared on the tarmac. Or again. A woman sobbing outside a beautiful city house, the exterior white as marble. Light rain falling, running into her tears. A business card drops from her grasp and is washed down into the gutter. If you're quick you can see the elegantly crafted writing on it, though the words won't mean anything to you. Yet.

Chapter One

Thursday, 9.54 a.m.

A cold wind scurries beneath the half-door as Jake stands in his outdoor shower staring at the familiar, now wintry landscape. A record is playing loud: maundering sounds escaping from his kitchen along with the steamy warmth of his house. There is ice on the cobbled courtyard in front of him, hard as iron, treacherous to negotiate in bare feet. The winter here grips you painfully tight, he thinks, it imprisons you, it makes you think of airy summer days like they are a story from someone else's memory.

Melancholy thoughts, and Jake snorts them from his nose along with the running water, rubbing his cheeks hard, and washing the soapy suds from his long hair and thick beard. Everyone feels gloomy in the winter. The days short and sullen, the sporadic splutters of icy rain, the nights starting early and then lingering, reluctant to concede the space to the morning. And what has he really to feel low about after all? His muscles tingle from his daily exercise, his head feels clear, his very own land stretches out before him into the pallid and sightless horizon.

It's no fun, though, switching off the shower and tiptoeing into the house on a day like this, an old towel wrapped around his hard middle, the frigid air clinging to the rest of him. There is quite a lot to cling to: he is tall, too tall he often feels, almost six and a half feet, and in the last two years his body has become broad and lean, with sinewy hillocks of muscle.

He cowers naked in front of the fire in the back living room for a moment, spinning slowly as if he were roasting, before he shrugs on his thick hooded top and pyjama bottoms. He remembers seeing Livia in front of this same fire for the first time, almost eighteen months ago, her rain-soaked clothes steaming, his own thoughts restless with curiosity and desire. At that point, she had been someone beautiful and inaccessible, a surprise that had brightened his existence from their first accidental meeting in a sheep field (he a city slicker clomping about uncertainly; she a local vet, who seemed as much part of the countryside as the meadow flowers beneath their feet). Livia still looks good in his clothes, he thinks, an old shirt hurried onto her body after a night-time shower, or lazily ahead of a morning's pottering in the vegetable garden.

The record finishes. It is Ravel's *Pavane for a Dead Princess*, slow piano echoing in the bleak. Jake goes to stop the hiss, and pours himself a coffee, carefully stirring in thick, dark sugar. He sips and feels warm inside for the first time. On the table in front of him is a postcard from a policeman, announcing that he will be visiting today at 11 a.m. Jake has no phone, no internet, and is miles from any postal route, so is a hard man to make an appointment with. He still loves that in the main. He now gets any relevant mail routed to the local shop – called, in a twee attempt to appease tourists, the Jolly Nook – in the nearby village of Caelum Parvum, and tries to remember to collect it once a week. The policeman, Chief Inspector Watson, knows Jake and his strange way of life, but also knows that Jake will always make time for him. They became close during a murder investigation, following the death of a local woman, and have stayed in complacent touch ever since. That particular period is still fraught in Jake's memory: the investigation had spiralled, an innocent old man – another sudden friend of Jake's – died, and together he and Watson had discovered a pattern of violent sexual assaults in the area dating back decades.

Jake has a few moments before Watson's arrival and tidies in a desultory fashion. Clothes drying above the stove go into three baskets, one each for him and his two regular house guests, Livia and her daughter Diana. He frowns for a second. The arrangement still feels temporary, and he wants it not to. But he and Livia can't quite agree on what permanence should look like, or whether a newly nucleated family like theirs can really prosper in such a place of awkward solitude.

Jake had been given his home as a legacy from a dying uncle, a gift to help him renounce the world and its entanglements. Little Sky – a glorious farmhouse, half from the eighteenth century, half newly designed, set in countless acres of land – had lured him from the city, as Uncle Arthur had intended, become a haven, a soft pastel expanse of peace, a world entire of tumbling fields and ancient hedges and deep loamy soil. The windy shudder of banked trees often the only sound to Jake's ears. The welcome of natural quiet. But it asked the insistent question still: was renunciation, complete rejection of all that is ugly and necessary and modern, ever fully possible? He reckons he doesn't seem to be making that good a job of it.

The sounds of stamping outside the door seem to answer the question once more. Jake can hear muttering, imagines the fussy removal of gloves, the inefficient search for pockets to put them in.

He opens the door ahead of any knock. 'Good morning, chief.'

A wizened face wreathed in smiles, nose reddened by that unforgiving wind, grey hair poking unruly from beneath a black woolly hat.

'Jake, my boy, delighted that you're in. I didn't much fancy an immediate tramp back across your fields.'

'I got your note right enough. And you know I tend not to have many other places to be.'

'I did know that. But strange things can happen around here. And who's to say that your lovely companion hadn't lured you away somewhere.' Watson was fond of Livia, whom he had known before Jake in her role as the local vet, a figure of warmth and positivity.

Watson walks past Jake into the kitchen, the heat embracing him instantly. He leaves his boots by the stove to dry, and in stockinged feet – a lurid red, Jake notes – pads across to one of the two nearby armchairs. Jake had soon realized, in a rural winter, that much of life can be conducted in the kitchen, near to food, and heat, and boiling water, so he has made the room – which is big and clean and welcoming – as comfortable as possible. He still spends most evenings in his thriller library, though, which has its own fire, and the palpable comfort of thousands of books as well.

Watson is long and thin as a poker and extends his legs so his feet are almost touching the stove door. He sighs exuberantly. 'Oh, but that's better. I thought my toes were going to fall off out there for a moment. It's not civilized, you know Jake, living somewhere that you can only visit by walking. It's like something from the Victorian period.'

Jake smiles and pours coffee. This is a version of a conversation the two had been having since the beginning of their friendship. He grabs another record from his kitchen stack, which totters awkwardly on a table in the corner and which he is always meaning to arrange more carefully. More piano, he thinks, and selects something by Liszt, his *Ave Maria*, then dips the volume so the sorrowful tinkling barely rises above and through the sputtering of the wood in the stove.

The two men, at ease, talk of this and that, the weather, the season, some of Watson's more routine work. The latter leads Watson where he wants to go, and he pauses, sits up and clears his throat with some unease.

'Jake, I know you're not one for talking proper shop, but I did want to see you for a reason.'

Jake had figured as much. He had been a detective himself in another life, a past that now only barely intruded into his present. A good one too, a cold case expert, a weaver of fresh narratives from old, broken threads. He had been rescued – as he sometimes saw it, when he bathed in the greenness of the lush land around him, or closed the door on an icy night for the comfort of a solitary fire – from a life of metropolitan crime. Arthur had made his new life possible, had given him not only the house but

9

the chance to narrow his horizons, embrace peace, avoid the murk and pain of lives shattered by violence.

Jake winces slightly, shifts in his chair. 'Knowing your lack of athleticism, shall we call it, I was fairly sure you hadn't come here for the exercise. What do you want to discuss?'

'It's a grim one, I'm afraid. A child snatch, something more or less inexplicable, happened maybe fifty miles from here.' The county Jake lived in was long and broad, filled for the most part with farms and tiny villages, and Watson's jurisdiction was almost unmanageably large. 'I've been working it these last few weeks and, you know at this point the trail is cold and the prospects bleak.'

'Parents?'

'Of course we've looked at them very carefully. But nothing suspicious. It was an IVF baby, a girl called Laura, the love of their life who arrived when they thought they couldn't have children. Now five, from all we can tell a happy and cared-for girl. I know that doesn't mean much, and we've both seen it mean nothing, but there's literally no evidence that they have done something here.'

The stove grumbles, and some wood dislodges itself. The record comes to an end, and Jake reaches forward and flips sides.

'What do you want from me? You can work this as well as I ever could, and I'm not a copper anymore, as we established last time.' A wry smile for them both, an acknowledgement of what had happened in the past, and how that inquiry into murder, suicide and spate of historic rapes had been solved mainly by Jake acting free from the restraints of official investigation.

'Oh, I know all that. But there's one piece of evidence.

10

It may be nothing, it may not even be evidence. But it's nagging at me, and I thought you might help me understand it. I even broke the rules a bit and brought it with me.' He reaches into his pocket and withdraws a transparent bag, which contains nothing more than a small, tattered business card in the corner. He hands it to Jake, who looks at it circumspectly. One side is blank, the other has two words in black and bold, printed with careful calligraphy: *NO TABOO*.

Chapter Two

Thursday, 11.22 a.m.

Jake's hands clench as the memory unearths itself. His voice is uncertain, clinging inside his throat. 'Where did you find that?'

'A few hundred yards from the snatch, half screwed up, like it had either been discarded or fallen from someone's pocket. There were no litter bins nearby, so no reason for it to be there. Nobody could explain it easily. So it became a piece of evidence. Is it ringing any bells for you?'

Jake has been taken back probably five years, to when he was already well-established as a cold case detective. He was living in the city with his then-wife Faye, and they had just had their second miscarriage. He hated that he measured the phases of his past relationship by each failed pregnancy. But he did. Each tragic event had formed a tightening, a choking, a steady and incremental strangling of their happiness. He couldn't think about his marriage without thinking of the pain. That was a miniature tragedy in itself.

Life at home was volatile back then. Sometimes he and Faye were pushed together in grief; sometimes it drove a thick, grim silence deep between them. Sometimes they could ignore it, as you would an ugly painting in the corner of the room, and they laughed and loved and told themselves that life was fine. At other times they knew that what they had wasn't working, and would never work.

All that meant Jake was spending more and more time in the office, his cases welcome distractions, however awful the events that preceded them. He had two on his books at the time: one was itself a child abduction, the other a murder of a homeless man, five years apart and by all accounts unconnected. On the second case, some stray DNA at the scene had led Jake to the murderer, a former soldier with a long record of violence, but he was too late to arrest him. By the time he had chased down the right identity and location, the man was dead, a suicide by hanging, the body cold and purpled by the time it was discovered.

The stolen child – a boy of eight, James, scruffy thatch of blond hair, smile wonky at the corner in all the photos he had seen – was never found. A cold case that stayed cold, as so many of them did. James joined the company of ghosts, the images of the unavenged victims, that clustered forever on the edge of Jake's consciousness, even now.

'The thing was, chief, I got a call one night, late at my desk. I was tying up the murder-suicide, still probing at the file of the missing kid. I remember it well: a panicked voice, shrill almost, and it blurted something, then hung up. An untraceable number, probably a burner phone.'

Watson leans forward, hands flat against his knees. 'And what was the blurt?'

'Find no taboo.'

'That's pretty hard to fathom.'

'I know. And I didn't fathom it in the end. In fact, I mostly thought it was a crank, except for the fact that it came to me on my personal phone, and that number would not have been easy to get. The internet was no real help, everybody I asked looked baffled. But I marked it in the files as an unanswered question.'

Watson nods. 'That's why your name came up when I looked into it. Was that as far as it got?'

Jake sips his coffee, his mind racing back into his past. 'I kept nagging at it, with little hope. There was a conspiracy theory we eventually dug up in the darkest depths of the dark web. It claimed that a collective of wealthy criminals somehow operated together, to provide illegal services to the elite. It was fairly wacky stuff, and sat alongside all the other usual rants about Jewish bankers, lizard people, royal paedophiles, microchips in vaccinations, and so on. Anyway, we discovered one chat where the phrase "they have no taboos" was there in italics. My Searcher, Aletheia Campbell, found it for me a year after the call, but there was nothing further to do with it.'

'And did your caller mention the cases you were working on?'

'Nope. It could have been to do with my soldier, it could have been James. It could have been neither. It could have been, it probably was, nothing.'

'And yet here's my card all these years later.'

'Which could have nothing to do with Laura at all.'

14

'True, true. But you and I don't like coincidences, or we wouldn't be good at our jobs. Plus, saying it's a co-incidence doesn't help me go further, so it isn't useful to me.'

Jake nods. That was true in detective novels and in real life. Coincidences do happen, but they are not helpful in building the story that is at the heart of making sense of the world: all criminal investigations are narratives that have to hang together; randomness is a terrible danger to them.

'I'm sorry I can't be of more help. I'm not sure there's much there really.'

Watson is silent. The record has finished. The stove is still for once. Outside, the wind whispers through the bare, ruined branches. A guttural croak of a solitary bird.

'Would you speak to your old colleagues again for me? I've gone through all the normal channels, and didn't get further than your file note.'

'I don't know, chief. I'm not one to get involved, and I've already had too much police business since my retire-ment.'

'You're still just about in your thirties, a gifted detective, so I won't allow the word "retirement". But I'm not asking much, just a call, a chat, a shot in the dark. I won't let this little girl down if I can help it.'

Jake's mind flashes at once to Diana, Livia's eight-year-old daughter, a bright and charming and innocent presence in his life. The thought of her in danger, of her being sullied by the vile rankness of adult desire, revolts him. He shakes his head ruefully.

'Of course, I'll help. But I don't have much hope. You better give me a couple of days, and then come back here then. If I get anything sooner, I'll call from the Nook. Can I make you lunch before you go?'

Watson gives a wintry grin. 'Now you know I never turn down free food if I can avoid it.'

Jake boils some potatoes he had been growing in his greenhouse – one of the several additions he has made to Little Sky in his time there – and makes a salad with some spring onions and pickled red cabbage. He serves it with some local cheese – sharp, salty and crumbly – and a glass of warm cider. Sleet spits at the window as they eat, the sky darkens and glowers, and Watson soon hastens on his way back to the road.

Chapter Three

Jake tidies up and then flops once more into his armchair. After a few moments, he feels oppressed by the mithering heat of the kitchen and decides to go for a walk.

Little Sky came with a vast expanse of land, mainly in the form of gently undulating fields. A miniature world to get lost in, big enough that he can do a five-mile run every morning and remain on his own grounds. The highest point is behind the house, humps and hummocks of thick grass making an unhurried descent towards a building that began life as a farmhouse in the distant past. It was extended into an L-shape by Jake's uncle and is a pleasant commingling of old and new.

Facing the courtyard between the two wings is a large lake, enclosed on one side by a wood, with a narrow beach at either end. In the middle is a small island, which Jake seldom visits but is a marker for him on his daily swims. Each morning, since the very first summer days of angry red dawns and simmering heat, he has swum in the wild water, naked and somewhat liberated. It is both a pleasure and a penance he imposes on himself. In these times of clenching cold, he doesn't make it all the way across like he does in summer, but he manages enough each day to convince himself of his own vitality.

From the beginning Jake gave names to the various landmarks based on characters in the crime books he loved, his other inheritance from Uncle Arthur. Thus Poirot Point prominent at the back of the property, Agatha Wood, Reacher Lake, Chandler Brook, large fields called Velda, Bosch and Wimsey, Wolfe Orchard, and so on. A foolish conceit, but one which he still enjoyed. By the lake, he has built a sauna, which he uses especially at night, sweating in front of hot red coals in the smokily lit gloaming, before plunging gaspingly into the unseen silkiness of the water.

Today he walks past the sauna and begins skirting the lake. Daylight is already slipping away, the mottled greys of the heavy sky bleeding imperceptibly into black. As ever, he basks in the quiet: the breeze lingering in the reeds, the frisky scatterings of leaves, the relentless slip-slap of the water on the bank. To his right loom the miniature houses on stilts he had built for his chickens. He can hear self-satisfied cooings and cluckings as he approaches, as they bury themselves in the straw for warmth.

Some sleet falls in his face, beading his beard, but he keeps on plodding forward. He knows the way even in the deepening dusk, feet following paths worn into the land by his routine movement. He is remembering old cases, old failures. James's mother had implored him to

18

find her son, even after the trail had gone cold following years of fruitless investigation. He can still see her face, harrowed by a grief that would never be assuaged, her eyes unlit by hope, the sour note of desperation emanating from her like a stench.

She had wanted answers, even if they were terrible, final, devastating answers. The uncertainty was worse than anything else, he knew, and he had not been able to remove it. He imagines that Watson was feeling something similar now, and quickens his pace as if to enact some sort of resolution on his part. He would do what he could to help, even as he doubted that it would be enough.

He has looped back towards his house, which nestles in a glimmering pool of light against the surrounding darkness. The wind picks up and he hears something, faint, then stronger. His name screamed out, not in anger but in play, in joy. He can make out the two figures standing in the courtyard shouting for him. Livia and Diana, here for dinner, waiting for him to come home. He picks up his feet and runs towards them.

Chapter Four

Thursday, 6.40 p.m.

Dinner over (venison burgers and jacket potatoes, both cooked in Jake's covered firepit just outside the kitchen window), and the house peaceful. Sounds of snow flurries and creaking timbers. The night outside black and wild. They are sitting in the library: Diana watching something downloaded on her iPad, cross-legged on the rug near the fire, straight-backed, headphones on, a model of concentration in her motley pyjamas; Livia, curved and floppy, her head on Jake's chest as they sprawl on the ancient sofa in the corner.

Jake still feels a flutter of nervous excitement at Livia's proximity: the smoothness of her brown skin, the wild fruit smell of her hair, the sheer physical reality of her body, its welcome heft and texture. Their relationship had so nearly not happened, due to his isolation, her work as a vet and preoccupations as a single parent. And then – more perilous still – one night of bloody adventure when they had been confronted by a man bent on harming them. That could have broken their bond, but instead it reinforced it, and they knew they had fostered something between them worth cherishing.

It isn't easy, though, making things work. Their lives are not particularly compatible. Jake has no structure, no responsibility; Livia has her job (long hours on occasion, hard work) and her responsibilities as a mother. She can't simply live with him, like him, breathing in the freedom of the land and sky. So they have to compromise: he stays more often with her than she does with him, he leaves quietly in the mornings, he gives her space, allows her to visit on her own terms.

Tonight he tells her about Watson's request, his own nagging memories of the lost child. She tells him about a new source of work for her. There is a huge country house fifteen miles away that had been mouldering for decades, owned by impoverished aristocracy who were gradually forced to reduce their activities until selling up became the only tenable option. The property had been bought by a rich businessman, keen to keep horses in the vast stables once more.

'His chappy, his chief of staff or whatever, came to see me. I'm going to visit next week, and if it looks doable, I'll become their vet.'

'Isn't there someone more local?'

'A couple of old sorts, but he said his boss wanted someone younger and hungrier.'

Jake pats her arm. 'That's you, young and hungry.'

'Middle-aged and keen to grow my practice, at least.'

'Can you spare the time?'

'I think so. At least in the beginning. I've always loved

horses, I'm good at treating them, and I don't think they're looking at creating some kind of advanced racing stables. I'll just have to be able to be in contact a bit more.'

Jake felt a tug in his stomach, a flutter of apprehension. 'What does that mean for us?'

She digs him gently in the ribs. 'Oh, calm down, you old worrier. I'm not ready to move in here yet anyway. I'll just need to be at home a bit more of the time to check messages, but I do that already. And when I'm here, the calls bounce across to Daniel. Don't get all edgy.'

But this was always the problem. Jake had managed to renounce much of modern life: he had no phone, no internet connection, no TV or radio. Little Sky was completely disconnected from the modern world, apart from the electricity and water supply, the former quite illegally. It was a deliberate and joyful black spot. But that was no way of life to support a busy professional woman, or a growing daughter. Daniel was a vet from another village, with whom Livia had a reciprocal relationship of cover, a common practice in large areas served by single operators.

Jake is still musing. 'At some point, we'll have to work out how we can live together. If you want to, I mean. My little island from the world has its problems.'

'Paradises always tend to fall, don't they?' She strokes the back of his head gently. 'I know we need to come up with something, but I don't want to rob you of this, or take it away from Diana and me. Let's keep going as we are. If that suits you . . .'

He can do nothing other than agree. But it is a source of anxiety to him, something shapeless inside that he knows will linger, unassuaged. They go back to their books.

After a while, Livia shepherds Diana to her bedroom, where they read together until she is ready to sleep. Then Livia returns, a gleam of pleasure in her eyes. She and Jake strip, and steal outside, their middles wrapped in towels, to the sauna, which is hot and dim and inviting, a contrast to the icy whistling of the wind. They giggle as they hurry to shut the door and disrobe once more. It is breathtakingly, almost painfully hot. They stretch out beside each other on the hot wood, which smells clean like fire. He loves watching the beads of moisture run down her skin, collecting in the soft valley of her stomach or in the dim tangle of her hair below. She is penny-coloured in the faint glow of the lantern, he is obstinately pale, ghostly.

Livia yawns. 'I like this bit, and I like the bit after when you take me inside and then, well, take me a different way. It's the icy plunge I dread.'

'Miss that bit out then. Hold my towel while I jump in the lake, and then we'll go in together.'

'And have you seem all tough, and me all weak? No chance. Come on.' She slaps his thigh. 'Let's see you shrivel up before you fill out again.'

He follows out of the door, the cold air clutching at them. She slips into the gloom, last glimpse of bewitching hips, and then he hears a splash and a squeal. He leaps in beside her, gasping, before helping her back onto the pier. The wood is gnarled and slippy beneath their feet. They wrap themselves in towels, and head to a bedroom far from the sleeping child. It doesn't take them long to warm up after that.

Chapter Five

Jake walks to the village, his practised lope covering the yards with ease. Walking is what he does now; it is like eating or sleeping, a part of the natural rhythm of existence. Distance, in his mind, is mainly a function of how far he can carry himself, which shrinks his environment to the closest ten or twenty miles around him, but at the same time makes him appreciate how wide and vast such a patch can be.

The day is bright, the sky blue, the air so cold his breath crystallizes before him, like a cobweb suspended by nothing. When he reaches the river, running high and flowing in sluggish sulk past him, he notes the sentinel presence of the heron. His heron, he likes to think: a regular companion on his roamings. As if in acknowledgement, or perhaps disdain, it billows open its wings, a powerful flutter of greys and blues, and with aggressive languor launches itself into the air, flying low over the surface of the water until it is lost in the distance.

Jake is heading to the Nook to phone Aletheia, his old Searcher. The title was used informally to describe those in his branch of the force who could trace information, physical and digital footprints, left – often unheeded – by people: where they spent their money, what websites they visited, when they were picked up on CCTV cameras, how they communicated with others. Aletheia was an artist at it, a sort of virtuoso, picking up trails, pinpointing the intersections of target with the outside world with pixel-perfect precision. Jake had relied on her in his cold case work, as did others across the police and military intelligence, and he knew she would help him if she could.

From the outside, the Nook looks like a sad and anachronistic enterprise, a flagging market for tat and over-priced essentials. But it is actually the heart of the village. Inside are all of life's provisions and most of its luxuries: locally brewed cider and beer; meat and fish caught in the area, sometimes from the farmers, sometimes from the poachers; fresh vegetables; a hodgepodge of preserves and pickles made with offhand skill by Sarah, the owner. At night it becomes a pub of sorts, a cellar opened to locals for a drink, payments settled incomprehensibly by a system of monthly accounting. On long summer evenings, the air sultry and warm, you could sit in the garden on the soft, springy grass at the back, and listen to the happy sounds of family chatter, the friendly bellows of children playing alongside the murmurings of small groups of adults.

Sarah from the beginning had helped Jake. Her own children had grown up and left the area, and then her husband had suddenly died, his hard life as a farmer taking an early toll. She responded with calm and resolution, had made the Nook just about pay, and was an unflappable presence in Jake's life.

When he opens the door, the bell tinkling quietly, she is standing at her regular position behind the counter, her feet on a pile of old newspapers to give her elevation and keep off the chill of the stone-flagged floor. She has a pile of receipts before her. She smiles affably, and carries on her tallying.

Jake moves past the till and gives her a quick hug. He can feel her bones beneath her skin, a momentary sense of her frailty.

'Good morning, my friend,' he says quietly. 'Are you well?'

'I'm not falling in love with adding up yet, I must admit. But otherwise not too bad, my old duck. You look like you're up to something and in want of a favour.'

'I am indeed. Your phone.'

'Nothing to stop you connecting your place up with a phone, as I've said before. I know, I know, your daft uncle – God rest him – wanted you to keep away from the world, but I'm not sure you really want it yourself, do you? It's not much to offer a lovely young family either.'

As Jake had been thinking along similar lines, he winces a little. 'Don't start. I won't argue the point. But as of right now, this morning, I do need your phone, so can I use it?'

'Course you can. It's always there for you. Something important, that might involve us in fuss again?'

'I really hope not.'

'You really hoped that last time.'

With a nod of her head, she motions him behind her,

26

through a doorway into the kitchen. He settles himself in an old armchair, wiry stuffing poking out of the thick cushion seat. It is surprisingly comfortable. He grabs the phone and thinks carefully so as to remember the right number. Sarah bustles in, and puts down a homemade cheese scone, split and thickly covered in butter, rocks of salt glistening on the surface, along with a glass of elderflower cordial.

'You need feeding up.' He doesn't. He is as strong as he has ever been, the outdoor life, and daily exercise, limbering and toughening his body. But he knows the pastry will melt in his mouth and is happy to accept.

As he chews, he dials the number, and imagines Aletheia in her normal lair. It would be gloomy, windowless, the greenish light of the screen pulsing back from her glasses, the noise of air conditioner and computer a steady hum in the background.

She picks up, and sounds pleased to hear from him. They talk briefly of life, her mother, a sickly soul for whom she cared when she wasn't working, Jake's own semi-wild existence.

'But you only ever come to me for a favour, Jake, so you better cough to that now.'

He scratches at a stray piece of fluff on the arm of the chair. 'Do you remember when we looked into that strange phrase "no taboo"? Nothing really stuck, but you did dig up something odd in an online forum somewhere. I wondered if that was everything then, and if anything had happened since.'

The airiness seeps from Aletheia's voice. She becomes businesslike, even brusque. 'Nope, nothing ever came of it, and we dismissed it as another crank conspiracy. There's nothing live or active in the files, I'm afraid. Look, if that's everything, I have to get back to work. Even more cases, you know, especially now that certain people aren't here to help clear them.'

Her laugh sounds forced as she hangs up. Perhaps she was busy, but she also sounded rattled. Jake sips his drink, musing. He can hear Sarah's hobnailed boots clomping on the stones in the shop as she hefts crates of vegetables. He realizes he should help, and moves out of the kitchen. Some are heavy enough – the squash, the turnips, the hothouse potatoes – to make his assistance worthwhile, and he is soon happily occupied. The unfamiliar trill of the phone interrupts them, and Sarah goes immediately to answer.

'Jake, it's for you, a woman called Aletheia.'

Jake drops a box of kale on his toes, mutters a swear word, and takes the phone. Aletheia sounds slightly out of breath.

'Jake, I'm on a very secure line. I can't talk now at any length, but I think we should meet. Can you get to the city in the next couple of days? Shall we say Monday at two, somewhere well-populated?' She names a restaurant inside a converted church, which is buzzy and busy, and serves breakfast all day.

'Al, do I need to worry? This is all a bit dramatic.'

'I want to be careful, that's all. We'll speak Monday.' With that, the connection is broken. Jake helps Sarah tidy up, then strides home, the wind blustering his long hair, his expression rather worried.

Chapter Six

Monday, 7.15 a.m.

Monday is also the day Livia is set to visit her new client and his stables, so they both leave from her cottage first thing in the morning. It is small – especially compared to Little Sky – but comfortable, all blackened beams and twisted lines. It looks like it has been snuggling into the landscape for generations, sharing colours and softness with the surrounding soil. The camouflage of custom. Inside it has the colourful chaos of all homes with young children in them: toys spilling haphazardly from boxes and cupboards, stray socks clinging to the sofa, lidless pens and pencils strewn on the table.

Jake likes being here. He and Diana have a friendly, playful relationship. She was a product of a largely unwelcome liaison at a party, and she has never known her father, a feckless figure from Livia's past who expressed no interest in her. Jake, who had so painfully failed to be a father himself, did not seek to replace him; he just wanted to be a friendly addition, a net benefit to her life. He did not crave complication, and nor did she.

Together they pack Diana off into a friend's car, with waves and blown kisses after a number of false starts. School is several miles away and the residents of outlying farms and the tiny villages pocketed across the valley, share lifts whenever they can. The house is suddenly silent. Jake tidies up, or at least tries to stem the flow of messiness, while Livia washes her hair.

When she emerges from the bedroom, she is smartly dressed: dark jeans, a thick chocolate jumper, and a long wax jacket of a similar colour. Her hair has been pulled back in a ponytail, framing her heart-shaped face, hints of burnished bronze at its ends. She looks practical and beautiful at the same time, he thinks.

She smiles all the way up to her green eyes, clear and bright as a cat's.

Jake straightens up. 'You look very professional.'

'You know, money likes to see money. These guys could be a real godsend when it comes to guaranteed income for me.'

'You never told me the name of the owner. Who is it?'

'I only had contact with his man, but by using modern technology – shock, horror, I know – I worked out who he's working for. A guy called Sam Martinson, big businessman, used to own a bunch of newspapers. You heard of him?'

'Sure. Nothing good, though. He got out of newspapers before the internet really hit, just about when I was starting as a copper. God knows what he does with his money now. But you only ever heard of him when he was doing something awful.'

30

'I didn't think the place would be owned by the first nice multimillionaire in history. I doubt very much I'll see him anyway.'

Jake reaches out to hold her in his arms, her black hair tickling his face and catching in his beard. 'I'm fairly sure there were stories of him being handsy at the very least, so be careful.'

'If he is, I can deal with it. And, believe me, a stable of sick horses and manure everywhere is no place to do anything like that.'

'I don't know: I can see you in a pair of tight jodhpurs turning a few heads.'

'I'll save that for here then.' She wriggles out of his embrace, patting him tenderly. They kiss briefly, faint taste of coffee on their lips, and then she is gone. He hears the cough and roar of her old Volvo as she drives off.

He knows he needs to get going: a trip to the city is no straightforward journey from here. He grabs a book he has brought from home: a novel by Jill Paton Walsh, continuing the Lord Wimsey-Harriet Vane series by Dorothy Sayers. Wimsey is, Jake thinks, his favourite amateur detective: dismissed by many as fey and posh, but actually a tough, determined figure, scarred by the traumas he has seen in warfare, desperate for something beautiful and redeeming with a brilliant woman. He thinks of Livia briefly, and shuts her old oak door behind him.

The sky has the pallor of winter, the colours muted like watered-down paint, washed-out umbers and ochres. Jake is wearing old jeans and a thick hooded top, his brown boots scuffed and weathered. He walks a couple of miles to a deserted and windswept bus stop and waits for a while. The cold nags at his face, but he has learned to ignore it, his hands clenched in his pockets, his eyes darting all around the landscape.

From the stop to the train station to the city itself takes all morning. He reads quietly throughout, tries to keep himself distant from his fellow travellers, ignoring the rise of the noise of civilization in his ears, the self-involved chatter, the insistent drumbeats leaking from headphones.

The restaurant is in a side street off the old meat district, formerly a place of slaughter and shambles where the iron tang of blood hung immoveable in the air for centuries. Now the area is more or less refined, but still wears proudly a faint sense of disreputability, as if it is still a place where unmentionable things might happen.

Aletheia is sitting in the corner of the former church, in a booth made from old Victorian pews, gnarled and varnished and welded together. She is in her forties, dark brown skin, black hair speckling faintly with grey, a prominent nose set in a rather beautiful face. The roof cambers above them, lightness somehow trapped in worked stone, the vast vaulted spaces absorbing all the chatter of the diners.

They order food – steak and eggs for him, waffles for her – and coffee. The small talk fails immediately.

'Why are we meeting like this, Al?'

Her face furrows, fainter lines in its smooth surface. 'Because I'm careful. And one side effect of my job is knowing how important it is not to leave too many traces behind me.'

'So there is something about the phrase "no taboo"?'

'It's not just a phrase, it's a company, or some sort of business entity. At least, I think it might be. I'm not entirely sure how it works, but I reckon it is a thing, a well-protected, well-financed thing that looms in the background, that I've never even got close to fully identifying. I've been pursuing it off the books since you left, nagging at it, and I now know enough to be very wary indeed.'

Their food arrives. Jake grinds pepper, sprinkles Tabasco sauce over his eggs. Aletheia nibbles the corner of a strawberry.

'Does this go back to our last conversation about it?'

'It does, yes. Remember I dug up that reference on the conspiracy website? I kept searching, and there was nothing. So I tried looking at it another way: I tried to find where it wasn't.'

Jake shakes his head. 'You always were a baffling genius. I don't even begin to know what you're talking about.'

Her smile is fleeting. 'So, I took as a premise that the reference we had was completely correct: that there was some large criminal enterprise that could offer anybody anything and that it was influential enough to keep itself totally secret. Those two things should be paradoxical: it should be one or the other, big or secret, or we're talking about something very unusual.'

'I see, I think.' He sips his coffee, which is strong like at home.

'My idea was that, even if I couldn't see it, something that big and strong would be visible in its impacts. Like in space, you can theorize the existence of a star by the effect of its gravitational pull. I needed to look for evidence of pull.'

'Did you find any?'

'Yes and no. I opened up the whole database of unsolved crimes, and started looking for commonalities: sudden closures of files, suspects lost, cases kicked to the cold files like you had, CPS advice being reversed. Evidence of elite cover-up, of something untouchable escaping the system. As you can imagine, it was a deluge of information, but I wanted to see if I could get some sort of shape out of all the noise.

'The problem was, a couple of weeks in, I got a visit, a knock at the door of the office. And a man walks in, about fifty, tall, unpleasant looking really, very well-combed black hair, like a newsreader from the fifties. I remember his eyes: one was grey, the other was brown. It made him look otherworldly. Anyway, he had Jeannette with him, you remember her?'

Jake nods. She ran the entire Research department of the Metropolitan Police; a tough, brittle woman who kept fairly aloof from the rank and file.

'She said he was a senior government adviser. They started by giving me the old flannel: what a great job I was doing, how important I was. And how they wanted to promote me, to give me a liaison role with MI5, given that so many of the cases I was working on had security implications. More money, a bit more autonomy – not that I needed that.'

Jake is aware that Aletheia had always been used to operating with very few restrictions. He motions for more coffee. 'That doesn't need to sound suspicious. You do deserve a promotion.'

'Don't I know it. I wasn't that suspicious at first for that reason. And then, offhand, at the end of the conversation, I was told that my last run of searches had set off a red flag somewhere, meaning that they could impact on a live investigation crucial to national security. So I was asked formally what it was about. I said that it was speculative, trying to establish the existence of an as yet undefined criminal conspiracy.

'Their faces didn't move. The man leaned forward, his breath smelt of mint, strong mint, his voice was slippery, gentle, creepy really. He grabbed my wrist until my hand started to throb. I've never been touched with such force, honestly. I was bruised for a week. He told me that investigations into that sort of conspiracy can be ruined by nosy parkers. I remember the phrase, "nosy parkers", which I've not heard since school. He said that was what I needed to show discretion about, the sort of discretion I would have to have in my new role.'

She breathes out. Jake could see that she had been genuinely frightened.

'I was a bit of a coward, Jake. I could see what was happening, that the squeeze was being put on me. But I love my job, I deserved the promotion, and I convinced myself that they could be protecting a real investigation. That might still be true, I guess. Anyway, I let go of my official interest, and kept plugging away on my own time without much luck. So here I am, more money, overwhelmed with work, but more closely monitored. Then you pop up, blithely using the phrase I've been trying to keep off my systems, and I thought I better warn you.'

He is quiet. The hum of the restaurant returns to his ears, mingling clinks and chatter. He explains what Watson had told him about Laura's disappearance. She exhales contemplatively, a picture of concentration.

'So are you warning me off?' he asks.

She gives a smile that is almost a wince. 'I would never do that, even if I could. What I'm saying is that you have to be careful, that's all. And you should warn your policeman friend, too. It may not be worth his while.'

'He's hunting a missing child. I think anything is worth his while for that.'

Aletheia gives an expressive shrug. 'Well, I wouldn't want to stand in the way of it either. But remember that old saying we used to have when we were doing anything to solve a case: "All right, I can see the broken eggs, now where's this omelette of yours?" Remember that? You wrote it on a Post-it for my desk. I've still got it. I'm just saying, make sure you get an omelette out of all this.'

'And you can't help?'

'I didn't say that, did I? I said we need to be careful. You never know, you could get home and the girl will be found and our conversation never needed to have happened.' She pauses, as if making a decision. 'I can do two things. Give you this.' She pushes across the table a small package in a cloth bag.

'I know you're living your isolated life. But this is a phone that works anywhere, untraceably. It's government kit, if you know what I mean. When you contact me, only use this; there's a number for my special phone saved under my name.'

Jake places his hands on top of hers, his knuckles bloated and scarred from boxing, her fingers surprisingly slender. 'And the other thing?'

'I can put you in touch with a friend of mine, Martha Kline. She's been dabbling around the edges of conspiracy stuff for years; she used to work for the security services. She helped convince me that No Taboo did exist. I'm not saying she's always right, or even always completely sane, but she knows some things. She now writes detective novels for a living, so I think you might get on. Give her a call, see what you make of her.' She hands over a small slip of paper, then leans across the table and softly kisses Jake on the edge of his beard.

'Don't do anything rash or obvious. Let me know anything you dig up – and keep me out of trouble as well.' She stands and looks around. 'I'll let you pay for lunch, or breakfast or whatever the hell that was.' She walks outside, and in a second is swallowed by the meandering crowd.

Jake sits for another coffee and thinks, a figure of perfect stillness amid the hubbub. Aletheia's fear had disturbed him, as did her willingness to act in spite of it. He exhales, drops some folded cash on the table, then he starts the long journey home.

Chapter Seven

Monday, 10.53 p.m.

Late that evening, Jake is walking cross-country. The buses
have stopped running at this hour, so it is something of
a hike. He doesn't mind. It is clear at least, but very cold.
He can hear the crackle of frost as it is forming beneath
his feet, feel the trees and hedges around him tense in the
chill, as if they are contracting themselves into position,
braced and unyielding. There is scarcely any noise of
animal movement, no tell-tale rustles of life in the black.

He is playing a torch beam in front of him, confident
of his way. The stars above are clearly defined, a scattering
of rice grains on a dark surface. He wishes he knew more
about them, and regrets the fact he has never learned. In
his old life, he never saw the stars, enshrouded as they
were by the glare of city lights and the invisible mist of
emissions. Now they are there every night, a joy and a
reassurance, and yet he has remained ignorant of exactly
what they are called, and why. He wonders if Livia has a

book on it. Or even Diana, he supposes, children being at PhD level when it comes to stars and planets and the like.

He feels the unfamiliar lump of the phone in his pocket, and it bothers him a little. He is being drawn back into the world again. And based on what? A business card, a half-remembered conversation, and a foreshortened search for where something wasn't. Jake resolves to speak to Martha, and then reveal whatever he has learned to Watson. He can do no more.

After a couple of hours walking, he reaches the outskirts of Parvum. To his left, looming, faintly illuminated by two forlorn lights smoking in the freezing air, is the local church, an Anglo-Norman affair. It is solid, a hulk of hewn stone, a monument to obstinate survival. It is guarded by similarly ancient yew trees, hunched over with age, their spindly branches interlocking like a roof.

Ahead of him is the road that runs through the village, quiet enough even in the day, but now utterly silent and dark. The only other lights he can see are from the cottages and slightly larger homes that are set back from the road. One is Livia's, but he moves quickly past it without looking in. It is late, and he doesn't want to bother her or Diana. He is relieved to see her car, a sign she has returned and is safe inside, and that is enough for him.

At the bend of the river, he moves off the road and on to a grassy field, his feet tingling with the damp and cold. A solitary owl hoots, another of his regular neighbours, an aloof familiar of his night-time wanderings. And then finally the lights of his own house loom inviting. He goes straight to his library and lights the fire, which he always tries to prepare before leaving the house. It catches instantly with a scratchy sound, the flames hungrily rising.

He then moves to the bookcase opposite, where there is a secret compartment built into the wall, accessed by opening a fake Sherlock Holmes book. Inside are some papers, a pile of journals, and a gun, oiled and clean and reassuring in a threatening sort of way. He puts the phone next to it and closes the compartment.

He is feeling a little restless, as he often does when he has been back to the city. As if his mind and body need space and time to return to the rhythms of his normal life. He rolls a small joint, taking the weed carefully from a large bag in a box he keeps by the sofa, and smokes it down in five deep breaths, relishing the muzzy rise of altered senses within him.

He runs his eyes over the ranks of novels on the four walls. Arthur's thriller library has titles from all over the world: noirish little Scandi things with inevitable pictures of a snowscape on the cover, tales of stoical cops in violent Scottish cities, lurid American paperbacks full of fast-talking wiseacres, stories set in classical Rome or modern Venice or Sicily. Italian detective novels, he thinks, whether modern or ancient, are always filled intriguingly with the fetid whiff of state and police corruption. After some happy snooping, he sees the name Martha Kline in magenta letters and takes it back to the sofa. A bit of research, he thinks, and a chance to escape the preoccupations of his mind once more.

Chapter Eight

Tuesday, 6.32 a.m.

He wakes the next morning, still in the library, stiff and cold. He should have gone to bed. The dead fire is a pale, ashen rebuke. His mouth is dry, and he can smell the bitterness of his own breath. He shivers and stretches, his shoulders crackling and complaining. He rebuilds the fire, and lights it, then wanders to the kitchen, where the stove is warm but close to expiring. Soon, it is sputtering to life once more, filling the room with heat and noise and life.

Jake drinks some water from the tap, brushes his teeth, and changes into his running things. He puts some coffee on to heat slowly in his absence. Outside, there is a thick frost on the cobbles, friable layers like icy moss, which he negotiates carefully. Soon he is on his familiar track, the ground hard and unyielding. It is early, the winter sky a deep navy colour, the sun merely an implication beneath the horizon, reluctantly bequeathing enough light to silhouette the naked trees in the distance.

He had enjoyed Martha's book, which had kept him up until the early hours, with a needless extra joint. It was a comic caper of a thing, about a gang of well-intentioned protesters trying to draw attention to the incompetence of the State by committing thefts of national treasures without getting caught. It was a sort of anti-detective novel, the police being either bumbling and benign or sinister and inimical. He wonders what sort of use she will be to him.

Jake completes his run, lungs grumbling, eyes bloodshot, and has a short, and shocking, swim in the lake. Then he showers outside, rubbing scented oil into the aching muscles of his legs. He doesn't want to leave the house for fear of missing Watson's arrival, so decides to devote some time to home improvement. Livia will perhaps drop in if she can spare time on her afternoon rounds, and it is a day to avoid unnecessary journeys, as the temperature continues to drop further, and snow clouds, pregnant and ponderous, begin to thicken above his head.

He has a workshop, of sorts, in a small outbuilding across the courtyard, and he heads there after surveying the vacant fields for any sign of Watson. Little moves in the sere landscape, apart from the trees shuffling their branches in the distance, and a bird of prey hovering in the white sky, at this remove no more than a comma on a blank page. The door heaves across with a faint shriek, and he moves quickly to light the wood shavings in the bottom of the stove. They curl and taper in the burgeoning flames, and soon provide some heat.

Jake has few practical skills, but is stubbornly trying to acquire some more. Much of the work around Little Sky he has carried out with his own hands, slowly, clumsily, gradually improving in confidence after each modest success and averted failure. He grimaces as he picks up his tools: his previous mentor had been the man whom he eventually caught as a serial predator, so he is now very much alone in his endeavours.

His current project is the construction of a treehouse for Diana. He intends it to sit above a campsite in Agatha Wood, as a place of refuge and enjoyment when she wants to escape Mum and her new boyfriend. He has some drawings on a table: the proposed construction has several levels, and spans two oak trees that are growing close together. He wants it to be accessible by a rope ladder, and then have a zip wire down to the ground for swift departure.

He is currently cutting planks of wood to fit the structure in his design, and the workshop smells pleasantly of oozing pine and the smoke from the stove. He is using some material he had left over from the sauna construction, and he happily settles to a morning of measuring and cutting. The finished planks are leaned against the far wall as a sign of progress.

His work goes uninterrupted, with no sign of Watson, and he stops only when he realizes he is hungry. He returns to the kitchen and fries a mess of eggs and ham, and makes another pot of coffee. He takes his food and drink to the bench by the lake, and stares at the flat, untroubled surface of the water, as smooth and black as oil.

That lost child case of his bothered him, now he has started to think of it once more, as many others still did. He wonders if there was a conspiracy behind it, or if it was – more likely – just another example of the sordid and contingent misery of real life, the suddenness of brutal accident that lay behind almost all crime. The result of an unplanned decision, perhaps, taken in the grip of a mundane emotion like anger or lust. That was what made crimes so hard to trace, in fact: they were often based on a devastating act that came from out of nowhere. It was why so many went unsolved, unmourned by all but the victims or their family, a statistic, a blot on an official record, but nothing more. Life always went on, pieces were always picked up, memories were always dulled by time and practice.

The initial investigation into the snatch (well before his involvement as a cold case man) had been conducted with purpose and determination, but no success. James had been playing in the front garden of his home with his mum. It was a suburban street in the middle of the day. It would have felt that life was more or less passing its inhabitants by; that sense of contagious inertia that comes during work hours when people are at home, no buzz of the busy, nobody checking or observing. The road was almost deserted, an occasional, anonymous car bumping past, but nothing more.

James's mum, Elizabeth had been called inside to her phone. Jake had seen the call log from her provider: it was her husband Mike, James's dad, and he had apparently told her he had forgotten about a meeting and would be late that night. They spoke for two and a half minutes. Elizabeth told him something funny James had said that morning. They clucked about his charm, his innocence, and said they loved each other. They left the call happy. When she went outside straight after, James was gone and she would never be happy again.

The police had combed the area, pored over CCTV, and

looked into the backgrounds of everyone who had come into possible previous contact with James. To no avail. His anguished parents had had a week of media attention, the father grimly stoical, the mother visibly bereft, before fading into the background, part of the intermittent cultural and media memory that feels no true sorrow.

The file had jumped into life – and hence on to Jake's desk – when a man called Simon Peters had been arrested for child abduction and murder three years later. He had been known to have operated in the area as a serial predator, though there was no physical evidence of James in his home. Jake had visited him in prison, where he was being held before his trial. He couldn't forget that day, a hot, mithery affair in late summer, the visiting rooms close and dank and smelling of unwashed misery. Peters had been no help, disdainful, not interested in bettering his lot in return for cooperation.

Jake thinks he had pursued all channels, but perhaps he had missed something. Was Peters part of a conspiracy? It seemed wholly unlikely. He had hanged himself in solitary confinement two weeks later.

Jake shivers. The day has got even colder, the sun now hiding beneath a blanket of cloud, light snow falling sedately all around him. He sees the bright flash of movement on the other side of the lake, and realizes it is Livia on her bike. He can't quite make it out amid the swirl, but imagines her face taut with concentration, her fringe jouncing in front of her eyes as she keeps her legs pumping.

He goes halfway to meet her, his feet sliding a little on the fresh fallen snow. She is wearing a long, thick black puffer jacket, and black waterproof leggings. Her hands when he reaches out to clasp them are icy tendrils.

'Liv, what are you doing coming to see me today? You should get off your round and go home.'

Her face is flushed with effort, redness suffusing beneath her brown skin. 'You know I can get about in all weathers. Plus, I had to get a message to you, it was left this morning with Sarah. Watson's had an accident, Jake – he's in hospital.'

Chapter Nine

Tuesday, 2.55 p.m.

He takes Livia inside and gives her a hot drink to warm her up. A saucepan of thick milk from a nearby farm, with a bar of dark chocolate melted into it. She knows little more than the simple message left by a colleague of Watson: that he had been involved in some sort of incident, and he was in hospital, knocked about but not in danger for his life. He was set to be there for a few days.

Jake hangs up Livia's coat and waterproof leggings next to the stove. They start to steam immediately. Underneath, she is wearing a thick jumper, and a pair of thermal long johns. Jake can't help but smile, even amid the bad news.

She notices. 'Are you laughing at my deeply unsexy leggings? You can tell it's cold, when I get these bad boys on.'

'They're like something an elderly American prospector for gold would wear in winter. In the nineteenth century.'

She comes up and places her pubic bone against his, face dramatically sultry for a second. 'That was the look I was going for.'

He traces his hand across her thigh and bottom. 'So do you have underwear beneath this underwear too?'

'Why don't you come and find out? I have a little time, and you can borrow my car this afternoon to go to the hospital.'

'That's the sexiest offer I'm going to get all winter.'

Various underclothes are soon scattered on the floor, and armchairs used exuberantly, if not for their original purpose.

Later they are sipping their drinks, wrapped in a blanket by the stove. Jake has opened its door, so the heat hits their faces direct, a soothing sting, and a pleasant smell of woodsmoke fills the room.

Livia is still smiling. 'I won't tell Watson that you were so lacking in concern for him you got yourself distracted by little old me and my sexy prospector knickers.'

'It would have been rude to you to fail to be attentive. Plus, we don't get that much time on our own, so I'm sure he'd understand.'

She snuggles against him. 'Are we worried about him, that this might be a sinister accident?'

'Who knows? I'll go find out and talk to him. People have accidents, which might have nothing to do with concerns they raise with ex-detectives.'

'When you put it like that, though, it does sound suspicious.'

Jake then tells her everything he had learned from Aletheia. Her eyes widen. 'I know you have to help a little. But you've got to promise me to keep out of this beyond

48

that. We got involved in something last time, and we put Diana in danger. We can't do that again.'

Jake nods, though he is far from sure he will be able, or willing, easily to extricate himself. To change the subject, he asks her about her new client. She is immediately alive with interest and fervour, clearly excited by the prospect of such work.

'The house is beautiful, old and huge, with these vast grounds stretching off in all directions. I hate to say this, but it's even grander than Little Sky.'

'How dare you!'

'Well, it is. It's called Purple Prose, though, which is a far worse name, so at least you have that. Anyway, I was given the tour by the guy, Josiah his name is. A former military man, now chief of staff, ran everything with precision. I didn't exactly like him, too cold, too austere, no life in his eyes. But the horses, Jake, the horses. Six of them, all beautiful and strong. They said I could bring Diana around sometime to ride one of them.'

'Do you think you're hired?'

'Oh yes, he was very efficient on that point. Agreed my terms and everything. I'm going to do a full physical for all the animals next week. It's such good news.'

'I'm glad one of us is getting some good news. Come on.' He pulls away the blanket from her, and she stands, naked, the shadow of the flames flickering on her familiar flesh. He throws the long johns to her, which were drooping from a chair, and digs around for his own clothes. 'You better get back to work. You said I could borrow the car to see Watson?'

'Of course. You've got the keys.' She is wiggling into her layers once more. 'I wish I could give you a lift on my bike, but I think you're too big for a croggy.'

49

'What's that?'

'You know, a crossbar ride – didn't you call it that? One person riding, the other being carried along . . .'

'I don't think we called it anything.'

'I can't help your lack of education. Give me a kiss then and I'll see you when you drop the car back.'

She opens the door and the cold air enters, a scamper of snow with it. It is mid-afternoon, and the night is already closing in. Livia needs to get to a nearby farm and then home again before evening takes away all of the light. Jake can hear her cursing exuberantly as she manoeuvres her bike and skids across the cobbles. He puts on a jumper, then his running jacket, and heads out into the gloom.

Chapter Ten

Tuesday, 4.15 p.m.

Livia's car starts robustly and he is soon on his way. The nearest town, Meryton, lost its own hospital ten years ago, so he has to go quite a distance to the even bigger town beyond. The hedgerows, stripped as they are by the season, still manage to enclose the lanes tightly as he drives. The wind is shivering the landscape, and the austereness all around looms like a peril. Winter afternoons are depressing affairs, lightless and lifeless, and he feels a shapeless dissatisfaction with the situation: Watson harmed, ghosts from his past on the rise, his own ability to build a simple life with the woman he loves under modest question once more.

Hospitals are never places to ease depression. And certainly not on dismal afternoons like this one. The car park is wet and windswept, filled to capacity, so he has to wait before awkwardly contorting the Volvo into a tiny space next to a bin for medical waste.

After some considerable period of baffled exploration within the hospital itself, Jake eventually tracks Watson down to the right ward, trekking a distance through gunmetal grey corridors, measled with signs and posters and exhortations to better health. The hospital smell – a wretched combination of antiseptic, boiled vegetables and unwashed bedpans – assails his nostrils; and the sight of so many unwell and helpless people bothers him, as it always does. It is a place of decay, of entropy, of bodies breaking down. The only briskness comes from the doctors and nurses, an obvious defence mechanism that stops them from being dragged under by the collective weight of all the corporeal failings around them.

Watson is in a bed by the window in a room shared with two others, both apparently unconscious. A curtain is half-heartedly drawn around his bed, flapping petulantly in an unseen breeze. Jake approaches quietly in case he is asleep, but Watson immediately turns to look at him. His face splits into a smile beneath two blackened eyes, already fading into purples and greens at the edges. Bruised hues. His wrist is in a thick cast. There is padding around his ribs.

'You look terrible.'

Watson grasps his hand, his skin papery and dry. 'You should've seen the other feller.'

'What the hell happened?'

Watson winces at the memory. 'I'd just had lunch at the Oddfellows Arms, you know just outside of Meryton, and was walking back to the car. I'd parked it in a lay-by. Out of nowhere came this blur, knocked me into a hedge, must have been going thirty or forty miles an hour from nothing. The doctors say I was lucky to get away with a cracked arm, some damaged ribs, and this clown face.'

Jake sits down on the chair next to the bed, which is sticky with drying disinfectant. 'Do you remember anything about the car?'

'Just that it hurt when it hit me. It might have been dark green, it might have been a four-by-four, but I failed in my role as policeman, obviously. No licence plate, no driver. Nothing.' He dry swallows, his lips contoured with bloodied cracks. Jake helps him to a drink of water.

'Was it deliberate?'

'That's the question, isn't it? Well, they didn't stop, and they came from nowhere very fast. It felt targeted. But you know how some folk drive on country roads round here: they know them like the back of their hands, so they think they can't hit anything. Perhaps they mistook me for a stray deer.' He sighs thoughtfully. 'But I've been lying here, running it through my mind, and I can't help but believe I was aimed at. And you can imagine how that makes me feel.'

Jake is wondering whether or not to tell him about his own discoveries since they last spoke, and decides to do it. He explains what Aletheia had told him, the spectre of 'No Taboo', and its impact on her investigation.

Watson is silent for a moment. 'So if we buy into a conspiracy theory, which I almost never do, this was a warning, was it, or an attempt to shut me up?'

'It could be. Or it could be another of those coincidences. What are you going to do?'

'I'm not saying I believe there is anything hugely sinister going on. But there's no harm or shame in being a bit more careful. No more blind searching through computer records. I don't know, Jake. Do you think that a combination of money and bent officials could conceal something like this?'

'Not really at first blush. But I can't rule it out now. Anyway, I came here to say that, whatever it is, I can't have anything to do with it. I have Livia and Diana to think about, my whole life. I got out of the business of getting involved.'

'I still have a missing little girl to think about.'

'Does that mean you're not backing away after this?'

Watson bristles, his grey eyes flaring beneath their blackened hoods. 'Of course I'm not. I'm going to carry on till I find her or lose hope. And I want your help.'

Jake looks around him. The other beds remain peaceful, their bodies as motionless as corpses. A nurse in the distance is tiredly picking her teeth, a cleaning orderly wearing large headphones is mopping the corridor in negligent fashion. 'I know you do. Look, I'm going to talk to the writer Aletheia suggested, and I'm going to try to get a look at my old files: the dead soldier and James. See if anything jumps out now. And then we'll talk. But unlike you I'm not a copper anymore and there has to be a line somewhere.'

Watson lies back against his pillows, his voice almost wistful. 'Oh, there's always a line. You just need to make sure you're on the right side of it.'

A silence builds against the background murmur of hums and bleeps, the living bustle of all hospitals. Jake squeezes Watson's hand. 'You look after yourself. And keep away from busy roads. I'll be back to visit in a few days.'

'I should be home by then. They'll make me take a rest up for a bit, but I'll keep things going on the quiet.'

'We can both do that, at least.'

With that, Jake leaves, smiling at the nurse as he passes

54

her, and gets immediately lost in the complicated one-way system of corridors. Eventually – after brief, but not unrewarding, stops in Radiology and Administrative Affairs – he finds an exit, and starts the long, dark journey home. When he gets to Livia's house, the lights are off and the place feels cool and unoccupied. She must be out somewhere with Diana. He leaves the car halfway up the drive by the side of the kitchen, looks through the window at the cluttered emptiness within and trudges home.

He goes straight to the library, picks up Aletheia's phone and messages her to send the files to the Nook as soon as she can. That doesn't commit him to much, he thinks; just to rereading, to plotting, to seeing if anything occurs to him.

Chapter Eleven

Wednesday, 7.05 a.m.

An icy morning, the sky caught between the paling of dawn and a blue so deep as to feel endless when you allow yourself to stare at it. Jake's door bangs, rattling against its hinges. He is up, warmly dressed and drinking coffee by the stove. A record is spinning in the corner of the kitchen, *Carnival of the Animals* by Camille Saint-Saëns, a strange and dramatic thing that becomes oddly soothing when played low like this.

He opens the door, and a man is standing with his forehead leaning against it. He half-falls into the kitchen. He is dressed in navy waterproofs that rustle as he enters. His long brown hair is tied in a ponytail and carries beads of moisture from the frigid air outside. His eyes are brown and sleepy, but hint at a spark of mockery within.

His name is Rose, who – despite a background as a small-time drug dealer and general rogue – is one of Jake's friends from the area. They had not always been so: Jake had been suspicious of Rose's earlier relationship with Livia, as well as his apparent willingness to work with terrible people in the dope business. But they had become closer during the investigation into the death of a woman named Sabine – another of Rose's former girlfriends – and had found themselves, perhaps surprisingly, on the same side. Rose had nearly died helping Jake, which is something that bonds people. They now fished together most weeks, Rose always complaining about the early hour, but never missing a day.

Jake hands him a cup of coffee, which he gulps greedily.

'What's this shit you're listening to, Jake? Honestly. It's like you're trying to play the part of weird loner.'

Jake waves away the protest. It was an old and regularly expressed criticism. 'Shall we get moving? I've got stuff to do today.'

'That doesn't sound like you. You're one of the few people who works less than I do.'

Jake shrugs on a thick hooded top and then goes outside. The puddles near the lake are thickly iced, opaque and purplish in the dim light. Their breaths mist in front of them. Jake trusts Rose to a point, but not enough to tell him the whole story, or the involvement of Aletheia. But he explains about Watson's search for the little girl, and how it might relate to an old case of his.

He chooses his words with care. 'So there have been these rumours of a high-end collective, a sort of club, who provide illegal services, and their name has something to do with the phrase "no taboo". That mean anything to you?'

'I hope you're not asking me because I'm a criminal myself?'

'That's precisely why I'm asking you.'

57

Rose nods equably, and puzzles for a moment. To his left a crow barks petulantly and flaps away. There is the contrasting rill of a songbird in the hedge, liquid and sweet.

'I can't say it means much. There've always been people who can get you things, no questions asked. I suppose, in my own humble way, I've been one of them. But you're talking about something more organized, are you?'

'I don't even know. It could be that, money no object, you want something hard to get or morally wrong – drugs, I'm guessing, pornography, girls, maybe even kids – then there's a place to go: like an elite concierge service but for illegal things. But I've not got much to go on.'

'Let me ask my most elite and disreputable friends.'

Jake grabs him by the arm and checks their progress. They are now by the river, heading towards a backwater where they fish regularly. 'If you do, please be careful. If this is nothing, it doesn't matter what you do or say, but if it's something, you don't want to draw attention to yourself.'

Rose clasps Jake's arm in return in mock-seriousness. 'I understand. I'm no hero, as we all know.'

After a few minutes they have reached a small lagoon formed by an island in the river around which the water flows sluggishly. Fish are harder to catch in the winter; they are slower, more lethargic and keen to conserve their energy, reluctant to leave the sanctuary of the banks. The sun is up, a glare of light but not much heat. It bounces off the river, shattering into a thousand shimmers, each rucked line of water a sparkling jewel. Jake hopes it might warm things enough to enliven the fish. Rose meanwhile has something else. He proudly pulls out a jar of turmeric and waves it at Jake.

'Our secret weapon.'

'Are you planning to season the fish we won't catch today?'

'No, I read that this might liven them up a bit, give them a scent to get excited about.'

They are using bits of sweetcorn and dried berries as bait, and Rose sprinkles the box liberally with the yellow powder. A faint smell, a hint of captured summer, floats in the air.

'Do you really think that will work?'

'Do I really think we'll catch a giant perch today, no I don't. But I've always been a tryer.'

They settle down on two tree stumps, and stare quietly at the water. After a while Rose carefully raises the subject of Livia, and Jake explains her new prospect of work at Purple Prose.

Rose casts his line, settles back expansively. 'I've definitely heard of that guy Sam Martinson. He's a bruiser all right. But he has the money to be, or maybe that's how he got the money in the first place. I'd tell her to take care around that house. You hear stories in Meryton of people going to work there, and coming back pretty appalled. They're paid off to be silent.'

'If they're paid off to be silent, how do you know that they're appalled?'

'People always know, don't they? And I have one of those trusting faces that make folk tell me things. Anyway, tell Livia to look out for herself.'

'She always does, but I will.'

Their eyes settle on the water, Jake's face lined by a persistent frown, a sense of foreboding he can't entirely shake.

Chapter Twelve

Jake and Rose stay for three hours, but the fish don't come out to join them. The cold is piercing and deep. The grass in the shaded area beneath a nearby log stays white and brittle with frost. The two men can feel the chill seep into their clothes and decide to make a move. Rose had left his car at the nearest point on the road before walking across the fields to Jake's house, so he is able to gather up the fishing equipment and sling it into his boot.

Jake refuses a lift and waves goodbye, before marching up the lane towards Parvum. He tries to call Martha, the thriller writer, from Sarah's phone, but she doesn't answer. He leaves a brief message, promising to call again tomorrow.

Livia is at home, between work calls, and Jake happily stays for a coffee with her. He has been trying to encourage her to read detective fiction, with mixed success, but he has today caught her with one of his Agatha Christie's,

The Murder of Roger Ackroyd, eyes screwed half-shut in a moue of concentration. She's on the epilogue, and puts it to one side with some reluctance. 'I like a clever solution, and a surprise ending, and when someone you like turns out to be not quite as you think. And it's nice – and not like real life, I know – to read about something where all the suspects are in one place. Straightforward, you know.'

Jake agrees and takes her in his arms by the stove. Her hair always smells like cherries, and he drinks it in, as she presses firm and reassuring against his chest. Her ginger cat, an aloof female called Cyprian, marches stately figures of eight around their legs, tail twirling like a conductor's baton.

They are kissing and Jake is leading her towards the sofa when a knock comes at the door. Livia gently disentangles, rearranging her vest and trousers. The room is warm, a fire roaring, gusted by the wind pouring down the chimney.

She opens the door and nods instinctively in recognition at the visitor. He stamps his feet on the mat, dislodging crystals of ice from his otherwise immaculate boots. They settle on the ground like snow.

Livia is momentarily flustered. 'Hello, do come in, I wasn't expecting to see you until next week.'

The man who enters is of middling height, solidly built, with black hair cut austerely short. It is greying at the temples. He has the gait of a soldier, square shoulders, symmetrical steps. His eyes are almost black. He doesn't smile in his greeting.

Jake moves towards him, and Livia turns as she closes the door.

'Jake, this is Josiah from Purple Prose stables. The man who runs things there.'

Josiah is dressed with visible care, not formal exactly, but precise. He is wearing dark boots and trousers, pressed with a crease, and a thick, padded windcheater. Jake, in some contrast, is in old jeans, scuffed brown boots and a jumper with a hole in one arm.

Josiah's hand, when Jake grasps it, is icy cold. His handshake expectedly firm.

'Josiah, this is—'

'Jake Jackson, I believe.' His voice is a quiet rasp.

'How did you know that?'

Josiah smiles. 'We do our research very carefully on anyone who comes to work at the big house. And I believe you attracted some notoriety a year or two ago in the apprehension of a serial rapist.'

'I think notoriety might be overstating it.'

'I don't know: "the Good Life policeman", the man with the long hair and beard desperate to avoid the world, but instrumental in ending decades of terror in the sleepy countryside. A charming story, and one which reflected well on you, of course.'

Jake forces a faint smile. 'As you'll know if you read the stories, I don't spend much time with the news of the day, so much of the bluster passed me by.'

Josiah reaches past him to stroke Cyprian, who purrs with throaty satisfaction at the attention, allowing him to pick her up. He puts his nose to hers and inhales deeply, as if to share the air for a second, before setting her down once more.

Livia comes to stand beside Jake. 'What can I do for you Josiah, nothing wrong with the horses, I hope?'

He has been staring out of the window, but brings his attention back to her. 'No, dear me, no. I'd be swiftly on the telephone if that were the case. I wanted to bring you the contract to sign as soon as possible, and to extend you an invitation.' He hands her a sheaf of papers, which had been carefully folded under his arm.

'I wasn't aware we were going to need a contract.'

His voice is flat. 'You may not have worked for someone with the profile of our employer before, I imagine. They are standard non-disclosure agreements, nothing to worry about. I'll leave them with you to bring to the house.'

His eyes catch Jake's. 'Which leads me on to the invitation. Mr Martinson would be delighted if you would both come to spend an extended weekend at the house, as guests of his for an informal gathering.'

Jake is already shaking his head, his hands raised in a protective gesture. 'That's kind, but, as you know, I'm not much of a mingler these days. I'm sure I'd be no great addition to any party.' He looks across at Livia, who is standing still, her arms folded.

Josiah's expression is unchanged, neutral as a clockface. 'Mr Martinson, knowing your background, thought you might say that. So he instructed me to insist, and to make the point lightly that he regards people who work for him, and their families, to be an extended part of his family. Your attendance is not a condition of employment, but . . .' He shrugs faintly, and runs a hand through his hair. His skin is smooth and pink, his nails trimmed with precision.

Jake looks once more to Livia, whose eyes are in turn searching his. Her face brightens artificially. 'When would the party be?'

Josiah reaches into his coat and brings out a stiff envelope. 'All the details are here. You will be working, I believe, that day at the house. The suggestion is that Mr Jackson here joins you in the evening, and you then stay on with us. It is a beautiful house, as you know, and I don't think it would be presumptuous of me to suggest you would not be bored.'

Livia takes the note and puts it on the table. 'Please tell Mr Martinson that we will do all we can to be there.' She gestures at the mess around them, which threatens to topple out from the shelves and cupboards at the edge of the room. 'We just need to deal with the childcare issue.'

Josiah bows. 'I'm hopeful that you will find someone to look after your little one. Diana, isn't it?'

Jake bridles slightly, though takes trouble not to show it. 'More necessary research for your boss?'

A wan smile, which somehow makes his face seem more grave. 'Hardly. I can see the name on the pictures on the wall there. Perhaps I'd make a detective myself, like Sherlock Holmes.'

There is a brief silence. Livia fills it by offering Josiah a drink, and looks quietly relieved when he declines. He shakes their hands once more, his still no warmer.

'Thank you, that's kind, but I must get back to the house. I'll tell Mr Martinson that he can expect to see you both.'

He bows, stiff-backed and formal, and silently shuts the door behind him.

Jake takes the contract from Livia. 'Don't worry, I can take a look at this. I was almost a lawyer once. And I can play the dutiful spouse role too. We could even look at it as a romantic break: me and you, an old country house, rolling grounds, sputtering fires.' He reaches for her and envelopes her in a hug.

Her voice emerges spiky from the soft folds of his jumper. 'That's total bollocks, I know, but thank you. I know you'd rather not get sucked into any social scene, but I do want this job, and think we should say yes. We'll make the arrangements work.' She half-shudders. 'What a creepy man, though. It feels like he brought the ice into the house, doesn't it.' She runs a hand down the side of his body. 'Good job I have you, the Good Life policeman, to warm me up.'

No other knock disrupts them for the rest of the morning.

Chapter Thirteen

Thursday, 9.45 a.m.

The next day, another frozen one. Jake is beginning to appreciate the majesty of winter in this deep part of the countryside. The combination of icy crispness and distant horizons, the beauty of bareness, of absence. The trees stripped of everything but their fragile skeleton. The ground hard and unyielding. The purity of the cold.

He has worked out after his run, using the punching bag he made from a giant old flour sack, which hangs heavily from a low branch of the beech tree next to his house. His hands sting and throb.

He knows he should have a shower and call Martha again. Instead he arranges himself beneath the beech, and stares upward at the sky. Through the spidery maze of branches lies nothing, no clouds, just distance, expanse. This is the silence he craves. Although life with Livia is pleasurably messy, he doesn't regret the times he spends alone like this, enjoying the freedom to be absorbed by a landscape that is indifferent to him. Aloof like the sky is.

And this may turn out to be a problem in the end. Take Livia's new job: she will want to be on regular call, available to the stables, as well as all her other professional responsibilities. It is already making demands on their lives, take that invite to Purple Prose he is now trying to put out of his mind.

It is a telling reminder that Livia cannot just come and escape forever to this haven of quiet. Nor can her daughter, who has to go to school, see her friends, eventually have her life endlessly diarized by phones and computers, the electronic warders of modern existence.

Jake can't imagine life without his new family, but he can't imagine it without this sort of solitude too. He closes his eyes and hears nothing but his deep breathing. The hard earth is like a block of ice on his back as the thin light of the sun diffuses all around him, and it eventually chills him so much he has to get up. He showers quickly before heading to the village.

Sarah is waiting with a box of files. 'Specially delivered for you, by a very strange man. Jumpy as a pair of frogs on honeymoon. Anyway, he knew who I was, and told me to give them only to you. As if I would rather auction them off to the highest bidder.'

Jake could see Aletheia's neat handwriting on the top of the box: *All the relevant files as promised.* He takes the box from Sarah, and places it quietly on the floor. 'Thank you for helping with this, my friend. I'll bring them home this afternoon. But while I'm here . . .'

'I know, I know, you need my phone. Ridiculous, but go on.'

He sits on the familiar armchair and dials Martha's number from memory. After several rings, he hears a loud, clear voice.

'Hello, hello, who is this?'

Jake explains who he is and his connection with Aletheia. 'Oh yes, the hairy policeman. I've read a bit about you as well.'

Twice in two days, he thinks. This is what fame must be like. He tries his own flattery. 'I enjoyed your book.'

'Which one?'

'I can't remember what it was called now. It was about a caper.'

'They're all about capers. That's my what-you-might-call genre of choice.'

'The cover was yellow and red, I think.'

'Literary critic on the side are you, too?'

Jake feels he is losing control of the conversation slightly.

'I want to talk to you about something serious, about a possible organization involved in committing serious crime.'

'Go on then.'

'Can we meet in person? I could come and see you.'

'Didn't Aletheia tell you? I don't meet many people in person. I'm not a great one for meeting up at all.'

Jake frowns slightly. Sarah enters and silently puts down a cup of tea and some carrot cake. He waves it away, but she shrugs her shoulders in mock defiance and walks off.

'I'd rather do it face-to-face, actually. That's how I always used to work.'

'But neither of us are working now, are we? I have my life, and it doesn't involve appointments. I'm sorry.' A ringing silence down the line. 'Well, I'm not that sorry actually.'

Jake almost hangs up, but blurts instead: 'I'm chasing down No Taboo.'

There is silence on the end of the line. An intake of breath. 'I won't ask you to say that again.'

'But does it make you want to meet me?'

Another pause. 'Quite the reverse. I'd run a mile, if I could. You don't seem really to know what you're doing here, do you?'

'That's why I'm talking to you.'

'Jake, I'm not going to meet up with you. But Aletheia gave you the phone, didn't she? I trust that more than normal lines like this one. We'll talk on the Signal app on it. Let's pick a time, and we can speak frankly and I'll tell you what I know. No contact until then. Say tomorrow, Friday, at 10 p.m.? I work better at night anyway.'

Jake tries to speak, but she talks over him. 'Don't worry your pretty Luddite head. Just open the damn app at ten o'clock and I'll contact you.'

She puts the phone down. He chews a piece of carrot cake thoughtfully. It all still feels so incongruous: sitting in a country kitchen, being shouted at by a conspiracy theorist about something he does not quite believe in.

Chapter Fourteen

Thursday, 8.50 p.m.

Jake has lugged the box of files back to Little Sky and is reading them in the library. Night has fallen fast, the fire is spitting furiously as the occasional snow flurry sneaks down the chimney. He has cooked a steak on the stove with some new potatoes and the last of his pickled cabbage. He is nursing a big glass of Rioja, which he has scavenged from the huge wine cellar in the corner of the basement. One of Arthur's many legacies was his basement store of essentials: tins of food, sacks of grains, bottles of water, wine and whisky. A surprisingly large bundle of cannabis. And there were some crates in a dark corner that Jake had still not opened yet. Little Sky could withstand a siege if necessary.

He turns first to the case of the dead soldier, which feels further apart from that of Watson's missing child. He figures he might be able to dispose of it more quickly.

The soldier – who was called Daniel Jones – had become

the chief suspect in the murder of Nathan White, a homeless man who had been killed four years before. White had been found with two appalling knife wounds, one to the stomach, the other a savage and forceful slash across the throat. What had been strange, and had confused the initial investigating team, was the likelihood that two different blades had been used. Both sharp, both lethal in the right hands, but the stomach blow had ultimately not been fatal. The hypothesis was that White had been finished off with the *coup de grâce* of the throat cut, but from a different knife.

The crime scene had been a mess, a literal shambles in the old sense of the word meaning abattoir: he had bled profusely in a dark alley in the east of the city, his body then mauled by rats before his chance discovery by a refuse collector two days later. The knives were never recovered. There were no witnesses. The file soon became dormant.

Jake had always felt galvanized by cases like this: something savage and inexplicable, the victim powerless and unmourned. Nathan White had never really stood much of a chance. His life was a catalogue of woes: he had never finished school, dabbled in minor drug-dealing, done a couple of short jolts for fencing and petty larceny, followed by a longer sentence for an assault in which he may well have started as the aggrieved party. He emerged from his last prison sentence to nothing, no money, no hope, just the address of a halfway house he had to attend. A few short months later he was dead.

Aletheia had accessed his prison records as well. White had been a fairly nondescript inmate, except for one incident in his last stay. Caught up in a prison brawl, he had

71

lashed out at a prison officer, which saw – after a period in solitary – his sentence increased to its full term. Typical Nathan White, Jake thinks: in the wrong place at the wrong time again. Luck never his to hang on to.

In the moments before his death, he had evidently reached out to grab his assailant, perhaps to plead for his life, perhaps in a futile attempt to fight him off. He had ripped some skin, which had caught beneath his fingernails, leaving enough recognizable DNA to test. The problem was that there was no match in the system, and the lead therefore cooled.

Fast forward four years, and a match did happen. Former Sergeant Daniel Jones, veteran of Afghanistan and Iraq, had been out of the army for almost a decade, and was apparently doing well. He lived in a nice two-bedroom flat in an attractive area, worked non-specifically in 'security' and had – to all those who knew him – moved on from his former profession of violence and conflict. One night, though, he had taken a woman home from a night-club and raped her. She complained to police the next day, tearful and outraged; he had immediately lawyered up and claimed it was consensual.

But his DNA entered the system. Two weeks later, the link was made on a computer somewhere, showing that he was a match for the Nathan White crime scene. And Jake had moved immediately. Jones had received prompt bail and was back at home when Jake went to find him.

Jake sips his wine, and closes his eyes. He doesn't need the file to prompt his memory of what happened next. He had reached the outside of the apartment block and followed in another resident staggering under a bag of heavy shopping. Jones's door wasn't locked, and Jake soon

72

saw why. He had kicked it open, stridently identifying himself. And he remembered his voice just stopping as he entered the living room. The muscled man, stripped naked, tattooed sleeves in dark blue and green against pale flesh, swinging on a homemade gibbet, eyes bulging, tongue-lolling, his bowels voided beneath him.

Closer examination of Jones's military file suggested a level of undiagnosed PTSD during his service itself, some prior accounts of unprovoked aggression that had been dismissed or forgiven. But the trauma must have damaged him, made him rage, and one day he had crossed paths with Nathan White – a chance encounter, a murderous coincidence, perhaps – and the rage had burst forth. Impossible to know why at this stage; both men were forever silenced. Case closed: a sad parable of what happens when men come home from war, or the essential inequality of modern society, but nothing much for Jake to do.

Jake exhales. It is late. His eyes ache. The wine tastes rusty and pointless in his mouth, a hangover in waiting for the morning. He can't face the other file at this time, another memorial to his own failure. He puts on a new record, something by Vivaldi with guitars and violins, which feels soothing and summery, like a breath of warm air, and starts to tidy the room. This is a force of habit he had adopted at the beginning of his life here. You have to have standards, he thinks, even if you are voluntarily in solitary confinement.

The thought sets off a spark in his brain. Nathan White in prison, sent to solitary for striking an officer. Simon Peters, the possible suspect in James's abduction, hangs himself in solitary. He flicks through the second file. Both events happened in the same prison. Different times, but not too far apart, even if the two men did not actually have sentences that crossed over.

Jake can feel his heart racing. Were the two cases, so superficially different, actually connected? And there was another link: those deaths by hanging. Two good suspects taken off the board before they could be further interrogated.

What was it Aletheia had said? She tried to look for the gravitational pull of something big, the influence of the thing, not the thing itself. Was that at work, shapeless to outside observers, but there, guiding the fate of these men? Jake walks to the table, his fingers tingling, and starts making notes. His wine is forgotten. After half an hour, he opens the secret compartment, takes out Aletheia's phone, and sends a long message, asking whether it is possible to find a connection in the past, in the prison system, that might reach forward into the present to help them.

Chapter Fifteen

Friday, 3.45 a.m.

He doesn't sleep much that night. No response comes from Aletheia. He tries to read – he is now on *Prague Fatale*, one of the Bernie Gunther books by Philip Kerr, vicious and brutal and beautiful accounts of private detection in Nazi Germany – but cannot concentrate. The storm abates, and he wraps up and goes outside, his feet damply bare in old wellies. The world in its aching iciness is still, as if all has been frozen and fixed into place. He can feel the expanse of the lake rather than see it, the silent night cloaking him softly like dark silk. The air is fresh in his lungs, the bitter cold somewhat cleansing.

Staring into the black, he worries again at the pattern out there that might connect all the cases, two children five years apart, a hanged soldier, and a murdered homeless man. At three in the morning, everything feels shapeless. A dissatisfying thought and, after a moment of fruitless musing, he wanders in to go to bed. Just before the early lightening of false dawn, when the night is fraying at its edges, pale blues and dark violets in the corners, he manages to sleep, his brain still restless and unquiet.

The next morning. No message back from Aletheia. He wraps up warm, and wanders down to Agatha Wood, where he is marking out the area for the treehouse. He hammers some iron pegs into the trunk of one of the trees, feeling a momentary sorrow at the damage to this living thing. He hauls himself up, gloveless, his hands reddened and stinging, to the first branch, which he straddles. He drops down a rope ladder and fastens it around a shorter outgrowth of wood. He clears out some stray twigs, easier to do at this time of year, during this season of bare desolation.

The tree is easily climbable, and he scuffles up to the highest point that will take his weight. There is a parting in the wood here, and he can see back across the valley to much of his land: the lake glinting placidly in the weak sun, his farmhouse, its chimney smoking strident against the sky, the rolling green fields beyond. All is peaceful. A hawk cries in the distance. A touch of savagery in the calm.

Soon he spots Livia's Volvo jouncing over the ground on her way to visit him. She often stops for lunch on a Friday, as it happens to fit the routine that takes her to some of the outlying farms in the district. Jake carefully manoeuvres himself down, the trunk still coated in frost, and jumps heavily to the ground.

He is waiting for her by Chicken City when she walks up, having left the car in an outlying field. It's another inconvenience, he thinks, that she can't call him or even travel along a road whenever she wants to visit him. Will she get sick of the hassle of it all? Life with a hermit. He hopes not. They have one emergency means of communication: there is a tree equidistant between their properties, Sherlock Beech (as he, obviously, has dubbed it), on which they hang brilliant bits of cloth as a summoning signal. They use it less now their relationship is secure, and they can plan more, but it is there as a pleasant reminder of their perilous beginnings. But does anyone in the modern world really want, he worries, a form of semaphore as a way of getting in touch with their boyfriend?

He puts the thought out of his mind and wraps her in a hug. She is coatless, but in a thick black jumper that swamps and swaddles her.

'Keep off me, I'm wearing a pair of dangerously sexy long johns, you pervert.'

He leans forward and tugs her trousers down to check. She squeals with laughter and pulls them up. 'Jake! It's too cold for that sort of thing.'

'At least you didn't say it was too public.'

'That's one of the things I love about here. We don't have to worry about getting naked in front of anyone.'

'Apart from the chickens.'

'Of course, it would be quite inappropriate in front of them.'

They walk hand in hand back to the house. Jake has been making soup all morning: kale and potatoes, together with onions that have been hanging in his pantry since autumn, and a venison stock he made the month before. He mulches some greenhouse herbs and walnuts with some sunflower oil and cider vinegar to make a pesto of sorts, and swirls it into the steaming bowls. It smells restoring, and he sets them down on the kitchen table. For music he puts on Samuel Barber's *Adagio for Strings*, from a recording of his longer string quartet by the Berliner

Philharmoniker. He feels he will never tire of this piece of music, at once melancholy and consoling.

They eat and listen for a moment, then talk about his investigation, such as it is. He explains his thinking on the files. Livia raises an eyebrow, a faint flash in her eyes, sudden sunlight on fresh fields. 'This sounds like you're getting involved, Jake.'

'Just doing some fact-finding, some research. Then Watson will have to take the risks. I'm not involved in any live inquiry.'

'I suppose not. What do you think this author woman will say to you? Do I need to be jealous?'

'I doubt it. It's one of those video meetings anyway, but she may be no more than a harmless eccentric. I'll find out tonight.'

Livia sips some coffee from a giant mug with a horse inexpertly glazed on the outside by a childlike hand. She crunches a chocolate biscuit with relish. 'And then we spend the weekend at my house. Diana wants to go riding, and I thought we could go for a walk while she does.'

'What a crazy life we lead.'

'I prefer the term "peaceful". Which reminds me: we have our visit to Purple Prose on Thursday: me in the day, and then both of us for the long weekend. Can you be home for four to keep an eye on Di? Just until we need to drop her off at Joanna's.'

'Of course. It will be lovely.'

And it would, he thinks. Further stirrings of domesticity, of true togetherness. 'You know I haven't looked after her on my own before.'

'I know. It feels like the right time, though, if you don't mind.'

'If she doesn't mind.'

'No, she's quite in love with you. They're reading *Stig of the Dump* at school and she tells everyone that her mum has brought a Neanderthal home with her.'

Jake laughs. 'I can't argue with that.'

Livia rumples his hair. 'Funnily enough, I used to go for the smart, clean-cut type, and now look at me.' Jake supposes he was clean-cut once, but in the last two years he has certainly embraced wild living. His hair falls down to his shoulders, thick and shiny; his beard is just about kept in order with scissors and an occasional razor, but still almost reaches to the top of his chest. In summer, he generally wears little more than a pair of shorts, his skin turning pine-coloured by the time the cherry blossom comes. In winter, he wears thick, warm jumpers and trousers that obscure his lean body. He looks like what he is: a man on the outside of civilized life, tending to his own interests, with little need to crook the knee to anyone.

'Would you prefer me if I smartened myself up much? Would you introduce me to more people?'

'As if you want to meet a whole bunch of new people, who I barely see now anyway. I feel bad enough about dragging you to some multimillionaire's house. No, I'm not missing out on a social life, and nor are you. Having a daughter on your own means you lose touch with most people.'

'At least you're not on your own now.'

'That's why I want you to look after Diana. The next step in our little family.'

'And at least one of your friends does like me. The fearsome Joanna, the journalist robbed of her innocence and ideals.' She had helped Jake with the investigation into the sexual predator; indeed, it was her research that had allowed him to connect the dots that led to identifying the man responsible. Joanna was a frustrated editor on the *Shire Gazette*: frustrated not because she craved the tarnished glamour of national journalism, but because she wished that the model for local journalism wasn't so irredeemably broken. She spent her days editing a website now owned by a faceless multimedia company, compelled to churn out nonsense for clicks and intrusive ads.

She was also a sort of sponsor of their relationship, a kindly figure who wanted them to prosper because she thought it was good for Livia. They had dinner together once a month, and Joanna often left clippings at the Nook of her favourite headlines for Jake's amusement. Her latest three were: 'Narrowboat on the loose', 'Sadness as bench falls over', and 'Appeal to return coat to man'.

He chuckles as he thinks of them. 'Are you sure she's happy to look after Diana until Sunday? It's very kind of her.'

'I've helped her out in the past, so I think it's OK. She's certainly honest enough to tell me to sod off, if it was a problem.'

'I wonder what she thinks of your Sam Martinson. I think he might have owned her paper at some point.'

'I'll ask her, and he's not "my" anybody, as you well know. Now, I have to get back to work in half an hour, so shall we stop wasting time talking, so you can convince me why I now like my men big, unkempt and hairy?'

'I thought you'd never ask.'

The music swells in the kitchen like a soundtrack as the wind howls outside. After a while they don't notice either.

Chapter Sixteen

Friday, 9.30 p.m.

Jake is in his library, fingering the phone nervously. It is a forbidding device, sleek black, flat, with a widish screen. There is a secure messaging system for text, and the Signal app already downloaded, and that is more or less it. Jake hasn't bothered looking for anything else. It seems to tap into some unknown Wi-Fi source, though. The whole of Little Sky is completely free of internet access normally, but somehow this device can function properly.

At five minutes to ten, Aletheia responds to his message with a photograph of a prison guard who had worked in the prison throughout the time that both Nathan White and Simon Peters had been there, and a link to a file about him. He is called Garland Smits, an odd-sounding name, Jake thinks, and he wonders where he might be from. His face is blank enough, pale skin with hooded eyes, receding hairline, a lugubrious, disappointed, dismissive expression.

Jake is about to open the file when he gets a notification

that Martha is online and ready to speak. He opens the app, and goes to sit on his sofa, a reading lamp just over his head, halo of light in the shadows. On the screen is a small, birdlike woman, with short hair spiked stylishly up. She is wearing a thin purple vest, and has a black tattoo wrapped around her upper left arm. The faint outline of muscle appears beneath it. She is sitting at a big writing desk of polished wood. He can glimpse the outline of her computer, and she is evidently using a separate, quite professional camera.

Behind her he sees what looks like the ruin of a library, tottering piles of books of different heights, spaced widely. He can recognize many of the titles from his own bookshelves behind him.

She is looking at his set-up too. She waves, a bit ironically he thinks. 'Hi there, Jake. Aletheia told me you'd be prompt and reliable, and let me tell you, I don't value the opinion of many people, but I do value hers.'

'Thank you, I think.'

'Some things before we start. First, well done on calling me from a library. I love the bookcases, I love the novels I can see. One day we can compare notes on who's your favourite crime novelist, apart from me. I'm a Rex Stout girl, but we can talk about that. Second, I do want you to know about who I am. So, I used to be on the police, and I did work with the security services. That's how I came to meet the fragrant Aletheia. But I had to leave, and do something else, which is how I came to be writing my crime novels, which you so kindly commented on yesterday. And no, I don't write bloody, complicated or upsetting books, not because I couldn't, not because I'm a weak and mimsy woman, but because I wanted separation from my old job, which was bloody and complicated enough. I wanted to escape, shrink myself, do you understand?'

Jake nods. He does understand. Shrinking his horizon was why he had come to Little Sky in the first place.

'Why did you leave the job?'

She frowns. 'Didn't Aletheia tell you?'

Jake shakes his head. 'She didn't tell me much, other than I should speak to you.'

Martha is silent for a second and then pushes back her chair. It rolls back, and he can see the bottoms of her legs are missing, cut off above the knees. She pushes herself forward again, businesslike. 'That's one of the reasons I left. Three stray bullets, close range, left my legs in bits. I was lucky not to bleed out there and then.'

He sips some water. 'What were the other reasons?'

'Oh, I saw some things, grew tired of some others. I got dismissed as a conspiracy theorist, someone starting at shadows after my terrible trauma. But let me tell you something, Jake. I'm no crazy person. Most conspiracies are – to use the technical term – fucking bullshit, as you know. The world is too fragile, too clumsy and too messy to be totally controlled by a cabal or a collective or whatever.'

Her voice hardens and quickens as she gets into the stride of her argument. 'But the world is also often too fragile to stand up to powerful people, to do what is right in the face of money and influence. So I believed, and I still believe, in what I call the conspiracy of impotence, of looking the other way, of complicity that can be disguised to yourself as pragmatism. JFK wasn't murdered by a brilliantly devised plot involving the FBI, CIA, the anti-Castro Cubans and the mob. But whoever did it relied on some of those institutions doing nothing, walking away, keeping silent.' Her face is slightly flushed, he can see a wobble in her throat.

'Have you given that speech before?'

'You bet I have.' She laughs. 'And that doesn't make it any the less true. Do you mind if I smoke some dope? Deadens the pain sometimes.'

She picks up a small pipe, lights it and inhales. She looks back into his eyes, as the smoke emerges in front of her. He sees her pupils dilate, black beads in her face.

'Don't worry about me; I'd join you, but I want to keep my head straight for all this. So what do you know about No Taboo?'

Her voice is a little more gruff, and he can detect the feathery lilt of a Northern accent, not too pronounced, but there, unmistakably, at the edge of her vowels. 'First, that I wouldn't talk to you about it except securely, and except for the fact that our friend Aletheia asked me to. It's not, as I was saying, a worldwide conspiracy, but it does have influence in shutting things down and letting bad things happen. So what is it? From what I've heard, it's somewhere between a members' club, a high-end retailer and an evil butler. At the more legitimate end, it can get you anything you want if you're willing to pay for it: rare wines, trips to forbidden parts of the world, experiences that most people could never dream of.

'But it doesn't stop with the legitimate. It can get you drugs, and not street rubbish, you know, cut with talc or laxative or bicarb, but beautifully produced and as safe as you can make it. Then it's heavily into the sex business, inevitably: boys, girls, trans, three-ways, group

84

stuff, whatever kink you like. Under-age too, obviously. Videos on demand or the real thing in the flesh. And that means it is in the trafficking business too, and the child abduction business as well.'

She pauses for a hit on the pipe again.

'So far, so awful but mundane. The problem is that some people have used it for even more dangerous stuff. That's how it lives up to the name No Taboo. Suppose you want someone knocked off, a business rival or tiresome lover; that can be done. But it also caters for what you might call people's capricious desires as well: say you want to know what it feels like to kill someone, actually experience the thrill of murder, then they could arrange it. Or you want to experience raping somebody without the risk of prosecution. No taboos. Whatever thing you can think of, it can arrange.'

'How do you know this?'

'I don't *know* it. But I've come across glimpses over the years, little hints of a larger operation behind something I was looking at. And one day we were tapping the phone of someone, I forget why, but an upper echelon criminal. Lots of agencies involved, a big deal. And he mentioned making use of No Taboo for business and pleasure. He said he heard of a woman who paid to be driven around knocking cyclists off their bikes. Seriously.'

'Why didn't you grab him and find out more?'

'The tap went dead after forty-eight hours. We find the man a week later upside down in a barrel somewhere near the mouth of the Thames. Of course, it could have been connected to something else, but . . .'

'Were you bounced out because you talked about this?'

She laughs, a harsh, invigorating sound. 'I was bounced

because I became a cripple, Jake. I had enough of investigating other people's problems, because my own suddenly
became rather fucking pressing. If you understand.'

'I'm not sure anyone would properly understand, but
yes, I reckon I can work out what you mean.'

At this point Jake decides to tell Martha everything
from the beginning. Throughout his narrative she rarely
lets her eyes fall from his. She makes no notes, gives no
visible reaction. Periodically, she grabs her pipe and
smokes, inhaling deeply, her face still fixed in a frown of
concentration.

When Jake finishes speaking, his throat a little raw, she
sits quietly, drumming her hands on the desk. 'All of this
makes sense, but there's not much to go on. You have to
let this Watson man, if you can trust him, focus on the
missing girl. The others we can think about in more detail,
more slowly. I actually wonder whether both your old
cases were No Taboo, and that's why you got called. A
strange coincidence, and someone seized on it. James's
abduction certainly has that feel of a professional, clean
job. No witnesses, grab the kid, who knows what for. And
your hanged soldier interests me. How is this for a hypothesis: a client wants to kill someone for pleasure; No Taboo
lines up Nathan White, the client stabs him in the stomach
but bungles the killing, and so it needs to be finished off
by a professional. Later on, he's sloppy and gets caught
in the system; they clean up the mess and suicide him.'

Jake scratches his beard, straightening a twisted hair
that immediately coils again. 'I can buy that, but there's
no evidence.'

'Only because you never – quite rightly – looked for
any. I think the prison link isn't a bad place to start. I'll

get Aletheia to send me her file, let's both look at it, and we'll speak again. You better message me a good time, but give me a couple of days.'

There is a silence. Martha is stroking her arm, oblivious for a moment. Jake coughs. 'By the way, I've never managed to get into Rex Stout – too dry and complicated for me, though I think the orchids are a nice touch. I'm going for Dorothy Sayers, the Wimsey-Vane novels. No argument.'

'Oh, we can have an argument, dear Jake. Just not now.'

'Thank you for caring about all this.'

Thin smile, more of a wince. 'Caring is one thing. Doing anything about it is quite another. Take care of yourself, Jake, keep things quiet for God's sake. We'll speak again.'

With that the connection is broken. Jake is alone again, a web of conspiracy before him in his mind. Was it plausible? He puts on a Mahler record, Symphony Number 5, mournful and portentous, and then picks up the Smits file and starts reading.

Chapter Seventeen

Saturday, 12.34 a.m.

Smits had been a prison officer for twenty years. Jake looks through his service record, which Aletheia has somehow accessed, and it is fairly mundane. Once he achieved rank, he moved to his current prison, a place with a maximum security wing to which the most serious criminals were sent: murderers, rapists, terrorists, hard cases and unrepentant recidivists. Within it was the solitary unit, a place both of detention and punishment.

There had been brutality claims against Smits over his career, but not many, and none that ever stuck. He was in charge of the solitary unit two weeks out of every four, and there he would have certainly met Nathan White, who went on to be murdered outside the prison, and Simon Peters, the paedophile who apparently hanged himself while still inside.

In his role, Smits would have had clear powers over the prisoners, the ability to speak quietly in their ears, bargain, cajole or compel. It was the perfect job to make contact with criminals and build a relationship with them.

Peters's suicide had led to a letter of reprimand on Smits's record. Jake reads it carefully. It concluded that he had allowed himself to be distracted from close observation of the victim and had failed to report a malfunctioning camera with due promptness. He was suspended without pay for three days, ordered to do remedial training, but soon returned to post.

This was suspicious, to say the least, the convenient way the death had gone unobserved on camera. Aletheia had clearly thought so. She had delved deeper into Smits's life, picking up his footprints with all her Searcher's skills. He had no mobile phone registered to him anywhere, but she produced a CCTV image of him clutching one as he walked from the prison. Clearly he only used burners, to avoid any scrutiny and to maintain the privacy of his contacts. Not the behaviour of an innocent man. He had a nice house in the suburbs with no mortgage and a Range Rover in the drive. His online spending was considerable: he liked expensive remote-controlled helicopters and drones, which he flew regularly in the park at the end of his road. He subscribed to two pornographic websites called Tied'n'Bound and Teen Fantasies.

Jake traces the inside of his mouth with his tongue, idly circling each tooth as he goes. His head aches, his eyes are sore. This guy was, to all appearances, dirty, and he was circumstantially connected to two criminal cases. But how did this help Watson with his abduction, and did it place anyone on the road to tracking down No Taboo?

There is one final piece of information in the file: a list of active bank accounts. Smits had several, which you would not expect for a hard-working public servant earning less than sixty thousand pounds a year. At the bottom of the page, a short note says that the subject holds safety deposit boxes in one location. Jake makes a note of that. Physical storage spaces always have potential for an investigator, if they can be opened, which at the moment he has no way of doing.

He shuts the device, and puts it back in the secret compartment. The fire has dwindled, is now a mournful glow of ashes. Jake opens a window and breathes in the air, which carries with it the departing damp of the very early morning. In the invisible distance he knows that Livia is asleep, lying on her stomach clutching a pillow with one hand, quiet apart from the occasional murmurous twitch. Tomorrow, he can visit her and her daughter, feel free and light, unburdened by the meanness and sorrow of life elsewhere, the griminess that clearly exists and has always existed. But he knows he can't leave that griminess alone now. He has to know more, help more. He resolves to visit Watson first before doing anything else, to see what else can be done.

Early the next morning he walks across the dark fields, footprints imperceptible in the hard frost, and borrows Livia's car before she is up. His own sleep had been fractured by angry visions. Before the sun was pushing back the last remnants of night, he was out running, driving himself onward, feeling the sweat flow and his heart throb. He had plunged into the icy lake with a cathartic shout, sprinted naked back to the shower, and felt energized once more.

Watson had been up a while himself. His house is big and ugly, built in the post-war period on the edge of Meryton. The front room had clearly been designated as a temporary office since his injury. A map has been attached to a bookcase, and billows when Jake walks in. He is ushered across the threshold by Sylvia, Watson's wife, a quiet and impressive woman whom Jake had only met once or twice.

'Jake, you can try to get him to slow down. The doctor said a week's rest, and I think he's managed twenty minutes.'

'He should just chuck it all in and retire, spend some proper time in the house.'

'All right, I'll be careful what I wish for. I'm making coffee, I'll bring it in when it's ready.'

Watson is sitting in a cracked leather armchair with a file on his lap. His hand is in a cast, and he moves gingerly. The bruises on his face have faded a little, the yellows at the edges now blending it into the normal pallor of his skin. He looks pleased to see Jake.

'Come and sit down. I've been going over all the information, and you look like you have more for me. I'd left a message with Sarah that you should come this morning – did you get it?'

'No, but I said I'd come by and check up on you, didn't I?'

Jake sits on the lumpy sofa and runs through everything he knows. They are interrupted once by Sylvia, who brings in two huge mugs of coffee on her way out of the house to go shopping. Watson sits still and listens, then summarizes the situation.

'Our problem is that there are two layers to this.' His voice is questioning, as if he is trying to work through his thinking as he goes. 'One is some giant conspiracy which may or may not be true and may or may not involve widespread corruption. I'm willing to believe it, for what it's worth, and we need to take a look at that prison guard. The more important layer for now is finding Laura. And I'm not sure how you've helped me much with that.'

Jake acknowledges the point. 'I've asked Aletheia to compare the James file with your Laura file, which she can access remotely. Maybe something will come up.'

Watson has an old-fashioned gas fire, which clunks and hisses, glowing angry orange. The room is warm and quiet, a homely place for reflection. For the next couple of hours, they sit companionably, Jake reading through the files and offering his thoughts as they arise. Watson is reading witness statements, and occasionally sends messages requesting information on his phone. None seem to return, until a loud bleep punctuates the calm. He winces as he grabs it. It's a text:

you win. call this number for what to do next

Jake has read it over his shoulder. 'Hurry up, chief. It might be important.'

'It might be a nutcase.'

Nonetheless, he presses the number on the screen and it rings. He puts his phone on speaker and stares at Jake, licking his dry lips. It is a recorded message, the voice slightly distorted.

'If you want to find Laura Wright, you should go to the cottage on the old Mill Road.' It gives some map coordinates, which Watson jots down.

It continues, no change in tone: 'She will be there unharmed. It's over. She can walk away, we can walk away. Go and take her back.'

The message ends abruptly. Watson immediately dials another number and gets through to the incident room at the station. Jake walks to the map and pinpoints the reference. It is a cottage in the middle of nowhere, near to a trickle of a stream that eventually flows into the river. They can make it in half an hour if they hurry.

Watson finishes speaking, and then looks up at Jake. 'You drive me. I want to get there as soon as I can. We're the closest, so let's go and check the lie of the land, and see if we can get her back. I can't drive myself, otherwise I'd go alone.'

'Don't be ridiculous. I want to be there too.'

He helps Watson on with his coat, a geriatric figure for an instant, before the energy of the impending discovery seems to relax his aching frame, speed his movements up. They jog to the car, Jake memorizing the route from the map. Watson's phone may not work as they get close to the target.

After five minutes, they both exhale, realizing they are too keyed-up for this long a journey. Jake is the first to voice the thought that has occurred to both of them.

'This feels too easy, doesn't it?'

Watson's face is set into a grim mask. Jake can see the white hairs on his unshaven cheek, lit by the morning sun that pours through the window.

'Maybe, maybe. But I promise you the last month has not been easy. It's been as hard as anything I've ever done. I don't know.' His breath whistles. 'Oh, you're right, of course you're bloody right: why now, why this way, and how have we won? I've got a horrible feeling about what we might find there.'

Jake is driving fast, or as fast as the old engine allows,

93

the car sliding on the icy road, but under control, a re-assuring roaring sound in their ears. They have moved from the more populated routes and are now deep in the countryside, the road so narrow as to be effectively one-way, and he fears another vehicle coming towards him at similar speed. They are lucky, nothing comes.

They reach a trampled verge of the road flat enough to take a car, and he shudders to a halt. He opens the window, bracing for the blast of chill air, and listens. No sound of vehicles, nothing in the air bar a bird singing quietly and mournfully. The scant wind flutters the remaining leaves of the hedgerow, puny and brown and lacking all life.

'This is, if the map's right, about half a mile from the cottage,' says Jake. 'How close shall we get in the car?'

Watson has clearly been thinking about that. 'There's three things possible here: one, this is genuine, and we have a terrified girl ten minutes away from being saved; two, this is a trap and we're going to blunder into something unmanageable; three, she's there but dead, and we have a murder scene.'

'Four, this is a hoax, and we're about to visit an empty house.'

'Then there's no point in worrying too much.' He calls his colleagues, their loud voices almost audible to Jake as they chatter back, full of contagious adrenaline. He hangs up. 'They're half an hour away. What do you think?'

Jake knows what they should do. He probably should not be here at all. He has a family just waking up an hour away, bare feet on the cold slabs of the kitchen floor, as they make pancakes for breakfast. He should be with them amid the happy clutter and productive noise. And in any case, they should wait for back-up, and take their time on something as serious as this. He shakes his head. 'We're here now. Let's just drive up and get her.'

Watson grins, tombstone teeth emerging. 'I had a feeling you might say that.'

Jake revs the engine, and they are on their way. He leaves the window open, his fingers tingling on the wheel. He goes a bit slower as they get closer, listening out for traffic. Nothing. He pulls into a lay-by, they get out, glancing uneasily at each other. They can see the roof of the cottage behind the hedge. Chimney smoke hovers, frozen into a column in the sky, scarcely moving. Still no other sounds.

There is a beaten-down path that breaks the hedge and leads right up to the building. From fifty yards away, the house looks uninhabited. No cars outside, no movement at the windows. Still no sound. And then Jake hears it. A faint keening noise, high-pitched; a sustained note in minor key. A steady, unbroken, unforgettable wail.

At once he runs down the path, a slight decline that speeds him forward, boots precarious but firm on frozen mud. Watson is two yards behind. Without a pause, Jake kicks the door, which flies open. The room within is dim, filled with old brown furniture, a flickering fire in the corner. And in front of it, sitting cross-legged, like a good child at school assembly, is a small girl. She is rocking, and making that noise he heard. She doesn't seem to notice his arrival at all.

He makes himself slow down and approach with care, and a soft voice. 'Don't worry. We're here to take you home. We're here to take you home. What's your name, lovey?'

She turns to look at him, her face puffy, eyes red with

tears, brown hair in a ponytail. 'I'm called Laura. What's your name?'

With a catch in his throat, Jake hoists her up and hugs her. She is light and trembling like a hedgerow leaf.

'I'm Jake. Don't worry. We're going to get you home to see Mum and Dad. You're safe. You're safe.' There is a pause, and then he feels her arms press against his shoulders, a clinch of recognition somehow that he is a figure of safety and reassurance. The eloquence of touch.

Watson is behind him, resting a hand on his back. Jake pivots slightly and sees him, tears running down his unshaven cheeks, the pulse of his throat showing the hammering of his heart. He is talking quietly, as if to himself.

Jake sets Laura down, realizing he has let his emotions get the better of him. 'Laura, who brought you here, and is anyone around?' The possibility of someone looming out of one of the unseen rooms with a weapon suddenly strikes him. He moves quietly, kicking open a door into a kitchen, looking up some silent stairs. Watson seems oblivious to any danger.

Laura's voice remains quiet, but her crying has stopped. She is stroking the thumb of her left hand with the forefinger of her right. She doesn't seem able to stop doing it; it is a compulsion, a quest for some comfort. 'They brought me here, but left. I heard them drive away. I was on my own.' She bursts into tears once more. 'They told me to sit here and not move. And I've not moved, I promise. I've done what I'm told.'

Jake hears Watson behind him, on the phone, marshalling the forces. Then he hangs up and presses another number. 'Kate? Can you hear me? Kate, I have someone who wants to hear your voice.'

Watson puts the phone to Laura's ear. Her confusion dissipates immediately, joy and relief flooding her face. 'Mummy? Mummy! Where are you? I missed you. Come see me!'

Jake is crying now too. He lifts Laura up and carries her to the car. He can hear the squeals coming through the speaker, as Kate and then her husband bellow their joy, their love, their disbelief. He can imagine how they are feeling: it is all a marvel, a miracle, an unhoped-for dream.

He opens the rear door and plops her down on the battered leather seat. One of Diana's discarded soft toys lies in the footwell. He reaches down and picks it up, a grey rabbit, dirty and discarded. Laura grabs it, hungrily, and starts stroking it with one hand, the other still holding the phone. Watson gets into the car beside her. He gently takes the phone, his quiet voice breaking through the hullabaloo at the end of the line. 'Kate, Kate, listen to me. Get yourself to the hospital. We have to take her there, but you can meet us.' Meanwhile, sirens shriek, and three cars emerge into the tiny lane. A blur of colour and combustion, a sense that the spell around the house has been broken, it is no longer a place of mystery and cruel confinement. Watson hangs up, winks at Laura, and gets out to meet them. Immediately, he starts directing officers to secure the building and search the area.

After a moment, he returns and gets in the back of the car. 'They can get going. I want to get her to her parents. Drive, as quick as you can.' He slaps the back of the seat, but Jake pauses before he starts the engine. His own heart rate has resumed its stable pattering, and he exhales thoughtfully. This was as good a scene as they could have hoped to find. The happiest of possible endings. The property was remote, he thinks, but seemed normal enough: no dank dungeons, no disconcerting neglect. Yet the sight of Laura before the fire had still startled and moved him, and he couldn't shake it. Her vulnerability lingers in his mind, that feel in his arms of something so fragile and breakable, as if he could count each of the slender bones in her body, their smallness and fragility.

She had been ripped from her home and family without explanation at a time in her life when fear and pain must otherwise have been complete strangers. She probably did not have the vocabulary, of word or thought, to understand and explain the peril she had been in. But she must have sensed it, that wordless, animal recognition of threat, the desperate anxiety of separation from her parents. Was that something you could come back from? Could you dismiss it as a momentary aberration, something shaken off as you do the lingering after-effects of a vivid dream? He hopes so. He looks in the mirror, and sees her face, impassive and pale. Time to take her home.

The journey passes in a blur, Laura quiet and distracted, Watson cautious of bombarding her with too many questions. And then he and Jake are both standing back in the windswept car park of a hospital, almost empty on a Saturday morning, but for the family embracing, and refusing to let each other go again.

Chapter Eighteen

Saturday, 11.45 a.m.

Later that morning, Jake is standing with Livia and Diana in the kitchen, trying not to cry again. Livia ushers Diana to the living room and her iPad, and returns to take Jake in her arms.

He gets control of himself. 'I'm sorry. What sort of copper breaks down like this?'

Livia strokes his beard gently. 'I seem to remember Peter Wimsey having a bit of a wobble.'

Jake laughs. 'I knew you'd love the Dorothy Sayers. In fairness, his wobble came from the experience of death and destruction during the First World War.'

'Yours comes from seeing one child saved, which reminds you of the children that went missing who you couldn't save. You've seen a lot, Jake. You need to acknowledge that. The bodies, the families, the ugliness. I'm not sure I'd love someone who bottled it all up, and drank it all into insignificance.'

'You prefer them to grow long hair and use it as an excuse to hide from the world.'

She pats his arm, strokes the hair there. 'As I think I said to you once before, my dear, I love the fact that you hide yourself away, except when you need to step up and do something. And even though we explicitly agreed that you would stay away from this one, I'm glad you didn't, and I'm glad it's over.'

'Is it, though?'

She pushes him with the heel of her hand, the tips of her fingers clinging on to his jumper. Her nails are faintly lilac and rough at the corners. Her voice hardens a fraction. 'Yes, it very much is. What else do you want to know?'

'I want to know why we were told we had won when we were nowhere near getting the girl. I want to know if there were some shadowy people involved in my old cases that I never picked up on. I want to know who this prison guard is. I want to know who else is involved. I can't just walk away.'

Her face is serious, green eyes cloudy. 'You came to this part of the country to walk away. And you promised me that you wouldn't do anything to endanger us. How could you think of sticking your nose into this?' She struggles to keep her voice calm, and glimpses Diana looking over her shoulder at them. Her next words are hissed, furious. 'We have a girl in that room who's already seen some things she never should have done. How dare you risk that because of pride, or curiosity?'

He reaches for her, but she flinches, as if struck. He feels hot, the back of his neck tingling. He breathes in. 'Liv, I was just thinking aloud. You're right. There's nothing more to be done, anyway. We've got the girl. I think they gave her back to make sure everyone loses interest, and maybe that's a deal worth taking.'

She nods, slightly mollified. But there remains a coolness, a deliberate sense of remoteness, like she is encasing herself in protective amber. Jake can feel it, and wants to break through it, but doesn't know what more to say. He rubs his hand along her arm, and realizes he is mirroring not only her, but the comforting gesture he had seen in Laura. Her fate was not something he could entirely forget or move on from.

Livia is staring at him, reading his uncertainty. 'Look, Jake, I know you, and how difficult some of this is. Just throw yourself into this weekend, and let's not think too much about anything else.'

He agrees with as much enthusiasm as he can feel, which is plenty.

'There's some real weather on the way, too, so we should try to get stuff done today if we can.' 'Real weather' to a country vet, Jake knows, is a serious business, so he helps to cajole Diana away from her screen. Bundled up, they head out for a walk to watch her ride, arm in arm, a nuclear family, still impregnable against the world.

And so the weekend passes happily enough. The snowstorm hits at five, the night already squat and heavy by that time, pregnant with wintry portent. It begins quietly, flakes meandering past the window, caught in the glare of the lamp outside. Gentle and reassuring. By six, it is a blizzard, whipped up by an arctic blast, a scene from a Victorian melodrama. They hunker down. Jake feeds the fire with logs he has cut, the irregular axe-marks a reminder of his labour. In the kitchen, Livia is preparing her famous Bolognese, and the meaty aromas mix with the woodsmoke for a scent redolent to him of home and happiness.

The next day, the countryside is a blank page. Four inches of snow have fallen, the most in more than a decade. Everything feels softened, cosseted, like the pillowy drifts had been tailor-made to obscure the hard edges of the world.

From the bedroom window, Jake can see the marks of animals and birds, refugees from the storm, up earlier than him to begin their weary labouring through the drifts. He can tell the tread of a fox, and imagines it slinking through the miserable grey of the dawn, thick tail dragging like a brush, in search of any creature not robust enough to survive the night. Or here, look, a heron, his heron surely, who must have stood stoically and aloof by the stream at the bottom of the garden as the cold winds blew. When he opens the window, he can hear the water flow at barely a trickle as the ice increases its inevitable grip.

A day of snowmen and snow angels, of ambitiously planned walks brought to a sudden and tearful conclusion. It is too cold for much more. Diana hopes to learn at any moment that school has been cancelled, but is disappointed. Further snow, promised gloomily by a weatherman on the radio, doesn't materialize, and the gritter makes its efficient way around the roads to keep them open. Jake decides to walk home while he can, just before dusk, so that the two can prepare for their working week.

His farewell clinch with Livia is as warm as ever, as if their dispute has been settled and put aside. He is not so sure. Thoughts of No Taboo warm Jake as he walks, feet crunching in the snow, collar pulled up, his eyes watering, his breath freezing at his lips. He decides to message Martha and Aletheia on his return, and visit Watson in the morning. Livia need never know.

Chapter Nineteen

Monday, 7.25 a.m.

The next day Jake is out of his house and on his way to telephone Watson from the Nook, when the Watsons' car, a red Audi estate, purrs up on the road just outside Parvum and stops. It is still quite early, the sky filled with the fire of sunrise, turning the river into a smouldering serpent behind them. The snow has frozen fast into place, and it makes the world seem even more still. In that bucolic environment, the car is an especial obscenity, a moving, spluttering intrusion, its exhaust fumes hanging in the chill air like an embarrassment.

Jake gets in with a raise of his eyebrows in mute greeting. Watson reverses and pulls into his old spot by the river, and quietens the engine. They are silent for a second, watching the nerveless progress of the water before them, steady and irreversible.

Watson is listening, as ever, to a classical musical station, and Jake recognizes the song, an aria from Puccini's opera

Gianni Schicchi, plangent and arresting, all attenuated strings and sorrowful thoughts. It is sung by a young girl called Lauretta, which feels appropriate. Before he can make any such observation, Watson turns and grabs his shoulder warmly.

'I've got an update for you, but first I wanted to thank you, young Jake.'

Jake demurs instantly. 'For what? I did almost nothing other than drive you to the cottage. Incidentally, I see your arm is a bit better.'

'My arm is good enough to drive this morning, and I couldn't bear being stuck at home. And listen, you being there got us to the girl quicker than we otherwise would've done. But there's also the fact that I came to you, you started asking questions, and a few days later, we get Laura.'

The timing had been nagging at Jake. 'Is there any evidence for that all being a factor, though, chief? All my investigations were very much *sub rosa*, unless you think Aletheia has been compromised, and I doubt that.'

'It's possible, isn't it? They had an eye on her before, after all.'

'In which case, don't we have to worry about her?'

'I can see from your face that you probably have been. I'm sure she knows the risk, and has been doing the right thing. The alternative is that they have come to notice your involvement through other means, perhaps by watching me, and are acting now to cut off any potential problem. I get the warning, then we get the girl, and the combination of the two means we lose interest.'

'And have we?'

Watson reclines his chair slightly. The soft voice on the

radio announces a piano piece by Sibelius, and the gentle notes murmur like the river in the background.

'That's the question, isn't it? We've learned just a little from Laura herself. She's been carefully examined, and I've spoken to her twice, very gentle, almost bland interviews, with Mum and Dad present. It will probably take weeks to get everything from her.'

'How much does she remember of what's happened to her?'

Watson's face screws up into a scowl, lines etched deep into his skin. He still hasn't shaved, and the white hairs give a ghostly aura to his flesh. 'Not that much. Which is probably itself suggestive. She can remember standing on the pavement outside her house, waiting for her mum to go back for her handbag. She remembers a van drawing up, or at least a very big car, and being pulled into it. She talked about the huge mouth at the back of it, which I think meant the open doors. Then falling asleep immediately. We think she may have been drugged.'

Jake breathes out. His stomach is lurching. 'What then?'

'It all gets very cloudy. She could have been kept on something to make her quiescent, or her brain could be refusing to acknowledge what happened. We know she has not been raped, thank God, and is physically in OK shape, a little malnourished, but nothing to worry about. She did mention a man with a camera, standing in red, polished boots. But that's about all.'

'I wonder how they picked her? Was it opportunistic, or were they watching her?'

'That, as ever, is an excellent question. My working theory is that they had a mobile operation, this van, with at least three people involved. One to drive, one to watch and one to do the grabbing. They could have patrolled the roads, day by day, until the chance came along.'

Jake had considered something similar. It wasn't very efficient, but it could have worked like that.

'Did you ever get reports of vans in the area, or on CCTV?'

'There's no real CCTV on their road. None of the people we spoke to mentioned a van at all.'

'And did her name connect to any of the other missing children cases?'

'Nothing. But we weren't really working on the basis that it was a serial job. There's still no evidence for it, apart from your conspiracy theory. That's one big line of inquiry for us now.'

'I take it the message you got on the phone led nowhere?'

'Nope. From a burner, could have been bought anywhere. I hate villains who are tech-savvy.'

'The fact of the message on a burner is indicative, though, isn't it? If it was a random snatch job, or a relative, it wouldn't have ended like this. There's a hint, an outline, of professionalism somewhere in this. I take it the house hasn't given up anything.'

'Only that it was empty, and just about habitable. A very good choice in some ways.'

Jake sighs. 'Maybe that implies local knowledge. Anyway, something to look at.'

The radio station has gone to adverts, and someone is jabbering about the value of life insurance for the over-sixties. Watson turns it down a little.

Jake looks across once more at him, searching his tired-looking face. 'So are you pursuing the case fully now?'

'We have to. A crime has been committed, a terrible

crime. And just because we got the girl back, it doesn't wipe the slate clean. She may never recover from what happened to her. And they may – they will, if you're right about No Taboo – do it again. No, the case is open. But the urgency is gone. My critical incident team is being reassigned, and it will be left to our normal resources to pursue. That's why I need my special assistant more than ever.'

Jake looks down at his legs. The threads at the frayed bottoms of his jeans have frozen stiff, and jut in different directions.

'I'm not sure I can. Livia has made it clear I shouldn't get involved, and she's right. When the girl was missing, there was a moral claim, I guess, against my retirement. Now that's gone.'

'What about all the children who might get grabbed in future, and might never come back?'

Jake smiles thinly. 'If I accept that argument, I could never have left the force in the first place. I can't shoulder that responsibility. Nobody can.'

'I can.'

Jake feels suddenly angry towards this kindly, insinuating man. 'Fine. You fucking keep on doing it. But don't patronize me as a friendly assistant, and don't pretend you understand who I am, or what my life should be. I helped, maybe it did something, maybe it didn't. But I'm not going to screw up my chance at a quiet life, just because the police in this county can't get things done on their own. You do your job properly, and you don't need me.'

Watson is silent. His jaw muscles clench, bulging beneath the stubble. Jake pushes the door open and levers himself out. The cold air slams into his face. He puts his head down and marches down the road towards the village, heedless of his destination.

In a few moments, the car crawls alongside him. Watson presses something and the window hums downwards. 'Jake, I'm sorry I pushed you. I'm not going anywhere on this. You can find me when you need to.'

Jake waves him away, sleet tearing up his eyes. The car drives off, loud reverberation in the empty lane. Nobody is around. Jake wonders where he is going, and looks up to see the looming spire of the church, a thick grey line getting lost in the white sky.

The path from the old wrought-iron gate is covered by the protective buttresses of the yew trees, so is clear and well-defined, a thin scuff of ice alone making the walk precarious. Away from it, the graves slumber under a woolly quilt, the tombstones all topped by swathes of snow, neat and tidy and as uniform as death.

Jake heaves open the wooden door, which is rippled and stained with age. It has weathered the years more painfully than the stones, but is there still, and sturdy. He is not religious, not remotely, but has always had some sort of affinity for churches. He likes their scale, their abounding emptiness, their contrasting manifestation of ambition and futility. He likes the fact that so many people must have thought the labour to create them, their persistent assault on gravity, was worth the while. He likes their quiet, too, their withdrawal from the swift and noisy passage of ordinary life.

Nobody is inside, and the temperature is scarcely higher than the winter scene beyond. His breath steams. He sits beneath the crucifix, the morning's dull light enriched by the stained glass all around him. He stuffs his hands inside his hooded top and thinks.

Part of him resents Livia's demands on him, of course, but another part accepts their good sense. If he wanted to be an active policeman, to assume the responsibilities of the role, to live in the wider world, he could have clung to that life, and all its attendant benefits and dangers. He could have stayed in the city. He didn't. He had rejected it. But at the moment he knows he is still somehow trying to face in two directions, and it is difficult, profitless. Livia is herself from that wider world as well, and is luring him into it in every other respect. A world of phone lines, and internet, and blipping devices, and parent-teacher evenings, and holidays abroad, and listening to the news on the radio. He had been relieved to abandon that some time ago.

Jake runs his hands through his hair, where tiny ice crystals have been forming. What price life with Livia? That was the question. Did he have to accept that it came with responsibility and noise and obligation? He stands, joints creaking, looks up at the altar. He wouldn't be the first person, he thinks, to have a crisis of faith within these thick and unforgiving walls.

Some sporadic, almost lethargic, snow falls as he makes his way home. He stops by the Nook to pick up some bread and cheese for lunch. Sarah is standing at her regular position in an impossibly thick maroon jumper that threatens to overwhelm her. She notes his purchases on his account, and then lets him know of a phone message.

'From a woman called Martha. Told you to take your phone with you like a normal person, and call her right away. A right madam, if you ask me. And I suppose you won't tell me who she is or what she's on about.'

Jake shakes his head. 'Better you don't know. I'm sorry she was rude. I'll call her and tell her off for you. But thanks for taking the message.' He holds his hands up. 'And before you say it, no I don't think you're my secretary.' She raises her eyebrows, and then her face splits into a friendly smile.

He leaves and hurries home to make the call. What could Martha have to say that was so urgent? There was no way he could not find out.

Chapter Twenty

On his way back, even though he is in a hurry, he stops at Chicken City to check on the birds. He has left them plenty of grain, old vegetables, and crushed-up eggshells, but is concerned about their health in this weather. They seem fine though, bright and lusty reds and greens against the snow and steely sky. They cluck and crow a welcome to him as he replenishes their straw and water, and fills their feeders once more. He can see from the markings in the snow that they have been stomping around vigorously in the daytime. Before last winter, he had carefully insulated their houses with old cladding, and built boxes within them, so they had a straw-stuffed place to bury themselves and huddle at night. That seems to be enough to stave off the worst of the season.

At home, he quickly makes things comfortable for himself. He lights the coals in the sauna for later, throws some wood in to stoke the kitchen stove. Then he puts the bread and cheese on a wooden board with some local butter and apples from his store. Wolfe Orchard had been productive this year, and he has more fruit than he can reasonably eat. One thing he has learned is that, kept in the cool and dark, apples do stay edible for a long time. They shrink and become wizened, but they hold their crisp sugary flavour. It's a pleasant economy, he thinks, and it heartens him to reckon that it has been practised around here for thousands of years.

He boils coffee too on the stove, before pouring it into a thick white ewer, and precariously takes his meal to the table in the library. The room has taken the chill of the day, so he lights the fire, blackening his hands on the old ash until he wipes them on his trousers.

His phone device is in the secret compartment, and he can see a series of missed calls from Martha on Signal. There is a message too from Aletheia, which he scans quickly.

Smits has been investigated before. There's a special flag on his file, which suggests someone in the forces has an eye on him. Could be because they are watching him, could be because they are protecting him. Call me on this number to talk.

Jake decides he'd better call Martha first, as her request to speak had been more urgent. She answers the Signal call almost immediately, her pale face peering into the camera.

'Ah, the wilderness man returns. I just wonder whether you might have bothered, after dragging me back into the dark world of criminal conspiracy, TO TAKE YOUR

PHONE WITH YOU FOR THE FUCKING WEEKEND.'

'I was with my girlfriend, and she is not entirely a supporter of my investigative work.'

'I'm a reluctant supporter of your investigative work at best, but I'm saying to you that if you want my help, you keep your phone with you. I don't care if you were romping in the snow in a picture-perfect Hallmark card. I'm doing you a favour here, remember.'

Jake considers telling her to stick it. He is, after all, no longer in the business of being shouted out for procedural inefficiency. But he wants to hear what she has to say too much for that.

'Fair enough, but I don't respond brilliantly to being shouted at by conspiratorial novelists either.'

'You'd be surprised how few people do. Now firstly, congratulations on getting the girl back.'

'How did you know that?'

'Because it's been on the news everywhere, wild man. You know, the national media. A sanitized version, but enough for me to work out what's been going on. They gave her up, eh?'

Jake nods. He has cut up a piece of apple and cheese and is chewing it softly. 'Why do you think they did that? Do they know we're looking at them?'

Martha is tapping away at her computer. 'I still have an eye on some fairly shady conversations in parts of the internet that most people don't know exist. And there was some activity three days ago. Lots of code words I don't fully understand, but clearly a message of concern.'

'How did they rumble our interest?'

'I doubt very much they know about my interest, and maybe not Aletheia's, but they've clearly been paying attention to Watson, and he's been talking to you. I've seen their behaviour before: little Laura was not important to them in the scheme of things, they won't be traceable through her because she's young and addled, so why not do something to call off the dogs? Your involvement would be a complication, and evidently it was one they didn't want to worry about.'

'Will they move on to other things?'

Martha is drinking something in what looks like a martini glass. She raises it in ironic salute. 'Deadens the pain. And yes, it's early, but I didn't go to bed last night so technically it's also very late. Will they move on? I guess the other way of looking at it is that they already will have done. They're a business, if they are what we think they are, a sort of mafia enterprise, offering services all the time, many of which aren't moral or legal. So this won't stop them. In fact, they've let this one go to ensure that nothing needs to stop them elsewhere.'

Jake sips his drink. 'So what do we do? Just walk away?'

'Nice metaphor to say to a woman with no legs.'

Jake flushes deeply and starts stammering, beads of coffee catching on his beard. 'God, I'm so sorry, I didn't think . . .'

'Don't be a moron, Jake, of course I'm joking. Worth it though to see your honest little puckered face. So, what can we do? I want to have a think about that bent prison officer.'

Jake explains the message from Aletheia. Martha nods. 'Let's see what she has to say. I'll see if I can join any dots with him, though she's the real genius at that, as you know. Your Watson will no doubt find out some more info from Laura if he treads carefully enough. We can take some time, see if anything clicks. Meanwhile you can face wifey with a clean conscience.'

'I'm not sure I like the term "wifey".'

'I'm sure I don't care. Now that we're firm friends you'll learn to put up with my language, and I'll promise to tolerate your insensitivity towards my amputations.'

'It's a deal.' He laughs, and so does she.

They agree to speak again when something happens, and hang up. Jake feels a little restless and dissatisfied. He tries calling Aletheia and gets nothing. He messages her, asking for a call whenever she can.

After pacing the room for a few minutes, he decides to get some exercise. He had missed his morning routine while at Livia's. It is now early afternoon, overcast and without wind, a world steady and saturated in grey. He puts on some old shorts and a T-shirt and then carefully wraps his hands in bandages. He shivers as he stands beneath the beech tree, then starts to move gently on the balls of his feet, circling his shoulders, throwing gentle, looping rights and lefts, slowly warming his body. He sets a timer for four minutes, and begins throwing shots against the bag, jabs and hooks, each punch thudding into the stillness.

He does eight four-minute rounds, with a minute's sit-ups between each. Soon the sweat is flowing, and his body steams in the icy air, an evanescent shroud around him. His skin is red with the exertion, his knuckles cracked and swollen, a trickle of blood running down to his wrist. He jogs to the lake. Naked, he feels the cold on every inch of his skin. His feet touch the water lapping at the edge of the pier, so icy it stings, and he has to exercise all of his determination to jump in. A fleeting second in the air of exultation and wild regret, then a plunge into darkness, his heart pounding, before he surfaces, dragging in the breaths like he is clinging on to life. He floats there, suspended in the chill, while he counts to a hundred, then clambers out for a headlong rush to the sauna.

There he is soon sweating again, his mind refreshed, running over the events of the last few days. He feels he can square a promise to Livia to stay out of any danger, for him and them, along with keeping in amicable touch with Watson, Martha and Aletheia. In another universe, in another life, he knows he would demand to be at the centre of uncovering this probable conspiracy, of rescuing the vulnerable, of chasing down the guilty. Instead he feels his own sense of guilt for not being that person, or being that person no longer. Life has always been a compromise, though, he thinks. He now has more freedom than most, but still has responsibilities and cares and obligations. He rubs moisture from his arms, flattening the hairs down. The sauna smells not unpleasantly of sweet pine, faint smoke, and old perspiration. The heat is intense. He feels it cleansing him. One more dip in the lake and back to the house, he decides.

When he is dry and clothed, he tries Aletheia again. Nothing. He worries a little, but doesn't feel he can do much for now. He picks up a book and tries to distract himself in front of the fire for a while.

Chapter Twenty-One

Monday, 4.25 p.m.

The sunset is spectacular, the thick clouds magically clearing as the day reaches its end. The scraps that remain billow upwards, pillow soft, now draped in pinks and purples and oranges. Intense colours, as if the sky is throbbing with energy.

Jake can't help but go out for a walk beneath it. There is probably only forty minutes of light left, but he wants it all to fall upon him. The lake shimmers beside him for a while, absorbing the pastel tones above, before he has marched clear to the edge of his land. From there he always looks at Sherlock Beech, his signalling tree, more from habit (and homage to his past) than anything else. He is meeting Livia on Wednesday, she is busy until then, so he is surprised to see a speck of pink fabric shimmering in the gloaming, like it has been torn from the edge of the sky itself.

He hastens his steps towards the village, wondering why

she might want to see him ahead of schedule. Lights blaze from out of the window of her cottage, and her car engine is still warm on the road outside. Jake knocks on the door.

Livia bundles him in, half grab, half hug. 'Jake, I'm so glad you saw that bit of cloth. God, I wish you had a normal phone.'

He realizes for the first time that she could use Aletheia's phone in an emergency. 'What's happened? Are you OK, is Di?'

She pulls him along to the table in the kitchen, past Diana, who is drawing happily on the table before the fire. She waves at him cheerily enough. Cyprian the cat is prostrate in front of her, half twisted on her back, a doughy knot. She does not deign to acknowledge his presence.

Livia closes the kitchen door behind them, and points to a note on the table. It is written in elegant handwriting, in a fountain pen. 'This was in Di's school bag when she came home from school. She never even saw it, so has no idea when it was put in there.'

Jake picks it up. It feels expensive, the texture almost like card. It reads:

Tell your nosy friend Jake now to be careful.
For everyone's sake.

He puts it down and strokes Livia's back tentatively. 'On the one hand, it could be anything. On the other, it feels like something to worry about, doesn't it?'

There are tears in Livia's eyes. 'How can you be so . . . so calm? Someone got this close to Diana in school. How can this be happening to us?'

She does not push him away when he hugs her, but he

can feel the tension trapped within her. He wants to say that everything will be fine, life will continue as normal, the assertion of daily routine a source of solace, of re-assurance. He isn't sure he is able to guarantee that.

'My best guess is that this is the same impulse that got Laura back,' he says. 'They're just making any follow-up to their activities even less likely. They're telling me I have no place to be involved in it.'

Livia's voice is a whisper. 'They're right, you know. And who are they anyway?'

'That's the question they don't want answered. But I don't think we're very near answering it.' He gives an abbreviated version of his conversation with Martha, and Livia nods absently. Then she stares at him, cat's eyes gleaming threateningly. 'So, is this it? No more amateur investigation?'

He nods, and grips her elbows tight. The fabric of her jumper is soft and bunches between his fingers. 'I won't do anything further. I just need to get through to Aletheia somehow and tell her. I've dragged her into this as well.'

'That's good. Do you want to stay the night? I think I'd like the comfort of it. Not that I need a big hairy man to protect me, before you say anything.'

'Perish the thought. One thing has come from this at least. I have that phone thing, that Aletheia sent me. Why don't you use it when you need to?'

'Maybe only in the direst emergency. I don't know why I didn't think of it before. Though, and I can't believe I'm saying this, I think I prefer a world in which tying some old knickers to a tree is my preferred way of getting in touch with my boyfriend. It's somehow more innocent.'

'It worked pretty well tonight.'

Jake opens the kitchen door so they can keep an eye on Diana, and starts helping with dinner: homemade butternut squash soup, and bread baked with bits of bacon and rosemary in it. The smell is delicious, homely and comforting, sweetness mingling with savoury.

That night, Jake doesn't think Livia will want to make love, will instead be tense and watchful and preoccupied. But she approaches him as they go to bed with an urgency, an aggression, pushing him down on to the thick coverlet, grabbing at his neck with her mouth. Afterwards they lie back, panting, hearts throbbing in the dark, the spectre of danger both a palpable fear and perhaps some sort of excitement too.

Chapter Twenty-Two

Tuesday, 9.15 a.m.

The next day, Jake borrows Livia's car. He stops off at Rose's house, which is a big old converted barn, far too plush for someone without an obvious source of income. He is outside, polishing one of his ostentatious acquisitions, an old crimson Porsche convertible.

Jake walks up to him warmly. 'Sorry for interrupting your mid-life crisis there.'

'I'd flinch from the criticism, except it comes from a hippy who left his job as he was approaching his forties, and is now shacked up with the local beauty.'

'Not quite "shacked up", but you're right. And that's what I wanted to talk to you about.' He explains the threat that came through Diana, and gives a rough outline about what happened with Laura.

Rose nods calmly. 'I understand. You want me to keep an eye on her a bit. I can do that, for you and for her. She's too nice to have something terrible happen to her.'

'So is Diana.'

'I agree, though she'll have plenty of supervision at school, more than I could give her, and then you guys will be with her. Let me make sure on my travels I stumble across Liv more than could be coincidence. I'll maintain a weather eye for you, Jakey boy, don't worry.'

Jake tells him about Livia's proposed day working at Martinson's stables, and Rose notes the time she is supposed to be there before Jake himself arrives.

'Do you really think she is in danger?'

'Not necessarily from him, but I can't be sure. I just want to protect her.' He sighs. 'But I also have to assume that the threat will go away, right? Otherwise, why make it? Now, did you hear anything about No Taboo on these travels of yours?'

Rose stops rubbing the car and looks up at Jake. 'Not much, not much. I sell weed to an old rock star who lives maybe an hour away. I won't say who, because discretion is my thing, as you know. But I asked him straight about whether he'd ever heard of it. And he started spluttering and panicking. He's not a panicky guy, let me tell you. When he calmed down, he told me that it was a service that he knew about back in the nineties, but which he kept away from now, and that it would be better for my health if I didn't ask him any more questions about it.'

'Was he threatening you?'

'Not exactly. He was sort of convincing me of his own fear, I think. I got the sense he was worried about talking.'

'That sounds like our friends. Well, I'm not going to fight a war against them, so I reckon you should listen to your old rocker. Don't run any risks nosing about on my behalf.'

Rose drops the rag into the bucket, sploshing the soapy water over the ground. Jake moves his feet away automatically.

'Are you really going to walk away?' Rose asks.

'I might speak to one or two more people, but yes. I have to be realistic. I'm an ex-copper, hiding from the world, friend of a small-time cannabis dealer, living a quiet rural life with a beautiful vet. I don't think I'm much of a threat to a criminal conspiracy.'

He bids Rose farewell, and returns the car to Livia's house. They share a coffee and a ginger cake, pleasantly preoccupied with domestic matters, before she goes out on her rounds, and he walks home. Her trip to the stables is two days away, and he will have to be on hand to wait for Diana's return from school.

He gets back in time to do some work on the treehouse, completing the final sections in the workshop, happily concentrating in front of the stove that hums and crackles. Not entirely happy, perhaps, as he has the phone with him, and Aletheia is still not replying to his messages. He wonders if anything has happened to her, but can't think of an easy way of finding out.

He spends the afternoon in the greenhouses on Velda field. They were last year's project: two big, sturdy structures, taken together almost a third of the size of his own house. Inside each were three long beds of well-mulched soil, raised up on old wooden sidings, with small heaters embedded to keep the soil from freezing. On a day like today, when the sun manages to send the clouds scurrying to nothing, and the pale light of winter falls everywhere, it is surprisingly warm inside, and pleasantly so.

Most of the growing space is taken up with edible

plants, but he is also trying to grow flowers too, something of colour and frivolity without practical use. There is a bank of slipperwort in one corner, sprays of yellow globes bright against the green of the leaf, and different pansies in a riot of blues and mauves and reds, their petals frail and blotched with dark spots. There are early tulips and a flower called the poor man's orchid, which looks like a flock of butterflies taking sudden wing. Diana helped him choose from a seed book, and the bursts of colour have all the energy of a childish scrawl.

Jake weeds here assiduously, then moves across to pick some of the other produce that has burst into life all around him. He pulls several potatoes from the thick loamy soil, which clings to them, darkening their pale skin. Alongside them he adds beetroots, so deep a purple as almost to be black, onions, their brown outside mottled and cracking, and carrots, all knobbly and muckily misshapen, green tendrils contrasting against muted orange. He plucks mint by the handful, alongside some thyme and coriander.

A savoury smell fills the area. He stretches out on the grassy floor. It is like a gentle steam room, warming and consoling. He wonders if he can let No Taboo go. He knows he should, not least because he is unsure of his ability to fight against something so shadowy and unseen. Once he knows Aletheia is OK, he feels he will have to let the matter lapse, stay close to his new family, and try to navigate that precarious bridge between the real world and the seclusion he has come to rely upon.

That night, he eats a stew made from the greenhouse vegetables, with a flatbread he makes, roughly hewed and shaped with the heel of his hand. He still values these moments of hearty peace, perhaps more than ever.

Chapter Twenty-Three

Thursday, 4.20 p.m.

Diana knocks on the door of her mum's cottage, and pushes it open without waiting for an answer. Jake has been there for an hour, anxiously making sure he has prepared enough for the arrival of an eight-year-old. He has made cupcakes – a ridiculous thing to do, he thinks – which are cooling on a rack in the kitchen, familial scents of vanilla and butter. He has charged Diana's iPad and made sure the internet is working properly. And he has prepared the living-room table, a large, wonky, mahogany affair that has survived all the world's drips and scalds and scuffs for at least a century. Diana likes painting, and so he has readied the brushes and the paints and the paper.

He wonders why he has taken so much trouble, but knows the answer. He needs this domesticity to work. He is desperate for its success. He also wants Diana to like him and his new, intrusive role in her life. Children to him have been a lifelong unknown quantity. He has no siblings, no nieces and nephews to gently introduce him to the joys and perils of childcare. He and Faye desired to have children with such burning passion, such remorselessness, and then charted their absence with a sense of such pain, that they lost sight for a while of what they were actually seeking. It became an obsession that was all but all-consuming, an end in itself that did not arrive. And then they never experienced the incidental joys, the happy messiness of family itself.

He doesn't want to blow this moment, nor does he want – fat chance – to overload it with unnecessary emotional freight. Diana is oblivious to all of this, of course. She hugs his legs, and then ducks behind him to grab a cake, catching it between her hands as it cools. Jake eats one himself to be companionable. They talk, in casual fashion, about school and friends and what she might be having for dinner. She then beams, a smile of perfectly formed, small white teeth that fits perfectly in the middle of her face, and settles down to painting.

It is as easy as that. And why should it not be? Jake shunts an armchair across the room with his legs and curls up on it. He has left so many books in this house over the last year, and finds an Agatha Christie, a country house mystery where he can't quite remember who the murderer was, and reads happily. After a few moments, he gets up to grab another cake for both of them.

Their silence is companionable, punctuated by the occasional slurp of food or drink, and the happy noise of Diana gently crooning to herself as she works. The heavy ponderous sound of the clock ticking. Jake has his own bag packed for his stay at Purple Prose, an assortment of his best clothes, which did not amount to very much. There was a jacket of sorts, thick and scuffed and velvety, his least damaged and darned T-shirts, a cardigan, some dark jeans, some boat shoes and his cleanest boots.

He taps Diana on the shoulder as she is carefully cleaning her brush in a beaker of tap water. 'Time to get ready to go to Joanna's, lovey. I'm off to meet your mum at work. We're going to miss you.'

Diana has been through all the emotions of being excluded from an exciting holiday, and is now instead clearly fizzing with excitement, intoxicated by the prospect of another break in routine, of a rare sleepover with friends. Jake gets her to grab her carefully packed bag, while he tries to deal with the mundane details of locking up the house. She soon returns with a magenta Disney backpack, from which her favourite toy hippo, once luridly pink, now a washed-out lilac, is sticking jauntily. 'I've brought Hippy, obviously, and three books, though I don't know how much reading goes on there.' She is still in her school uniform.

They get in the car. Jake lets her in the front, where she snuggles down proudly before carefully locking her seat belt into place. She looks up at him. Her eyes are green like her mum's, but paler, and wider.

'Jake, I liked hanging out tonight. Thank you for looking after me.'

He feels a lurch in his stomach. He has enjoyed the sheer normality of it too, the functional, frictionless pleasure in feeling for a moment just like a father. He revs the engine, the headlights flicker on and they drive off into the snowy dusk.

Joanna's home is a beacon of light. It is an old Quaker

coffeehouse on the edge of a village. Clearly, nearby residents had objected to its abstemiousness at some point in the last century, or at least failed to take advantage of it, and it had become a family home, all big ceilings and draughty rooms. When they approach the door, they both can hear the uproar of early evening family life. A television blares, a toilet lustily flushes, two children demand to know where a hotly desired game has been left.

Joanna bustles up to the door, wiping floury hands. She is small, compact, heading towards comfortable middle age. Her face is wreathed in smiles when she sees them.

'Di! Jakey! What a pleasure to see you, especially you, little missy.' She fondly grabs Diana's cheek. 'Come in and join the chaos. Nelly and Teddy are around, making a mess. Di, go and say hello.' Nelly is in Diana's year, Teddy the year below, and they are all firm friends. Diana shows no self-consciousness, carefully deposits her bag, coat and boots on the stand by the door and enthusiastically scrambles up the stairs.

Joanna looks more carefully at Jake. 'Come in and shake the cold off, and have a drink before you go off on your little jaunt.'

She walks him into the kitchen, where a pot of stew is bubbling on top of a large black range, scents of meat and tomato. The table is scattered with flour, and there's also a bulging hunk of bread dough and a giant rolling pin.

'I'm making bread, and wish I'd never started the bloody thing. Here, let me get you a drink before I get my hands dirty again.' She has a saucepan of cider mulling on the stove, warming hints of apple and spices. She hands him a pewter tankard filled almost to the brim. 'You'll not

128

mind if I finish the baking off while we talk. Or my kids won't get dinner and then they get really unbearable.'

Jake takes a cautious sip, then a deep swallow, feeling the liquid warm him through. 'It's very nice of you to let Diana stay. We don't do this sort of thing very often.'

Joanna is picking flecks of dough out of the webbing of her fingers. Her face is reddened by the heat emerging from the stove. A radio murmurs soothingly in the corner, some news that Jake has no interest in catching.

'I'm sure, knowing you, this one trip is more often than you'd like, you old hermit. No, I'm glad you're supporting Liv. It almost makes you seem for a second like a normal couple, though you'll no doubt drag her off to your isolated lair again as soon as you can. And it's nice for Di to be around the kids too, hooligans though they are.' She pauses, head cocked like a spaniel, and is rewarded by the thumping of floorboards as children race headlong between rooms. Squeals of triumph and despair.

She grins once more. 'What's this place again she's gone to? Purple Prose, is it called? What a terrible name.'

Jake explains what he knows about Sam Martinson and his demands on Livia's time. He doesn't get much chance to finish his thoughts.

'Sam fucking Martinson? Dear me, what an appalling shit of a man. Ran our place into the ground. Not that we ever saw him. He just thought we were the monkeys to churn out rubbish which might fill the gaps between the ads. That was when newspapers made money from ads, of course. I haven't thought about him for years. I hope one of his horses kicks him in the knackers.'

Jake laughs. 'Apart from his refusal to respect journalism, anything else I should know?'

129

Joanna has been rhythmically slamming the dough on the table as she talks, knocking it into shape with vengeful pokes and pulls.

'Oh, there's always rumours about men like him. Hands on young girls' bottoms, exploitative housing deals, too close to government ministers. He owned some dodgy porn magazines at one point, I seem to remember. Every few years a rival newspaper group would turn him over, or some MP would go public with concerns about him ruining, you know, public discourse. All way above my head. Not someone I felt proud to work for. But, as we've discussed before, pride is not the lot of hacks like me.'

The dough has been transformed into a series of small loaves, expertly rolled and prinked, Joanna's pincer-like fingers having performed a strange and miraculous enchantment.

'Do you think I should be worried about Liv?'

'There are several thousand people whose houses I'd rather she be at. But I doubt he's much more than a powerful man who makes people do lots of dirty work for him. That's not a story, as we say in the business.'

Jake wants to agree with this. 'We'll come and get Diana at some point on Sunday morning, probably after breakfast. If that's OK with you.' He pauses. 'And if, for any reason, there's a problem, you can always mention it to Rose or Watson.' Joanna had known Rose for a while, and had interviewed Watson after the excitement of two summers ago.

She frowns, and smears flour across her forehead, white stripe merging into her greying temples. 'Why would there be a problem? Are you involved in something?'

130

'Not exactly involved. But some of my old cases have come back to life, and I want to be very cautious if I can.'

'If they turn into a story, you know where to come. I could do with another bit of journalistic exposure.'

'You're the first conscience-free hack I'll ever think of, I promise.'

'God bless you for that, Jakey.'

He stays for a while to see Diana settled and having dinner with her friends. Joanna's husband works nights and will not be around until the morning, but there is a real sense of family at the table. After half an hour of loud and charitable hospitality, he drives back to Livia's house.

There he moves quickly and efficiently, keen to see Livia again. He spends a moment refilling Cyprian's food and water bowls, enough to last a couple of days. She is a largely self-sufficient creature, like all cats, contained and regal, just aloof enough to make you question the extent of her regard for you. Jo and Diana could drop by and replenish her supplies on Saturday. Then he takes the phone and thrusts it deep in his pocket, puts on a black hooded top that stretches over his broad shoulders, grabs a roadmap and a bottle of water and heads back out onto the roads once more.

Chapter Twenty-Four

Thursday, 7.50 p.m.

It is not an easy house to find, despite its size. A freezing fog has descended, and Jake's headlights seem to illuminate mere absence. Thick wisps shift across the road, moving sedately in the frosty air. He opens the window and feels them oozing in, like half-frozen liquid, clinging to all they touch. He drives slowly and cautiously, relieved that few people would venture out in this perilous weather.

The entrance to the property is so discreet he misses it the first time. Just a modest wooden plaque saying 'Purple Prose', unilluminated, and a narrow turning. He takes it, and after some tortuous twists the lane ducks behind high hedging and then suddenly broadens into a long straight avenue lined with elm trees, their branches stripped entirely of leaves, weighted thickly with piled snow. They look like angry, starving sentinels in the yellowing beams of Jake's headlights, brooding and ancient and huge.

They are soon dwarfed by the house itself, to which

they lead in funereal procession. It presents a giant rectangular front, with windows in precise rows, perhaps twenty or thirty in total, as if in a child's drawing. To one side, the order and symmetry wavers into an old tower of different colour brick, darker and gloomier, which twists into the sky. Everything is lit from below, a strange blue-green light, which makes the walls loom, as if underwater.

Gravel crunches beneath the wheels as Jake gets closer. He wonders where to park in a place like this. He stops as the drive becomes a large circle, surrounding a huge ornamental fountain, which is also uplit. The water has frozen into place, stiff shards of cloudy glass, like something trapped in time. The naked statues grimace and gurn as if waiting for their bath to warm up.

He switches the engine off and opens the door. The cold hits him, stinging his face like a slap.

As he walks to the front of the house, the door framed by white pillars, it opens and Josiah emerges in stately fashion. He looks like he is expecting Jake.

'Detective Jackson. I'm relieved this inclement weather didn't cause you any difficulties. Do let me have your keys, I'll make sure the car is put away safely.'

Jake hands them over. 'It was fine so long as I took it slow. And it's not detective any more, as you know.'

'It is an honorific, like a military title, which I feel is suitable still. But we will not argue. Come this way. Ms Livia is awaiting you.'

Jake follows into the atrium, which is immediately at least twenty degrees warmer. A fire, a medieval caricature of a roaring blaze, dominates one wall, huge logs jovially crackling, and two twisting staircases wend their way towards an unseen floor. Josiah leads Jake to a small door to one side, which opens into a wooden-panelled corridor. At the end is another door, wearing its considerable age defiantly, thick and oaken. Josiah knocks deferentially and opens without waiting for a response. Jake follows him in, delighted to see Livia, who looks beautiful and flushed, her skin glowing as if newly minted, though her eyes seem mildly perturbed. She is standing next to a squat, powerful man who advances confidently, arms open wide.

'Detective Jackson, thank you so much for joining us. Though if I was asked to accompany Livia here, or anywhere for that matter, you'd be able to see the scorch marks from a low-flying plane.' His laughter barks. He is in his late fifties or perhaps early sixties, hair metal grey, expensively trimmed, no sign of stubble on his face. He has the body of a former athlete, now thickened at the middle, but with the vestiges of a mighty past still visible. His eyes are pale and set fractionally too close together, making his face seem too symmetrical; there is arrogance and calculation in his gaze.

Jake takes the proffered hand, prepared for the inevitable macho crush. It duly comes. 'Nice to meet you. And your name is?'

Another bark. 'I'm not exactly used to introducing myself. But you are the wild man of the woods, aren't you? Sam Martinson, in the flesh. Soon to be Lord Martinson of Wallingford, if my spies are right. And they are. Pleased to meet you.'

Jake turns to Livia. 'How are you doing, lovey? Is everything OK?'

She reaches out and squeezes his hand. Her touch is warm and firm. 'It's lovely to see you,' she says.

Martinson escorts them to chairs arranged in front of

his desk, and sags down onto his own large and ornate seat behind it. On the desk there is a green baize blotter, trimmed with black leather, a few sheets of paper piled orderly on top. Josiah stands silently, butlerish, in the corner.

'I'm not going to ask if you mind if I smoke because this is, after all, my house, isn't it? I hope you don't mind, at least.' Jake shakes his head slightly. Martinson reaches into a drawer and pulls out a thick cigar. He bites the end off, lights it with a taper from the fire, then inhales expansively.

As he speaks, smoke seeps from his mouth. 'So then, welcome to my humble home. I'm joking of course. I do realize how grand and beautiful it is. When you come to know me a bit better, Jake, you'll realize how much I admire boldness and big gestures.'

Jake leans back into his chair. The fire flickers in the corner of his eye. 'I guess you won't be the first tycoon to think like that. I think I probably have more modest tastes, to match my more modest means.'

Martinson winks. 'I don't know. From what I can gather, your place is pretty impressive. A big old patch of land with a beautiful home in the middle next to your own private lake. Maybe you're more of a tycoon than you think.' He chuckles, his hand drumming against the hard barrel of his stomach, which stretches the material of his shirt as he leans forward.

Jake raises a questioning eyebrow and is about to speak before Martinson continues. 'Oh, I know a little bit about you, Detective Jackson. I always make sure I have a dossier prepared about all my guests. Knowledge is power, I've always felt. And it's so much better if people know exactly

135

who they're dealing with from the beginning. Saves awkward questions later. No, your police career, your retirement, the legacy of your sadly departed uncle, and your recent heroics in catching that terrible rapist. All known to me. Saves on the need for small talk too.'

'You don't strike me as someone who prefers contemplative silence.'

Another chuckle. And his hand slaps down hard against his stomach, sharp as a pistol shot. 'How well we know each other already. Now, the house rules. No phones.' He raises his hands in mock surrender, his cigar smouldering between the heavy gold rings on two of his fingers. 'Not a problem for you, detective. I know you're free from the taints of modern technology, so I won't need to deprive you of anything. It's a little whim of mine – and you know what is odd or even insulting in a poor man becomes an excusable eccentricity in a billionaire like me, vulgar though it is to admit it. I like my guests to be present and undistracted when they are enjoying my hospitality. I've told Livia she can use my landline any time she wants to speak to her daughter, but otherwise to enjoy being disconnected for a while. A rare pleasure I don't need to lecture you about.'

Livia is stroking Jake's wrist gently. 'That's a rule we can live with,' she says, 'but are there any more?'

'Just that I would welcome your presence at mealtimes, and I may have a few games or distractions planned that I would love you to indulge me with. But first, tonight meet your fellow guests, and tomorrow explore the place. We can get to entertainments later. Now.' He looks at the Rolex on his wrist, chunky gold against a twisting nest of thick hair. 'Why not go to your room to refresh yourselves, and then join us for a late buffet supper? Josiah.' He clicks his fingers, imperious as a matador, his gesture – as everything else in this interview – ironically ebullient, as if he were both keen to impose his authority upon Jake while being able to satirize the exercise at the same time.

Josiah eases forward, as if on oiled rails. 'Do accompany me to your bedroom. And then supper will be served at half past nine.'

They stand and follow Josiah to a large door set into the rear wall. Martinson remains seated as they pass him. He doesn't move his head, but speaks, his voice unusually soft. 'I hope this will be a nice rest for you, detective, after your adventures chasing lost children. How lucky that you were able to find little Laura. It's such big, wild, sprawling countryside out here, isn't it? Hard to imagine that you could ever find anyone who didn't want to be found.' He looks up suddenly and meets Jake's eyes, his expression dark and fierce and challenging.

Chapter Twenty-Five

Thursday, 8.45 p.m.

Josiah has silently opened the door, and waits for them in the corridor outside. Jake feels that the heat of the place is wilting him slightly. He looks at Livia, who smiles and exhales. There is a thin sheen of perspiration on her brow, her fringe damp. Together they are taken up a flight of stairs, down a corridor – the panelling duck-egg blue, giant brass-framed pictures on the wall, of hunting pursuits and tetchy aristocrats – and through double doors into a giant room. A four-poster bed dominates its centre. Josiah raises an eyebrow by way of farewell and sweepingly departs. Their eyes lock for a moment, before they collapse happily into each other's arms.

Jake speaks softly in Livia's ear. 'How's your day been?'

She puts her arm on his chest for leverage and sits up slightly. 'The work was good. Lovely horses, who probably won't need me that much, but I gave them all proper physicals anyway. The atmosphere in this house is definitely a bit weird, though. You know what old Josiah is like, and hardly anybody else has spoken to me. Martinson came down to the stables after lunch, and clearly is very fond of his animals. He took one out, a big black thunderer of a horse, and he absolutely knows his stuff as a rider.'

'Did he make a pass at you?'

She snuggles in deeper. 'Only you find me irresistible, I think.' She reaches around and moves his hand to her bottom. 'You can't help yourself.'

He smiles and they kiss lingeringly until he makes himself get up and look around the room before things go too far. The décor is poised somewhere between shabby and splendid. The wood of the bed is ornately carved, tendrils of plants and petals of flowers etched into the surface, and the furniture – the giant wardrobe, the mahogany writing desk, a bureau with a beautifully shaped vanity mirror – is solid and antique. But there are signs of neglect: a bulge in the pastel-striped wallpaper, the tapestry at the top of the bed mouldering around the edges. A quiet fire slumbers, lost in a huge fireplace, throwing out insufficient heat to warm the whole room. Five sets of candles flicker mournfully.

A giant window looms at the far end, with thick heavy curtains partially drawn. Outside is a wall of blackness. A door is set into the wall on the right, leading into a bathroom. Jake takes Livia by the hand and escorts her in. It is full of creams and whites, marbled flooring, a giant tub with outsize taps. Jake leads Livia to a bench by the bath, whispers in her ear. A stray hair tickles his nose, scents of familiar fruit.

'This looks big enough for both of us.'

'Do we have time?'

He sighs. 'Probably not.'

They move back into the bedroom, and he notices a file on the table. It is labelled *Part One: Orientation*. There is a note from Martinson on top of it, his handwriting bold and jaunty: *I told you – always good to have a dossier to get you started. Meet your fellow guests.*

'That's a novel approach,' says Jake. 'What do you make of Martinson really?'

Livia is sitting on the bed, bouncing it slightly. 'I wouldn't go out for dinner with him if I had the choice, I guess, but he seems nice enough. And this looks like it might be a fun break for us. We've never been on holiday together. Perhaps because your whole life is a holiday.' Jake winces at the self-evident truth. 'So come and give me a hug at the very least, even if we don't have time for anything more.'

They lean back against the headboard together, content for the while, wrapped in an old embroidered blanket while they read the miniature pen portraits of their fellow guests.

Sam and Adele Martinson [*Sam is grinning wolfishly into the camera, his hand proprietorially on the shoulder of a skinny, blonde woman in a figure-hugging red dress. She has a large ruby necklace, and chunky jewellery on her hands. She is pale, around forty, her expression empty and conscienceless.*]

Your hosts. Sam is the owner of Purple Prose, formerly Bredon Hall, a sixteenth-century country house, set in a thousand acres of rolling fields and forests. He came 14th in the *Sunday Times* Rich List last year, with diversified business interests ranging from Saudi oil and gas to American supermarkets to – most recently – Chinese mining. He sold his major publishing house a decade ago, pocketing a colossal profit. Widely tipped to be ennobled in the New Year's Honours.

Sam and Adele have been married for fifteen years. She is his second wife. They met at work, when she was a PA in the office of one of his editors. She is a passionate horse rider and champion show jumper, as well as running a burgeoning property empire. She also collects figurines.

Jason and Rebecca Lamb *[A couple about the same age as Jake and Livia. They are both clearly affluent, in smart clothes, with deftly manicured hair and clothes. He has a tan that comes from regular holidays, supplemented by the occasional sunbed, and clearly takes his image very seriously. He is in good shape, though carefully sucking in his stomach for the photograph. Rebecca is mixed heritage, part of her family from somewhere in Eastern Asia, beautiful and steely-looking. She is an inch taller than her husband, which – from his stance – looks like something he minds.]*

This couple have it all. Wealth and success in the city, looks, and a happy marriage. They met a decade ago in the trading arm of Goldman Sachs, and competed to see who could take the other on a more expensive date. Rebecca won with a private jet ride to Rome. Semi-retired, they spend some of the time managing their stock and property portfolio, the rest looking for excitement and novelty around the world, whether it be running with the bulls in Pamplona, or big-game shooting in West Africa.

Jim Daisley [*Late fifties, balding, heavy-set, but immaculately dressed in an expensive suit designed to obscure as many physical blemishes as possible. The picture has been taken for a high-end magazine shoot. He is sitting at a poker table, cards thrown in the air, frozen in time, their sides as sharp as razors. His face is smiling, but there is a contemptuous twist to his lips he cannot conceal.*]

Jim is a legendary figure in the world of private banking. He is said to have advised everybody from German royals to the Pope himself. He was brought in as a special consultant to the government in the last financial crash, but his innovative ideas were ignored, and he resigned on a point of principle. His wife of thirty years, Paula, died in a car crash four years ago. He is fifty-eight and looking for a new challenge, if ever he can find one.

Fenella Jewell [*Mid-forties, pin-striped pantsuit, brown hair cropped short in a stylish bob. Ironically boyish-looking. Her hands are clasped on her hips, legs taut and wide in a powerful stance. Her eyes interrogate the camera, bold and insinuating. She has a single emerald ring on one finger.*]

Fenella inherited much of her money from her family. Her father was an American oil baron, her mother the granddaughter of the Earl of Dartmouth. From rich beginnings, she became richer, investing in land and the leisure industries. She was often photographed in the early years of the century, attending parties always dazzlingly and daringly dressed, accompanied by beautiful young men or women. She spends much of her time in California, but still keeps a large Mayfair house for the spring season.

Henry Franklin [*This picture is not posed. It is taken secretly, but with good quality equipment. A man is emerging from the front door of an Edwardian townhouse. He is tall and strongly built, broad shoulders and visible biceps in a tight, white T-shirt. It is early morning in summer, the light gentle, and his face is puffy from a lack of sleep. His hair is thinning slightly, but he still looks handsome.*]

A former university rower, Franklin is a solicitor with a prominent London firm. Now in his early thirties, he is married with two children. He has provided legal advice for a variety of projects connected to Mr Martinson's companies over the last five years, having been earmarked as a talent soon after he joined his firm. He is staying at the house all week, as an extended job interview for the role of legal adviser to part of the Martinson empire.

Charlotte Sampson [*A promotional image of some sort, either for a pop singer or something less salubrious. Charlotte is pouting at the camera, thick lips glinting, her hands clasped in front of her in apparent submission. Her clothes are not cheap, though, a black dress, slit all the way to the top of the thigh, nipples stiff against the fabric. There is intelligence in her eyes, and something that looks like controlled despair. She is tall, with copper hair.*]

143

Charlotte speaks three languages, and has travelled the world over the last five years, working as a hostess in hotels owned by a company connected to the Martinson conglomerate. She has regularly attended parties at the house, where she has always entered into the spirit of entertainment here. She is currently single, and saving to start her own entertainment brand.

Dr Hamed Doshi [*A distinguished looking man in late middle age, probably of Pakistani or Indian origin, hair thick black, speckled with dark grey. The image is taken from a website, presumably of his own private practice. He is sitting, with studied informality, on a desk, hands straight by his sides, pink shirt open just one button. A hint of coiled chest hair is visible. His clothes are expensive, his teeth suspiciously white.*]

Dr Hamed owns one of the largest chains of private health clinics in the subcontinent, as well as two popular practices in London's Harley Street. His background is in surgery, but he has also been careful to preserve his general medicine credentials. He has been the Martinson family physician for five years and is a regular guest at Purple Prose. He is twice divorced, and still, he likes to believe, rather eligible to the right woman.

Jake throws the file to the floor. 'That's a motley gathering you've brought me to. Is there any reason behind it? There's plenty of money in the group, I suppose. I wonder if any of them are much fun to hang out with.

Somehow I doubt it.' He looks at the clock in the corner. 'Come on, we better get changed.'

Livia has shrugged off her top and trousers and is lying, long-limbed and elegant, critically appraising the shape of her thigh, fingers pressed against a semicircular birthmark, as she regards him with cynical affection. 'Don't be a grump too quickly. I guess we can see them for supper now, and then keep our distance apart from mealtimes. We can still have a chance to relax. You better get ready yourself.'

He swiftly puts on his jeans, and a white, ribbed vest. Livia heads to the bathroom. There is a knock at the door, which makes them both jump. She disappears out of the room as Josiah truckles in and gives Jake a peremptory nod. 'Mr Martinson trusts you have settled in, and would like to see you in the library in twenty minutes. I'll return to escort you, as you might struggle to find it on your first evening.'

Before Jake can answer, he departs, the door shutting silently. Jake goes across to the fire, stabs the embers savagely with a poker. They flare, and he takes the opportunity to pile on some expertly hewn logs that have been gathered to one side. Thick smoke floods up the chimney, the room smells of camping and comfort. Livia returns, still in mismatched thong and bra, looking for her bag, which must have been brought up earlier in the day. She picks up the dossier where Jake had dropped it.

Jake puts down the poker. 'We might as well make ourselves warm for the night. Anything else in that file, Liv?'

Liv is looking at the final pages. 'There's a floor plan of the house. It seems to have a central section and two wings coming off, heading south. The library is in the west wing. We're in a line of bedrooms in the east wing. The space in the middle looks like a kitchen garden and lawn. It's a big old barn, I'll tell you. And then there's this, the last page – come over and look.'

Jake walks back to the bed, and sits down once more. The page has the heading: *PART 2 – to come . . .*

'Why does that fill me with fear?'

Livia is carefully pulling a black jumpsuit from her bag, and hops on one leg as she puts it on. 'It fills you with fear, my dear, because you are anti-social, and the thought of organized entertainment appals you.'

'Forced fun is the worst, as well you know.'

Jake has opened his bag and is looking critically at the clothes he has brought. 'I reckon I might look a bit like the man who's come to clean the gutters.' Livia helps him pick out a woollen check shirt and smartish cardigan which, with boat shoes and no socks, makes him at least mildly presentable.

'Now you've gone from manual labourer to too-old hipster, but that's the best I can do in the circumstances. By the way, are you going to confess to having a phone here?'

'I wasn't going to. I don't fancy coming up with an explanation, and I still want to get through to Aletheia if I can. I'll just hang on to it quietly for now.'

There's a knock at the door. Josiah holds it open, and Livia struggles into her heels. She loops her arm through Jake's and together they follow the silent man into the gloomy corridor outside. A portrait of an unnamed aristocrat from a long-gone past glowers at them as they go.

Chapter Twenty-Six

Thursday, 9.35 p.m.

The library is huge and dimly lit, the size of a largish restaurant. Bookshelves reach from floor to vaulted ceiling, rising up in serried ranks across the whole room. In the middle there is a sort of clearing, ringed by soft armchairs and reading lamps. It is there that the party has gathered. Strained tones of small talk, the clinking of glasses, the occasional bray of awkward laughter.

Martinson immediately disentangles himself from the group and replaces Josiah as their escort. Josiah in turn slides away into a corner, eyes restlessly covering the room and its inhabitants. Jake is taken by the arm a yard ahead of Livia. Martinson has a cigar in one hand, his face flushed with pleasure and red wine.

His voice is loudly self-confident, filling the room. 'Everyone, this is Detective Jackson, formerly of the Metropolitan Police. Just behind him is Livia, his partner in the romantic sense, here on the premises to look after my lovely horses. Jake, I took the trouble of sending you a short note about everyone, so introductions are rather superfluous.'

'I'd love to see that note about me.' This itself a booming voice, also full of confidence, from Jim Daisley, who has settled himself into a leather armchair and is swirling a glass of brandy. 'You always were happiest when you were printing malicious untruths, Sam.'

A nervous titter. Martinson appears unoffended. 'Let's just say, Jim, I've always been of the publish and be damned mentality, which means I'll be damned if I let you see your note.' A hearty laugh, which is shared by nobody other than his wife, Adele, who seems to think it falls upon her to support her husband's attempts at humour.

Martinson is still addressing the room. 'Let's just mingle and enjoy each other's company, and a late supper, and we'll see what tomorrow brings. Unless the night has any surprises, of course.' Another guffaw.

Livia is immediately taken up by the Lambs, Jason and Rebecca, leaving Jake alone with Martinson, who ushers him to one side near to a bookcase. The titles are hard to read in the low, flickering light, an impassive bank of inaccessible knowledge. Martinson puts his head close, so Jake can smell his breath laden with cigar smoke and the cloying sweetness of booze.

'I look forward to a proper chat at some point during your stay, Jake. I've always been fascinated by crime stories, you know. It's one of the reasons I got into papers, actually. Anyway, I'm sure you've got some for me, and I might even have a few for you. I'll find a time when we can get cosy away from the weather. I'd do it now, but I worry that the lovely Livia might get gobbled up by some of

148

these sharks you can see in the room. I look forward to a revealing conversation.' He gestures brusquely, indicating that Jake might join the party properly.

He immediately heads for Livia, who is in a conversation with the Lambs and Dr Hamed. Her smile for him is one of pained dismay.

'Jake, so glad you're back. I've just been hearing about what a boringly conventional view of fidelity I have. Jason and Rebecca here believe in share and share alike, and Dr Hamed refuses to accept that monogamy is part of the natural human condition.' Hamed inclines his head gravely. His hair is salt-and-pepper hued throughout.

Jake casually strokes Livia's arm. 'So is this less of a country house party, more of a swingers love-in?'

Rebecca is staring directly at him, nibbling an olive from her martini. Her hair is raven black and lustrous, bouncing the sparse light back from the chandelier overhead. She is lithe and strong-looking, clad in a black, tight-fitting dress. She is wearing make-up to accentuate her cheekbones. 'We'd be up for it, if you are. But I'm not sure the whole group is especially sexually liberated.' She gestures with a manicured eyebrow to Fenella Jewell, who is talking to Jim Daisley, or rather being visibly bored by him. His expansive gestures contrast with her defensive stillness, arms crossed, head bowed.

'Jim would give anything to sleep with Fenella, but her interests currently lie more in the same-sex area.' Her teeth gleamed at Livia. 'She'd want to peel you out of that luscious outfit or me out of this thing first.' She looks in the other direction, where a different small group has congregated. 'Meanwhile, our hosts are the model of monogamy. I don't say that Sam has never strayed,

149

especially when he owned newspapers. It's well known that journalists have the morals of monkeys, after all. But here, in Purple Prose, he likes to play the part of respected lord of the manor.' She finishes her drink, and holds her hand out without looking. A server, all in black, face modest and expressionless, fills it up from a stainless steel shaker. She sips deeply, and withers Henry Franklin – the ambitious lawyer, Jake remembers – with her gaze. 'The tall, boring-looking man over there, I don't know about, but he looks biddable at the least. I'd lure him back to bed myself, but I always think it's unfair on Jason. He doesn't mind a bit of boy-play, but I reckon it ends up leaving him just too little to do when it comes right down to it.'

Hamed has been rocking on his heels during this speech. 'Charlotte, the woman over there.' He gestures with his drink. She is in a striking red dress, cinched at the waist with a bright white belt, talking rather glumly to Josiah, who has strayed from his position by the wall. 'She looks to me that her availability might be – not to put too fine a point on it – professionally determined, so she may be willing for some sort of game with you, Rebecca.'

'Or you, perhaps, Doctor?'

'It's sometime since I had to pay for sex, my dear.'

'Oh, we all pay for it somewhere along the line, don't we, Livia? Come, let me introduce you around.' Livia casts a look over her shoulder, and is then manoeuvred towards Jim and Fenella. Jason trails after them, in a somewhat spanielish fashion, though he would not acknowledge that, Jake thinks, even to himself. He turns to Hamed.

'You sound rather cynical for a doctor, if you don't mind me saying.'

Hamed's eyes are flickering across the room. 'I find that it's always dangerous to romanticize doctors. Yes, we can save people, but we do it as much for ourselves as anyone else. The intellectual challenge, the hero complex, the chance to rival God for a brief moment. I think you'll find I'm as morally compromised as you, dear detective.'

'Or more, in fact.'

Hamed holds his hands up in mock surrender. 'Equivalence is never a fair game to play, I concede. Let me get you a drink. I always have Black Velvets when I am here. The combination of good stout and dry champagne is almost medicinal. Almost.' He grips Jake's bicep, and wanders off to summon a waiter.

Charlotte, meanwhile, approaches carefully, sidling up to Jake at an oblique angle, like a plane cautiously making a pass above an airport before landing. 'I always have a sense when people are talking about me. It's like justified paranoia. What were they saying?'

Jake tries to think of a way to gloss the conversation politely. 'The general tenor was on the subject of traditional monogamy, I think. I'd only just joined the group myself.'

She smiles and sips her flute of champagne. 'That was nobly done. But I bet the subject might have come up that I'm a whore, didn't it?'

Jake nods gently. 'The possibility was raised, yes.'

'Does it shock you?'

'I was a policeman in a big city for fifteen years. I'm not that easy to shock.'

'I won't deny it. I've worked very hard being an excellent whore, distasteful though it has sometimes been. And I have no intention of staying one forever.'

They stand together for a moment in silence. They watch

Adele stalk to one side of the room, whisper in Josiah's ear.

'You won't get much of a shock out of that one. Adele. Very cold and distant, one of those women who are always suffering from headaches and hissy fits, nothing ever quite right for her. Being married to a billionaire helps, of course. A few years ago someone wrote a big piece about some of her financial dealings since marrying Sam, mainly as a sort of slum landlord. How she had made millions – not that they needed it. She used to watch some of the evictions from her Merc outside apparently, just to check that the families were removed properly. Her own roots are humble, and she said she couldn't respect people who couldn't raise themselves out of the gutter.' She sips her drink again, face wreathed with disdain. 'Anyway, the paper ran the profile, which was less than flattering, and two of the journalists were involved in hit-and-run accidents three days apart; one's still in a wheelchair.'

'How do you know about it all?'

'I've spent a lot of time with a number of powerful men in the last few years, Jake. And they're all more or less the same. They all think that they're special enough to make you feel pleasure for real, and that you would happily sleep with them for the thrill not the money. And they all bore on after they've done their business, mostly about their work or their rivals.'

Daisley, standing next to Livia, looks across at them talking, and raises his glass. Charlotte stiffens for a hint of a second, and then looks away. A waiter, his face blank and beautiful, hands Jake a large glass of swirling black liquid. He sips it tentatively; it is rich and delicious.

Martinson suddenly advances to the centre of the room

and claps his hands loudly. 'Food, now! It's getting late.' Immediately, the doors swing open and a series of long trolleys are ushered in by other members of the silent, night-clad staff. There is a rib of beef, rare, the first few slices already shaved off by a fiercely sharp blade that has been embedded in the flesh. A whole bank of smoked salmon, coiled and pink. A series of miniature bowls containing all sorts of easily consumed food: spiced prawns, tiny shepherd's pies, fried courgette spaghetti. On the final trolley there is a tower of profiteroles sticky with glazed chocolate and gold dust, and a huge passionfruit pavlova.

'Eat, eat,' Martinson is exhorting. 'There might be a few vegetables around, but I can't abide vegans, so I better not see any tonight.'

Charlotte looks across to Jake. 'I know why I'm here in this carnival. But why are you?'

'My girlfriend has just started working for Martinson.'

'Oh the pretty vet? I saw her in the distance earlier by the stables. I love horses and ride them when I can, which is not exactly stereotypical for a prostitute.'

'I have to say you seem more bothered by your occupation than I am.'

Charlotte gives a silvery laugh and raises her glass to his. 'Fair point, detective. I am defensive, so I'll stop harping on about it. Go on, you rescue your vet from whatever dreary conversation she might be having with Daisley and Hamed.' The doctor, after leaving Jake, had made his way slowly around the room to Livia.

'Do you know him?'

Charlotte rests her hand on Jake's shoulder and squeezes. 'I know everyone, darling. Know everyone, am bored by everyone, but here I am, all tits and teeth, still very much the social animal. But don't you get too relaxed while you're here, some of these people are dangerous.'

'In what way?'

'You're the detective, you'll figure it out. But take some advice from a working girl: you must be careful about who to trust.' She pushes a stray hair behind her ear.

'Should I trust you?'

'You should trust nobody. Go, get something to eat.'

'Can I get something for you?'

'How gentlemanly. No, I'll probably find other forms of sustenance, if you know what I mean.' She has made eye contact with Jason, who nods her towards a door that might lead to a bathroom. She pushes Jake firmly away, and treads quickly out, her heels click-clacking like castanets. One last remark floats back over her shoulder: 'Nobody here is as innocent as they look.'

Livia sees Jake is alone, and disentangles herself from her conversation and joins him by the buffet. She grabs a few slivers of smoked salmon, he two miniature shepherd's pies, which clink precariously on his plate. They find chairs and eat off their laps.

Jake notices Livia picking delicately at her food, with small, feline mouthfuls. He smiles. 'Saving yourself for pudding?'

She grimaces. 'I've never been very good at eating in public, you know. It feels like everyone is watching every single time you open your mouth.'

Jake looks around. 'I've not spoken to everyone, but I don't reckon this is a room full of folk who spend their time worrying a lot about others.'

Livia wipes her mouth delicately, and sips a minute

amount of champagne. 'That's true. There's a lot of money in this room, and a sort of, I don't know, brittleness. Nobody is hearty or natural apart maybe from Martinson. Even that chap Daisley is more watchful than he wants to let on. It's like they're waiting for a sign, or maybe have forgotten how to just be normal. My friends, the luscious Lambs, are so desperate to be polyamorous and dangerous, it's almost sad. Then there's Doctor Hamed, nice enough, but a bit slick somehow, a bit too smooth. How about the vampish creature you were chatting up?'

'Charlotte? I don't think she was that vampish, but she's definitely a pro. She was very disobliging about Adele, and warned me not to trust anyone.'

'It's good advice, but odd that she needed to give it.'

They watch as Josiah marches smartly across the room to the door. Moments later, he returns, a man looming behind him in the shadows, but lingering beyond the threshold, reluctant to join the whole group. Josiah waves discreetly at Martinson, who immediately stands and heads to meet him. As the door is opened more fully, Jake catches a better glimpse of the new guest, his hair dark and longish, his face lean and taut, his eyes – oddly enough – of different colours. One of grey, one of brown.

Chapter Twenty-Seven

Jake and Livia are back in their rooms, the fire burning cheerily. Livia is running a bath. Thundering rumble of water, steam misting the mirrors. Jake is at the door, his face furrowed in concentration as he watches her tip various sweet-smelling unguents into the tub. Scents of vanilla and lavender fill the air.

She looks over her shoulder. 'So you think that mystery guy is connected to No Taboo?'

'It would be a hell of a coincidence if there was another person with odd-coloured eyes, who had nothing to do with anything. But who knows? I wish I could get in touch with Aletheia but she's not answering my messages. I just tried again.'

Livia turns off the taps, and the noise subsides. She shrugs off the plain white robe she has been wearing, and, swift as an otter, slips into the water. Only her head is visible, resting above a collar of foam, her face flushed with heat.

'What do you think it means then?'

Jake exhales thoughtfully, and then moves next to the bath, his hand making figures of eight on the milky surface. 'It might mean Martinson is connected closely to No Taboo. Which on one level wouldn't be a surprise, because he's the sort of super-rich power broker who absolutely would be part of something like that. The question follows: did he invite us here because of No Taboo, or is our presence here nothing to do with that?'

'Coincidences are unlikely, as you always say.' Livia blows some froth into the air. 'Does that mean we're in danger?'

'I don't think so. He's a public figure, we're guests at his house. I let Watson know we were coming too, so it's not as though we can just disappear into thin air. Martinson told me he wanted to talk crime stories tomorrow. Let me speak to him and try to gauge what he's up to. And let's see if we can speak to that man who just arrived as well, get a sense of what we're dealing with.' With that, he disrobes himself quickly and tries, unsuccessfully, to slide into the bath with the same elegance as Livia.

The next morning they both wake early in their unfamiliar bed. Morning light on snowy ground is always insidious, even before the sun fully emerges, creeping around the curtains, brightening every corner, cautious and intrusive as a thief. There is frost on the balcony, crystal and clean. Little noise emerges from the grounds, muffled and swaddled as they are in snow.

Jake and Livia dress quickly and head out, keen to explore outside. They encounter nobody on the stairs, though they see the back of Josiah heading sedately into a corridor in the distance. Breakfast is being cooked, the smell of coffee and bacon mingling pleasantly with the old smoke from the night's fires which now lie in powdery ruin.

Outside they walk briskly along a path that takes them towards an ornamental lake, which has partially frozen over. Geese slither on the ice, before plopping contentedly in, their bodies plump and serene. They call to one another, lilting squabbles. Jake and Livia pause to watch the water in the middle ripple and roll. Then they look back at the house. It is a vast edifice, obscenely squatting on the landscape, the two wings coming down from the imposing front, creating an incomplete square in the middle. Jake knows that Martinson occupies apartments on the first floor of the west wing, away from his guests on the other side. The library and dining room are in the centre. There must be tens of rooms, he thinks, that are musty and unused.

There is a chapel a few hundred yards away in the other direction. It is a compact, private-looking building that has aged almost entirely into its surroundings. In the early-morning mist, it is nothing but a grey smear. Jake and Livia skirt the lake on the other side and head down some steps into some more gardens. Flower beds lie empty and dusted with snow, their contents no doubt buried beneath, awaiting the warming arousal of spring. Some nearby birds whistle and twitter, flitting and resting on the bare branches of some apple trees that make up an orchard in one corner. Life is there in the natural world, but restrained, cautious, unsure that the sustaining future will come around once more.

Livia holds his hand tightly, their knuckles white, and swings his arm as they walk. 'I meant to ask you, did you ever call yourself JJ at any point?'

Jake snorts quietly. 'What possibly made you want to ask that?'

'Well, you have this quite butch name, Jake Jackson, which I like and all, but I wanted to know if you'd ever called yourself something snazzier. I don't know why I thought of it, probably saw someone going by the name of AJ or CJ or something on the internet.'

'Now that you mention it, I did have a late teenage period where I tried to get people to call me JJ. I thought girls might go for it more than Jake.'

'Did they?'

'Not really, no. Turns out your sex is cleverer than they look.'

She mock slaps him, and they walk on, their faces alight with the cold. They go down some more steps, and see the entrance to a maze, whorls of forbidding privet hedge about as high as Jake's head. In front of it is a bench on which Dr Hamed is sitting, hissing savagely into a mobile phone.

Jake and Livia hang back, but their path sweeps unavoidably past where the doctor is sitting, and he spots them almost immediately. He hangs up his phone and rises to greet them, his face still bearing the marks of agitation, his manner artificially pleasant in an effort to smooth the encounter.

He shakes both their hands, fingers stiff and cold. 'Lovely to see you both out and about so early.'

Jake gestures to his phone. 'I thought nobody was allowed these.'

'I have a medical exemption. I had to call a patient, and Sam gave me permission. I have to hand it back in though, absurdly enough.'

159

Livia sits down on the bench, and idly plucks a strand from the hedge. 'That didn't look like an especially harmonious doctor–patient conversation, if you don't mind me saying.'

'Money so often gets in the way of good medicine, in my experience. And money tends to make people angry too. If you'll both forgive me, I'll head back towards the house and finish the conversation there. No need to interfere with your wintry walk.' He strides away, and soon returns the phone to his ear, his other arm gesticulating widely.

Livia grabs Jake's arm to help her rise from the bench, and holds on to him as they walk. 'He wasn't a happy bunny, now, was he?'

'Doctors are just failed vets anyway, aren't they?'

She smiles, teeth as white as the ground beneath. 'I knew there was a reason I ended up with you, JJ.'

The path loops around, and into a pasture, a larger field that must be full of wild grasses and flowers in a more congenial season. They look back to the house, now more than a mile away, its silhouette stark against the lightening sky, smoke thrusting forth and merging with the high scatterings of cloud.

Livia nudges Jake. 'Let's head back for some breakfast. All this fresh air can't be good for you.'

Some twenty minutes later, they are striding across the virgin snow, back up to the main set of doors at the back, their hands and ears tingling, a flush of colour across their faces. They are met at the door by Charlotte, who barges brusquely past, her face tight with anger, tears prickling her eyes. She doesn't stop when Jake calls her name, but scurries towards the stables.

160

Behind her stands Josiah, his still face marmoreal. He gives the briefest nod of acknowledgement to them, and waits until they have stamped their boots on the mat.

His voice is smooth as ever. 'Mr Martinson would be delighted to see you in his private drawing room for breakfast, if you are amenable. Usually he likes to have his guests dine together, but he wanted better to make your acquaintance. I believe that his wife will also join you.'

'How lovely.' This is Livia, her voice bright and accommodating. 'Do we have time to get changed?'

'Mr Martinson's schedule is quite tight, and there's no need for formality when it comes to clothing.' Jake cannot help but notice that Josiah casts a look in his direction when he says this.

They allow themselves to be ushered through a series of doors and corridors, before Josiah walks them into a large, high-ceilinged room, alive with two roaring fires and now bright with the morning's sunlight. Martinson is sitting on the sofa with Adele, his hand resting proprietorially on her thigh. He doesn't stand, but motions them to the sofa opposite with an imperious shake of his hand.

His voice booms like a bittern. 'Sit down, you two. Let's have a spot of breakfast together. Coffee first?' A member of the waiting staff, blonde and magnificent-looking, eyes downcast, enters the room with a silver-plated antique coffee pot, and distributes the drinks, before removing a series of warming lids from a buffet laid out on a corner table. Fluffy scrambled eggs, well-cooked sausage and bacon, some corn muffins straight from the oven.

Livia plays the grateful guest. 'This is very kind of you, Sam. You have such a lovely place here.'

161

'I'm glad you both could make it. After breakfast, I thought Adele here could come with you to the stables to talk horses and get your initial report. And then Jake and I could have a chat about this and that. Sound good?'

'You're the boss.'

'Indeed I am.'

They rise to select some food, and Jake finds himself beside Adele, who is appraising him critically. He does the same in return. She is tall, certainly taller than her husband, her body athletic, firmed evidently by hours of horse-riding, but still filling out appropriately with age. By no means a stereotypical trophy second wife. Her expression is not warm, her voice rough and metallic.

'My experience of police is not a good one, Jake. Not that I've had a criminal past or anything. But I can make an exception for you if Sam wants me to. He and I are great allies in everything.'

'That's good to hear.'

The general conversation, when they resume their seats, stutters on, never quite settling into awkwardness. Talk of horses and houses, politics and newspapers. After half an hour, Adele leads Livia out to the stables, scarcely giving Jake another glance. Martinson watches her leave appreciatively, then sits back and lights a cigar.

'So then Jake,' he says smokily, 'let's talk about why you're really here.'

Chapter Twenty-Eight

Friday, 10.45 a.m.

Livia is still at the stables when Jake gets back to their room, and he decides to go for a run to clear his head. He limbers up outside on the driveway, the cold pummelling his bare arms and legs, his muscles slow to loosen. He feels old for a second, and stiff, and a little bit past it.

He forces himself into a steady jog, sensing each impact of the iron-hard ground like a shock through his legs, before he eventually settles into the practised comfort of his normal running motion. His breath is a thick fog in front of him, he can see the heat steam from his reddening thighs. In the distance, he spots Livia, patting the muscled neck of a chocolate-coloured horse, Adele standing, arms folded in an aloof pose behind her. To her left a magnificent grey is being led out for exercise, head proudly twisting and tossing against the bridle, legs high-stepping, thin as a child's pencil drawing, hooves clattering on the icy cobbles.

163

He finds a different path to earlier in the morning, and heads west from the house, a scant track leading towards fields that rise and fall like billowing waves endlessly into the middle distance. He thinks about his conversation with Martinson.

The beginning had not been surprising. Martinson had taken the time, as Jake thought he might, to brag a little more about his newspaper background, the stories he had published, the politicians he had humbled. He then confessed, as before, to an interest in crime and policework, the psychology of it all, and had invited Jake to talk about some of his old cases, many of which he had – disconcertingly – seemed already to know well.

Jake told a few old favourites, stories every police officer has, those stock tales of danger and self-deprecation that can be dusted off for any occasion. It gave him time to think about his next move. Eventually, he mentioned the two cases that he believed were connected to No Taboo, explaining the frustration of investigations that produce either no result or an unsatisfactory one.

Jake has been running for half an hour, his lungs sound, his heart strong. The exhilaration of exercise. He mounts a small hill with some effort, and is rewarded with a memorable view: a valley floor nestling beneath, the land paled with snow, trees coming forth like abandoned shipwrecks, their boughs twisting upwards towards the mute winter sun. Further away, he can see a village following the length of a stream that looks still – as if frozen – at this remove. The water gleams, a mirror in slow motion. The houses a disordered jumble of roofs and buildings, like toys scattered across a carpet.

Martinson's eyes had widened when Jake talked about

the abduction of James and the murder of Nathan White. He waggled his cigar near Jake's face, the ember burning sullen and smoky near his eyes.

'I thought you might mention those cases, Jake,' he said. 'You've got grounds to think they might be linked to things happening now don't you?'

'What makes you say that?'

'One thing you need to know about me is that I always know things. I enjoy the power of it. And I like involving myself in danger. Always have.'

Jake had swallowed, and committed himself. 'Do you know about something called No Taboo?'

Martinson had chuckled. 'Now why would I admit to that?'

'Who was the man who came last night to the house, black hair, odd-coloured eyes? Something tells me that he might have something to do with it all.'

Martinson clapped slowly, dense, thudding sounds that reverberated in the still room. 'Bravo, Jake, you're a good detective after all. Charles, who you so sneakily spied, is a business associate of mine, an important one. I may tell you more later, and I think you should probably meet. But tell me first: what do you know about No Taboo?'

Jake's smile had been rueful. 'Not much beyond that it seems to be responsible for a body of crimes that have never been punished. That it might have a connection to the abduction of Laura, which you've already told me you know about. And, now, that its links seem to reach out to this lovely place and to you.'

Martinson had stood up abruptly, and clapped Jake on the back. 'Fair enough. I just wanted to know what sort of interest you had in it all.'

'You're not going to deny any connection?'

'Jake, I don't think you give me enough credit, I really don't. I'm not a weak and passive suspect, to be investigated or drawn into things against my will. I am someone with a natural interest, shall we say, in what you and your inspector friend have been up to, certainly, and the ability to involve myself, supportively or otherwise, if I really want to.'

'Is that why Livia and I are here?'

His face was animated by a mischievous smile, his teeth capped and smooth and fraudulently shiny. 'Why is any one of us here, when you come right down to it? Now I have to go and make some calls; I enjoyed our conversation greatly.' Without another word, but with a hand planted firmly in his back, Martinson ushered him out.

Jake turns for home, which must now be four miles away and out of sight. His wet top feels chill in the icy wind. His feet are numb, his trainers sopping in the snow. He feels like the only moving part of a landscape in the frigid grip of stillness. There is no trickle of water he can hear, no preoccupied chuntering of hedgerow birds. Nothing. Even the trees, shorn of their leaves, offer no consoling susurration. Silence is like claustrophobia, and he picks up his speed as much as he can, the second half of a run always a bit quicker, a bit easier in his mind as each sodden step brings him closer to the end. Physically, this has been a satisfying experience; mentally less so. He remains as anxious as when he started, a sense of nagging impotence, or rather that something large and perilous is ever looming just beyond his grasp.

Chapter Twenty-Nine

Friday, 12.50 p.m.

Livia is waiting for him when he emerges from the shower, his whole body pinked and tingling and tired. She looks somehow delicate, her features soft in the washed-out light of the room. The place smells of old smoke and lavender from Jake's shower. A new fire has been started and is flickering in the corner, producing bright orange flames but no great warmth as yet. Jake dresses briskly and tells Livia about his conversation with Martinson.

She then describes her morning with Adele. Her expression is thoughtful as she blows her fringe from her eyes in ruminative fashion.

'She's a cold woman, you know. Hard, I guess. Very possessed of her own sense of authority, dismissive of others. A bit of a gossip as well. Franklin, that dull lawyer chap, she told me about his weakness for a high-end escort called, of all things, Monique. Apparently, he hoards cash so he can pay her without his wife knowing, visits her once a week, is in thrall to her completely. That picture in the dossier was him emerging from her place. All part of Martinson using leverage to keep him honest in his dealings. Hamed is Adele's doctor, but she's not exactly fond of him. Apparently he's desperately in debt and unsure what to do about it. I reckon Martinson uses that to make him biddable.'

'Anyone else get a mention?'

'Not much. There's something theatrical about this gathering, like we've been put together for a purpose, and she knows it. She's clearly not just a puppet or a trophy, by the way. I wouldn't underestimate her. She seems close to both Martinson and Daisley, told me that she has become part of their business interests over the years. She doesn't have much interest in the Lambs, and says they're only here for their own amusement.'

'Did you ask her about the guy we saw last night?'

'Our motley-eyed friend? Yes, and she got quite sharp with me. Said she wasn't here to talk about her business associates and that I should get on with my work. We spent the rest of the time talking horses.'

Jake has shrugged on a jumper and is now sitting by the writing desk. 'So what do you make of it all?'

Livia is silent for a moment. Her eyes dart around the room. 'You know I'm starting to get a bad feeling about this place. When I got back here, it felt like our things had been touched, looked through. Did you notice anything?'

Jake had felt a twinge of something when he had been changing out of his clothes, but dismissed it. He'd hidden the phone at the back of a drawer in the otherwise empty bureau, and it hadn't been disturbed. 'I know what you mean. I'm getting a bit unsure of it as well. What is Martinson's connection to No Taboo? There's clearly something. And he's almost proud of it, or defiant at least. Does he want us here to keep an eye on us?'

Livia perches on Jake's lap, her softness a pleasing and reassuring weight upon him. She looks him in the eye, her expression quizzical. 'Should we get out of this place? I've done my work, we've shown a bit of deference and willing. Let's get home to Diana, shall we? We don't need any of this. I know, I know . . .' She slaps him gently. 'You love the whirl of the big country house party. You probably want to see who the Lambs lure to their bed, chat some big business with whatever his name is, Jim. But sometimes family must come first, my little social butterfly.'

'Music to my ears. Let's go make our apologies after lunch.'

They start to pack their bags, their possessions spread out heedlessly in the haphazard manner of all people staying away from home, but are soon interrupted by a knock at the door. Josiah pauses for a mere second and then enters.

Jake gives him an effortful smile. 'Oh, I was just coming to see you, actually. We're going to head off after lunch. Liv is missing Di, and is worried about one of her other cases, so we thought we'd make a dash earlier than planned.'

A movement somewhere between a nod and a shake of the head. 'Mr Martinson has planned some festivities for the weekend, a game of sorts, at which he would value your attendance. He may be somewhat offended if he hears you are leaving so soon.'

Livia is bright and confident, falsely so, her face widening with determination. She lightly grasps Josiah's arm, and he flinches instinctively. 'Come now, he has a house full of people to play with. He wouldn't want to keep us here against our will now, would he?'

Josiah offers nothing in immediate response. His eyes

flick between them, cold and reptilian. He then opens the door, and begins to back out. 'I will inform him of your decision. Lunch is in the dining hall in twenty minutes.'

They arrive on time, having left their bags in the atrium by the front door. The hall is huge, with thick beams across high wooden ceilings, blackened with smoke and age, the space dominated by a large table of polished mahogany. Place settings are laid at the end near the window, which runs from the ground to the ceiling, the upper parts made with stained glass, ruby and sapphire, brilliantly backlit by the winter sun. Two fires roar on either side of the table. There is a sideboard running down half of one wall, of similar hue, laden with warming dishes. Hearty food once more: pies and bubbling stews, a fluffy mound of mashed potato, an array of neatly peeled and prepared vegetables. There is a huge antique tureen of mulled wine which is adorning the air with a comforting scent of cloves and orange and alcohol.

The other guests had clearly arrived a little earlier. They were all at the end of the table with laden plates, some mostly consumed. Hamed rises when he sees them, and motions a waiter to hand them pewter mugs of the warmed wine. Nobody else acknowledges their arrival until they sit down. Hamed sips his own drink, stretches his legs towards the fire. His plate is empty.

'I hear you're leaving us, what a shame. Things were about to get interesting.'

Jake swirls some wine in his mouth, relishing the heavy taste of fruit. 'Josiah mentioned something about a game, but didn't elaborate.'

'He can be oysterish that one, a closed shell. No, we are going to play a murder mystery game: you know, country house, corpse discovered, everyone plays a role. I rather think you might have enjoyed it with your detective background.'

'Alas, they have decided to reject our benevolent hospitality, the rotters.' The voice is loud from across the table. Martinson has entered, with Adele behind him, their faces as cold as the weather outside.

Livia turns towards him. He holds up a minatory hand. 'No, my dear, we won't pursue it. I never beg, and I won't make you justify yourself. You have your reasons to leave, just as I had my reasons to keep you. All thoroughly respectable, of course. No, you both run along if you must, we shall do our best not to miss you.' With that he settles into a large chair by the fire and waits for his food to be delivered to him.

The meal passes, laboured conversation, occasional silences punctuated by clinking cutlery. Jake and Livia are both keen to escape the awkward atmosphere as soon as is reasonable. As coffee is served, they stand to leave. Charlotte rises with them and begins to accompany them to the door. Her movement is checked by Josiah, who nods towards Martinson. He wags a thick finger. 'My dear, can I have a word with you? You can say your goodbyes from just where you are, no need to walk our mutineers to their car.'

Charlotte swallows, her eyes search out Jake's, alive in freeze-frame, pleading almost, and then subdued, resigned. A flare suddenly snuffed out. She shakes their hands, her fingers cool and slender. Her touch lingers on his, she gives his hand a squeeze, laden with meaning, perhaps, or nothing, he cannot be sure. Then she turns and heads back towards Martinson and the group, her shoulders bowed like a chastened child.

Chapter Thirty

Monday, 8.30 a.m.

It is good to be back at home, walking the land once more. They had passed a quiet weekend at Livia's house, after a noisy and welcome reunion with Diana. More play in the snow, more hunkering away from the world. The uneasy sense of strangeness they had experienced lingered in their minds, unspoken, then had been displaced mostly for the while, just a low hum in the background drowned out by Diana's joyfulness and the bustle of domestic life.

Jake had slept last night at Little Sky, alone in bed, having drunk slightly more red wine than he was used to. It didn't help him sleep, and he had been up before first light for a penitential run and plunge in the lake. The temperature had risen to just above freezing, and the wind had fallen off, so the snow was soft underfoot, almost slush, made luminously bright by the rising sun, first crimson then burnt orange fading into a mild and humble yellow.

He had planned as he ran, trying to establish what he would do next, and how he would – in the end – extricate himself from the situation. Laura was safe. His cold cases were just that: cold, frigid, beyond resuscitation. No Taboo was a problem for someone else, if it was a problem that could be solved at all. And yet. There was Charles with the motley eyes, the knowingness of Martinson, a houseful of brittle, amoral folk. That guard, Smits, made rich and powerful by his own malignity, squatting hidden within the prison system.

After his hot shower, steaming like a cauldron in his courtyard, Jake had dressed and sat down in front of the kitchen stove, whittling wooden pegs for the treehouse. But he couldn't settle. Which is why he is now tramping the ground on one of his lower fields, the river no more than a distant bootlace in the corner, discarded amid an expanse of mottled green dusted with white. A mist gathers in the bowl of the land beneath him, thick as swirling smoke. He sees a skip of movement, a magpie hopping on the wintry ground, the white of its belly merging with the snow, purple and black above like a priest's robes. He'd read once that magpies were thought to be unlucky because their plumage was not all black, their piebald appearance a sign they had refused to go into mourning for the death of Christ. Something unbelievable like that. Or was it that one magpie was bad luck, but two were a sign of fortune? He watches this living omen for a second, and feels a curious sense of relief when another drops down from the trees, a flutter of muted feathers. They scratch around companionably. Two for joy. He hopes it is a sign.

There is more weather coming, Livia had told him, the

rise in temperature was an illusion, a false hope that the stormy period was over. By nightfall they would be in the grip of the freeze once more. That makes this walk the more pleasant, he thinks, a temporary hiatus, stolen pleasure in the depths of winter. He inhales deeply, fresh ozone and the cloying scent of rotting leaves. The sweetness of decay. He has the phone with him, which he hates – it makes him feel connected, commonplace, tied to something that has become inescapable – but he still wants to hear from Aletheia, and to discuss how to leave all this with her.

It vibrates against his thigh. It is a message from Martha, curt and capitalized as he has grown to expect.

HAVE NEWS. URGENT. CALL AT NOON ON SIGNAL. YOU BETTER HAVE YOUR FUCKING PHONE WITH YOU. M

Jake gives a soft involuntary snort. He replies with a simple 'OK', and puts the phone away. He heads further south, crossing a bridge well away from his property, buttressed beautifully with soft curves carved out of crumbling stone. It had been built sometime in the eighteenth century for access to a manor house that must still be somewhere, tucked amid the shifting trees, out of sight. No longer a place of drama and greatness, what was once the economic and social centre of a small community, a monument to one rich family supported by countless poor families. The land around here is full of quiet corners, big old buildings, where the rich might still subsist, but not like they used to. Jake shakes his head. He is rich, of course, by any standards, so why should he sneer. But he

174

craves isolation and freedom, not the need to control or exploit other people. Maybe that's what keeps nagging him about No Taboo: it is something that overwhelms and corrupts, protected by money and power, something insidious and unhealthy that needed to be fought and exposed.

Walking breeds futile philosophy, he reckons, as the mind seeks its own exertion to match the efforts of the body. He has certainly been warmed by the exercise, his T-shirt damp against his back, rivulets of sweat being chilled in the cold air. He has, without caring much, found his way back to Parvum, the scent of woodsmoke ahead, a glimpse of a roof, the side of a cottage, a vegetable patch of turned, dark earth. Funny how these smaller buildings huddle into the landscape as if for comfort.

The Nook is empty, apart from Sarah somewhere in the cellar, noisily shifting and muttering. He raises his voice in greeting, and her face, reddened and welcoming, soon appears from below.

'Ah me duck, you're just in time to take some deer meat off my hands.'

'I'm not used to the hard sell from you, Sarah. Are you trying to shake this place up a bit? Shift some units? About time too. I keep telling you, you need a marketing strategy.'

It is a standing joke between them, Sarah's lack of commercialism, though Jake thinks she does all right in her quiet and methodical way.

'Let's just say this lot has not come from any official cull, but managed to appear on my back doorstep anyway.'

'You do know I'm a former policeman, don't you?'

'As if you blooming well let us forget it. Now my knees aren't being done any good half in and half out of the cellar, so yes or no to this improperly acquired meat, Mr Former Policeman?'

Ten minutes later he is back on the move once more, a big – needlessly big – haunch of venison on his shoulder. When Jake was very young, he had read a picture book about Robin Hood, beautifully hand-illustrated in pastels. One scene showed the outlaws carrying a deer on a spit towards a fire; it had always lingered in his memory as a representation of heartiness, of hunger satisfied, of the outdoor life. Something wholesome, he supposed. It makes him grin in happy recollection even as the venison digs into his shoulder, and hastens him homeward.

Chapter Thirty-One

Monday, 12.05 p.m.

Jake has spitted the venison and is waiting to roast it slowly over his firepit, letting it sit outside on the windowsill, cold as any freezer. The flames are too high for the moment, and he is building the heat carefully. When the wood is reduced to embers, white-hot and pulsing in the slight breeze, then he will let it cook for hours. The meat is lean, and he has affixed some pork fat to the surface, using sticks of rosemary to hold it in place. This will dissolve, basting and protecting the flesh, so it can cook slowly and succulently.

Meanwhile, Jake is in the library, staring at the phone, waiting for Martha to come online. He has a record playing quietly in the corner, Aaron Copland's *Appalachian Spring*, something inappropriately light and vernal. She is late, and he lets his mind wander. And then her face suddenly appears, at a moment when he is smelling his clothes, and under his arms. Her raucous chuckle announces her arrival.

'I'm sure you do smell a bit, wild man. Isn't wifey keeping a good enough eye on you? I'm sure, left to your own devices, you'd just become feral.'

Jake rolls his eyes. 'Hello to you. Do you have news for me?'

Martha is puffing at her pipe, eyes faintly bloodshot, voice a corvid croak. As she speaks, a wreath of smoke encircles her face. 'Yes, sir, of course, sir, reporting for duty sir. I didn't realize we had joined the army together on this.'

He can see the futility of an argument here. 'Why don't we start again? Good afternoon, Martha, I believe you have some information you'd be willing to share with me?'

'That's probably better. OK, two things, then I'll get off this link. It's as secure as anything can be, but I didn't get here by refusing to be cautious.'

'Not to spoil the mood, but that's exactly what you did. You're stuck in that chair because you refused to be cautious, I imagine. Some would even call that brave.'

She winces a smile. 'You're one of the only people who mentions the leg thing openly, you know, Jake. Either you are good at understanding disabled people who crave openness, or merely autistic and lucky. But, we're wasting time. I do want to be cautious. This is all pretty dangerous stuff. And when a woman with no legs tells you something is dangerous, you better well imagine she knows what she's talking about.' A pause. Another puff of thick smoke.

'So, the two things. First, Aletheia has – I think – gone dark. She's taken holiday from the job, taken herself off normal channels. She's clearly worried someone is prowling after her, or might be about to start. And I think she wants to dig some more about our unfriendly prison guard, Garland Smits.'

Jake sits forward, worried. 'You say you think that's what she's doing. Do we know?'

'She sent me one message, which looked plausible enough. I'm checking her out, in a roundabout way, to see if there's anything untoward. But that's why she's not returning your messages.' Martha's expression breaks into something approaching tenderness for the merest second. 'So try not to worry. I think she'll pop back up, but I'll do what I can to make sure she's OK. For both our sakes.'

Jake nods. 'And the second thing?'

'A body has been delivered from Purple Prose to the hospital. Some time yesterday afternoon. But none of the official channels are being used. No murder investigation. A pathologist is being brought in specially, but no name is on the system. All very odd.'

Jake feels a surge of something approaching shock, but also the vaguest sense of an unstated prediction coming true. He holds the phone tight. 'Who is the body?'

'I know lots of things, but not that. All I could find out was a body, fresh, coming from that house.'

Jake wonders who it might be. Charlotte is the first face that flashes across his mind. There was something always troubling about her. He would have to find out.

He clears his throat, and stops his thoughts wandering. 'How do you know what you do know?'

'Jake, I don't think – for all your remarkable empathy – you truly understand what I've done in the past. My job was to know things when they happened, before anyone could put in place things to turn them into bullshit. I still can do that if I apply myself. I still have my sources.'

Jake thinks, fingers restless on the arm of the chair. 'You know Martinson said something similar to me the other day: he prides himself on what he knows.'

'Let's just say that I'm not flattered by the comparison, but you have a point: no doubt all this is taking place at a level which most people – including bumbling rural ex-coppers – don't know exists.'

'So what do we do about it all?'

'*We* don't do anything. I'm the cripple, remember, you're the bumbling ex-copper. But I do think *we* – by which I mean you – should take a look. The autopsy is tomorrow morning at six. It'll be wrapped up by eight. I'll arrange for a hospital pass to be left at reception in the name of Rex Stout. Don't ask me how I can do that either. Just dig around as much as you can without getting caught.'

Jake is staring past the screen at the scuffs on the floor, meaningless gouges caused by careless shifting of the furniture. He catches Martha's eye. 'Humour me. *Why* should we do this? Why don't we walk away?'

'I'll forgive the metaphor this once. Because, dear Jake, whatever you think, or whatever wifey might say, we've already got involved. We are in this. As soon as you helped your chap Watson by considering that business card, as soon as you dragged in Aletheia, called me, saw the man with the funny eyes. As soon as all of that happened, we became involved. And now we have to get out properly. And that doesn't mean we can just run away and escape when things get tough. I know that's your MO, Jake, that's why you're where you are, but that shot is no longer on the board.'

Jake feels nettled, a flush treacherously rising to his cheek, but he can see the rough justice of what she is saying. He swallows. 'Can we not call Livia wifey, by the way? Livia is just as easy.'

Martha is puffing away lugubriously. 'Fair enough. And fair enough on you taking the criticism on the chin. You're an all right man to have an adventure with, I reckon. Look, let's end this chat now. Any texts we send, sign off with the name of a crime author, for verification. If we leave it blank, the other will know there's a problem.'

Jake grins bitterly. 'They did that in a John Buchan novel, but they used derby winners, horses, I think.'

'I never loved Buchan. Too blatant, too Boy's Own.'

'One day after we're done, we'll have to have a proper literary debate. You're talking nonsense as ever.'

'I can't wait for that, what a reward that will be. I'm all of a flutter with excite—' And with that Martha kills the call.

Jake throws the phone across to the sofa opposite, where it nestles against the cushion. He wonders whether he should call Watson, or Livia for that matter, talk things over, formulate a plan. But he thinks not. Livia would not welcome his continued involvement, he knows that. And he has not checked with Martha how much she wants her identity or involvement widely known. It would be hard to explain to Watson how he knows about the autopsy, without bringing her into it.

He spends the rest of the day outside, wrapped up in his thickest clothes, a woollen hat with an incongruous bobble atop, staring into his firepit, book on his lap, turning the venison. He watches the clouds gather, the vaulted expanse of the sky go from pale blue and limitless to grey and heavy and threatening. Darkness falls early, the wind starts to whistle around him, riffling the hair near his shoulders and his beard. There is slight succour in the glowing warmth of the fire, the smell of roasted meat, the sputterings of fat. But not much. After several hours, the roast is done: its surface charred and caramelized, smoke-stained, the meat still just about reddening, odd blooms of blood when he cuts it.

He walks to the village, despite the ominous skies, now invisible in the black of evening. He finds, as he expected he would, Rose holding court in the Nook, mid-blarney, a flagon of warm cider in one hand, a hand-rolled cigarette in another, his dark skin flushed, his expression filled with mocking pleasure, and he convinces him – after some gentle persuasion – to meet him back there at seven in the morning with a car.

The night outside the shop is clean and cold, oddly healthful in contrast. But it is a troubled Jake who trudges home to try to sleep a while. He wonders what body the morning will bring.

Chapter Thirty-Two

Tuesday, 8.25 a.m.

Rose waits in his car, reluctantly, in the hospital car park while Jake goes to pick up the pass from reception. It is quiet, though by no means empty. Two doctors stride purposefully, a man and a woman in shirtsleeves and suit trousers, their rainbow-hued lanyards bumping against their chests. Patients slump on various seats, as far apart as possible, their faces drained by the unforgiving light. One is reading a thriller with an austere landscape on the cover, two are staring at their phones absently. A fourth, in the corner, has given up on all possible stimulus, and glares at the middle distance, mouth tight in pain or perhaps anger. The smell of disinfectant and decay everywhere.

The receptionist is on the phone, and addresses Jake with no more than a raised eyebrow. Jake gives the name 'Rex Stout' and his desire to visit the mortuary, and she silently slams down a pass. She cups the receiver. 'That's the only replacement you're getting, be more careful with this one.'

He sees the card has a blurry image of an anonymous man with facial hair, a close enough resemblance to pass idle scrutiny. He makes a note to congratulate Martha on her efficiency, and hangs the pass around his neck. Rose drives him to a rear car park, where there is a door to the mortuary.

'Can't I come with you?' This is a variation of a conversation they have been having since Rose met him by the river just as a gloomy and frosty dawn was breaking, the black fading into purple, the stars sedately disappearing as if by the turning of a dimmer switch. The storm had held off, but the temperature had plummeted, the paths and roads coated with precarious blue sheet-ice that crackled underfoot.

'I only have one pass. Be a dear, and stay in the warm, put the radio on.'

'Remind me, why am I doing this again?'

'Because you believe in karma, and you want to make reparations for your criminal past?'

A pause. Rose strokes his stubbly face. 'Nope, definitely not that. Just get it done quickly. Hospitals give me the creeps, even in the car park.'

Jake slips out of the car, and hunches his shoulders as the wind immediately bites, the cold experienced simply as pain. He manoeuvres along the path and pushes open the door. Inside it is not much warmer, or more welcoming. The lights are dim, funereal even, casting shadows into the corners adorned with dying pot plants, centring on a reception desk in front of a set of closed double doors. Everything is painted in shades of grey.

Jake can't see anyone on duty. He presses a button but hears no sound in response. He is about to see if the doors are unlocked, when they open and a man shuffles in, short and slightly overweight, his thinning, yellow hair pushed across his head, his belly fighting a battle with his shirt and winning, glimpses of pallid flesh above his belt line. When he looks up, Jake sees his big blue eyes amid a sea of sagging skin, the bags beneath thickly pronounced like they might hold water from above.

Jake hazards a smile and is met with nothing. He clears his throat, and briskly waves his pass. 'Morning, morning. I'm here to take a quick look around, no need to bother anyone. I just need to see your latest paperwork, and match it to your most recent arrivals?'

The pass is casually examined. 'Mr Stout, is it? Hardly sounds like a real name. Well, nobody told me about an official visit. Who are you anyway?'

Jake gets into character, someone personable enough to be convincing, boring enough to be forgettable. 'I'm a consultant to the hospital, not a doctor consultant, an efficiency consultant. I always disappoint people when I say that, I'm afraid. Ha, ha. We're here to look at how the Trust might save money, and I need to see first-hand all of the processes, including, I'm afraid, what you might call the terminal one. No need to disturb your day too much, Mr, erm?'

'Dennis, John Dennis.' He scratches a contemplative flake of dandruff from his hair, where it joins the liberal gathering on his shoulders. 'Morgue attendant. You've just missed the autopsy doctor, but he'll back in an hour or two.'

Thank God for that, thinks Jake. 'No worries. I know

how busy you all will be. I'll just look at the paperwork and be out of your, er, hair well before then.'

Dennis has already sat down in front of his computer, his wrist flicking the mouse with practised motion. He waves airily behind his head. 'Your name sounds like a fake one, but they don't pay me enough to care. If your pass lets you in, have at it. Recent paperwork is on the first desk, waiting approval. I'll just be out here.'

Jake nods and edges past him. His pass works, and he pushes through the double doors into an anteroom of the mortuary. The sterile smell of embalming fluid greets him, caustic in his nostrils. He looks through the slim files on the table.

The first two are from earlier in the weekend, cases where both had died in the hospital itself: a liver failure and a huge cardiac arrest. The third is more interesting, but also confusing. It has only been partially completed. There is no name on it, just a peremptory dash of the pen. The originating address is somewhere called 'The Lodge', which Jake remembers as an outbuilding of Purple Prose, originally a place for overspill on big weekend events there. No other identifying information has been added to the front sheet.

The next sheet contains a drawing of a blank human body, on which someone – presumably, he thinks, an attending paramedic or doctor – has drawn in two lines indicating stab wounds, one in the chest just beneath the collarbone, the other, dramatically, across the neck. The phrase 'massive blood loss' is written beneath in hasty biro. The final sheet is titled 'Preliminary observations'. It is mostly blank apart from a note saying: *Per instructions from File 827, no comments, death recorded as congestive lung failure, following long-term treatment.*

186

Jake feels his hackles rising, even in the dank chill of the room. The sheet indicating stab wounds would have come in with the body, he reckons. After that point, the corpse must have been examined by somebody involved in the conspiracy, paid off, probably the autopsy doctor, who was yet to return to finish the job. As it stands, the file had not been properly purged, but it soon would be, leaving only the bare reference to a death by natural causes. Jake sidles to a photocopier and runs off a copy, which he folds into his jacket pocket.

He looks around him. He can see the crown of Dennis's head through the doors, the bluish blur of the screen in front of him. He checks the clock, watches the jerky insistence of the second hand: he has only been in here twenty minutes, so he has a little more time, he thinks. He moves to the next room, which is even colder, but brightly lit, a vision of the clinical and the sterile. In one corner is a drain, presumably to remove the unwanted fluids, but the whole place is clean, almost violently so. One whole wall contains a series of huge drawers, a body bank as they used to call it, where corpses are stored until they are taken off for burial.

Jake looks down for the reference number on his version of the file. He finds the relevant drawer and jerks it open. It slides smoothly out on castors. There is a body bag, which he carefully unzips, but he can tell from the shape already what he will find. Nothing. It is empty. Whatever corpse there was there, if there was one, now it's gone.

Chapter Thirty-Three

Tuesday, 9.20 a.m.

Jake stands with his hands on his hips, lips pursed. It is not that surprising, he supposes, if a cause of death is being hidden or altered, that something surreptitious would need to be done with a body. The carnage of a stabbing is above all obvious, a long gash across the throat, or a puncture wound to the chest, with its halo of contused flesh, purpled and obscene. It is not something to be explained away or ignored. And yet, to all intents, it has been, by an organization with a long reach indeed, to pluck evidence from a hospital, and have records altered without qualm. Once the file was clean and in the system, the death registered, no doubt the body could be quietly buried with nobody any the wiser.

The ticking of the clock prods him, reminds him that he is standing somewhere he shouldn't be, and he carefully closes the body bag and slides the drawer back into place. He tries a couple more drawers at random, revealing the pale cadavers of the recently deceased, the colour of fish belly, their expressions blank, hair combed down into place, huge and catastrophic scars down their body where a pathologist had intruded into their final repose. Death is always a mess, he knows, a calamity of smells and sights, and always an assault on dignity. The living body, for all its flaws, is a feat of engineering, of majestic usefulness, it makes sense, it has shape and solidity; robbed of life it becomes no more than a slab of flesh, something animal, a sack of viscera already on the turn into putridness.

There is a small bag in the corner of the room. He picks it up, it has almost no weight at all. Inside is a dress, long and black and expensive, its upper half savagely ribboned. The work of a knife, he thinks. He pauses, and decides to take it, folding the plastic into its smallest shape and slipping it beneath his jacket.

Time to get out of here. He walks into the anteroom, checks there is nothing else to investigate, before heading back out through the double doors. Dennis is still at his screen, now spooning yoghurt into his mouth from a square Tupperware container. Jake glances over his shoulder: his screen shows several tabs open, videos from YouTube and less salubrious sites, at least one of which looks rather pornographic.

Dennis clears the screen, but laconically, as if he refuses to be embarrassed by his online activity. Jake raps the desk in farewell, before pausing as if he has just recalled something. 'Oh, one thing, there's a reference somewhere to File 827 in one of the recent cases. I couldn't see that file anywhere. Mean anything to you?'

'Mr Stout, if that is your real name. I'm a scut worker,

a drone, a loafer and an idler. I sit here, get free internet, the occasional ignoble thrill of touching and cleaning up after dead bodies, and lots of time to work on my novel. I don't make managerial decisions about file systems. I've never heard of File 827. If it's not there, I can't help you.'

It was a long shot, anyway. 'No worries. What's the novel about?'

Dennis's lazy, ironic expression sharpens for an instant. 'It's a spy story, but set in the future, a world where a dictatorship controls everything, but a mole from within threatens to destroy the hard-won order. Sort of *1984* meets *Tinker, Tailor, Soldier, Spy*, if you can imagine such a thing.'

'I can indeed. You keep at it. Thanks for your time.'

With that, Jake pushes open the back door, an expected blast of frozen air striking his face. Rose is idling the engine in one corner of the car park, and Jake quickly marches up and slides into the passenger seat.

'Hold on,' he says, placing a hand on Rose's arm. 'I just want to see if anyone comes along.' They wait a tetchy ten minutes, while Jake explains what he has seen.

It only makes Rose the more keen to go. 'This is some deep shit you're getting into, Jake. I don't like the sound of a cover-up like this. I can't see the point in waiting to get dragged into it further.' He starts fussing with the mirrors, checking all around him. 'And whose dress do you think that is? The prossie you mentioned before?'

'Elegantly put. It must be a strong possibility, though, mustn't it? Someone from the house, a woman, killed probably as part of a game. Remember they mentioned a murder mystery; I don't think it would be too much to think it was a real one.'

190

'This sounds like the No Taboo thing we're all supposed to be scared of. I don't like any of it. I think we should get out of here.'

Jake nods silently. Rose revs the engine – the car is a sleek Land Rover Discovery, loud-bodied and powerful – and the wheels slide in the slick slush before gripping as they jerk forward.

They make the journey home without speaking much, Rose turning the stereo up, strange, hypnotic beats he has mixed himself, which make an eerie soundtrack in the ash-grey landscape. A flutter of snow begins to fall, dancing in the whispering wind. Rose drops him off at the edge of Parvum, his usually placid expression furrowed. 'Jake, you don't need me to say this, but I really think you ought to be very careful about meddling here. I hate to sound like Liv, but what the fuck are you doing? You don't need this. I don't need this, for that matter.'

Jake leans through the car's open window and shakes his hand. 'I know, but I don't think walking away is going to cut it. I'm stuck here, unless I can find a way out. I won't bother you though. You're right that you don't need it.'

A mirthless smile. Rose returns the pressure of the handshake. 'Ah, I never shy away from a scrap, or a bit of intrigue. If you're stuck, I'll help, but for both our sake's let's only do something if you have to. And make sure you keep Livia well away from this, or you'll be back to being hermit man again.'

Jake nods, and stands back. Rose speeds off, throwing a splutter of dirty liquid in his wake. Jake wends his way carefully through the village as the intensity of the snow increases. It is beautiful and silent: the join between house and land, road and field, human and nature, blurred and obscured by the fall. Livia's house is empty when he lets himself in, the fire in the living room a muted glow, but still warming and consoling. He makes himself a coffee and sits by it, feet towards the embers, his mind active and troubled.

Livia must be on a long round of visits, so he decides to head home. As he locks her door, the key stiff and awkward, he turns towards the road. A big black car is parked twenty yards away, its engine purring, windscreen wipers flicking insistently. As he heads up to the river, it revs and moves past him slowly. The rear window comes down, and he gets a glimpse inside. Charles, the man with the two-tone eyes, stares back impassively, holding his gaze, faint movement of his head sideways. Next to him is Fenella, whom Jake remembers, the arch woman from the house. Jake can recall little more than her dismissive attitude, her aristocratic disdain for those around her. Charles is holding her hand, thick fingers clutching at something cool and slender, and her face looks pale and pained. The haughtiness is still there, a smoulder in the eyes, but it has been tempered, diluted by a more powerful emotion. Fear, perhaps, or shame. Jake moves towards them, but the car increases speed and turns the corner and away, the engine noise slowly diminishing, absorbed by the surrounding softness.

Chapter Thirty-Four

Tuesday, 11.45 a.m.

Watson is waiting in the courtyard when Jake gets home, his long frame wrapped in a thick black coat, leaning under the eaves to get away from the snow, hands deep in his pockets, an angular shadow. He is whistling tunelessly when Jake reaches the house, face breaking into a smile at his arrival.

Jake busies himself in the kitchen immediately, stoking the stove and leaving its door open to warm the room quicker, brewing a strong pot of coffee. That delightful combination of homely scents. He grabs a record too, something to settle languorously in the background, a performance by the New York Philharmonic of some Dvořák, which starts with the sad strains of the *New World Symphony*. Watson is watching him with his usual half-sardonic expression.

'Have you been up to much, since we last spoke, Jake?'

Jake hands him a steaming mug of coffee, a swirl of

thick cream on the top. He settles onto an armchair, wrapping his arm protectively around his slender knees. 'Just the question I was going to ask you, chief.'

Watson sips reflectively. 'Not much good news to report, I'm afraid. Young Laura is coping well, which is one positive thing at least. We think the damage to her is limited. But her parents have said they want us to stop questioning her so she can get on with her life. I don't entirely blame them. It puts our investigation into her abduction into a holding pattern, to put it mildly. In fact, my instructions are to let it drop and focus on other things.'

'Instructions? Has someone been telling you what to do?'

Watson bridles, shoulders stiffening. 'I resent the implication of that. No, I perhaps shouldn't have said instructions. I meant it's been deprioritized due to a lack of available evidence. It's a decision we all have to sign up to, and I'm going along with it as well. Reluctantly, but – to be honest – I'm not too sure where to go to next. She's not given us anything when it comes to her attackers, we got nothing from the house, which was clearly just used for that one occasion to drop her back. No prints, no DNA, nothing.'

'Have you looked more broadly at No Taboo? You're the one who found the business card.'

Watson lets the question hang while he contemplates the answer. A sudden sway of hectic strings, a note of plangency, rises from the record player, and then subsides once more. The stove spits and murmurs to itself. Watson holds Jake's gaze.

'I've done what I can, but I want to be frank with you,

194

Jake. Either this whole conspiracy is real and above my paygrade, my ability to handle. In which case it's probably best left alone. Or it's a mirage, something not actually there, in which case there is nothing to be done.'

Jake breathes out. 'So that's that.'

'You don't approve?'

'I didn't say that. I do feel that there are malign forces around the place, though. I think we've seen enough signs of that.' He is careful what he can tell even as close a friend as Watson, without compromising Aletheia and Martha. But he sketches out his thoughts on the atmosphere of Purple Prose, the presence of the man with the odd eyes, his reappearance outside Livia's house. 'And then, chief, I hear – I won't say how – that a corpse appeared from Martinson's place, but the body has gone missing from the hospital.'

Watson drains his cup. 'And where, if I might ask, did you hear that?'

'I can't say, but it's a good source.'

'But where does it take us when it comes to Laura, or anything else? I do trust your instincts, Jake, always have done. But I want to know what I'm getting into. I tell you what, I'll ask about that body quietly and let you know. You tell me if you get bothered by that piebald chap again. Other than that, do we leave it there?'

Jake's face betrays little emotion. 'I guess.' They share a moment of contemplative quiet. Jake slaps his hands against his knees. 'Now, the last time you came here around this time you were looking for lunch – can I tempt you again?'

'I thought you'd never ask.'

The meal is a simple one. Jake finds he likes strong-tasting food above all now. It is cold venison carved waver-thin from his roasted haunch, pink and smoky and delicious, served with small onions pickled in red wine vinegar so they are lurid magenta and eye-wateringly sharp. He cuts thick slices of bread, and slathers them with butter, scattering thick crystals of salt on the top. They drink ale he keeps in a barrel, delivered to the nearest road and then rolled painstakingly the couple of miles to his door. It is cool and dense in flavour. Watson savours every mouthful, and bids a companionable farewell, his slender form quickly absorbed by the growing storm outside.

Jake carries the remains of the coffee pot to the library, and takes the phone from the hidden compartment. He sends a message to Martha, outlining all that has happened. He pauses contemplatively and signs it 'Conan Doyle'.

He stokes the fire, picks up a piece of wood and his whittling knife, resuming his shaping of pegs for the tree-house, allowing the shavings to fall into a small basket. They are useful for firelighting, and he likes the way they ripple and contort as they are consumed by the flame. He has put on a Grieg piano concerto in the background, minor key plinking that focuses his sober mood. The phone beeps in unwelcome fashion. Martha is responding.

THAT AUTOPSY SIT IS ALARMING. LEAVE WITH ME. AM NOW LOOKING INTO THE CHARLES CHARACTER, AND HOPE TO DIG SOMETHING UP. MEANWHILE, ALETHEIA HAS SOMETHING. SHE WILL MEET YOU AT BLUNTISHAM CHURCH, TOMORROW AT 10am. APPARENTLY YOU KNOW IT. TAKE CARE. LOVE, ALLINGHAM

It is good, he thinks, that Aletheia is back in contact, albeit vicariously. It must be something significant too if she wants to meet in person. He picks the knife up again. Funny how his mum had always referred to worrying as 'whittling', the anxious working away at something, often without purpose. Funny also that he has now thought of her for the first time in what seems like years. She and his father had died in a car crash, a sudden tragedy that ensured at least they were never separated in old age. It had given him some financial independence, and emotional resilience, but it had also meant he had little experience of family at all in his adult life. That is what he had craved with Faye, and then thought he had relinquished by coming to Little Sky. Family was the opposite of freedom, but it was also the opposite of loneliness. The inevitable trade-off. Images of life with Livia and Diana flicker before him. His family perhaps.

Another beep. A further reminder why he has relished his escape from technology. But he looks immediately in any case.

ONE THING: THAT 'FILE 827' IS A STANDARD CODE FOR NATIONAL SECURITY OVERRIDE. IT MEANS THAT NO FURTHER QUESTIONS CAN BE RAISED ABOUT BODY. DEEP CONSPIRACY. BUT AS WE SUSPECTED. I'LL KEEP DIGGING. TEY

The 'Tey' reference perplexes him slightly. He looks around the room, novels filed in period groups and alphabetical order. Over the last year or so, he has lazily disrupted the system, returning books to the wrong section, but there were so many of them that the basic structure still persisted. He finds a Josephine Tey in the Golden Age section, and plucks out *The Daughter of Time*, which seems to be about a policeman investigating the murders of the Princes in the Tower by conducting research from his hospital bed.

Jake takes a look out of the window. The blizzard has intensified once more. He walks around the house, locking doors. He might as well hunker down with something to read. The wind whistles down the chimney, the fire dips and dithers, never still, and he occupies his mind with a conspiracy from five hundred years ago, instead of the one he is being forced to confront in the present.

Chapter Thirty-Five

Wednesday, 10 a.m.

Jake gets to the church at Bluntisham early and by a circuitous route. The storm has blown itself out once more, but it lingers as the merest hint on the edge of the horizon, a sulky, furtive presence filled with threats to come. The day is achingly bright, the light tart and sharp, lemony sun-glare bouncing off white snow, unsoftened by a sky that is broad and clear and deep.

Jake's breath hovers in front of him as he tramps across the ground. His walk is long and cold, his boots trudging in snow that is nearly a foot deep in parts. The world is devoid of people; it is tundral, hostile to the very notion of life. A bird of prey circles aloof in the sky above the field, but there is nothing to drive it downward, no reason to swoop.

He knows the church well. It contains the body of Sabine, the woman whose death had prompted his investigation eighteen months before. He had sat in the graveyard when it was mossy and soft, thick with greenery. Now it is as austere as death itself, hard and solid and unforgiving. The Anglo-Norman architecture is still imposing, a presence in the landscape, the eye drawn to a shape hewn from the stone itself, a rose window that is more than a thousand years old.

Jake circles the building cautiously, senses tingling. The ground is covered with fresh, untramped snow, so he can feel confident nobody has arrived ahead of him. The church door opens with a shudder. The prospect inside is gloomy despite the bright light, reflected off the snow, now pouring through the two main windows. The stained glass makes it bleed red and yellow on the flagstones beneath.

Jake's breath smokes even inside. The modern heaters that are clustered around the end of every other pew have not been switched on, and wouldn't be until half an hour before a service. Even then the elderly congregation would keep coats and scarves on, creaking uncomfortably to rise for each hymn. At this time of the morning it is a place of seclusion and emptiness, perfect for a meeting.

He settles in on a pew by one of the huge supporting pillars, a feat of medieval engineering that still leaves him astounded. Close-up, he can make out, glistening in the frosty light, the cuts that have modelled the block, each one a tiny step towards the overall creation, an act of care and patience, the artistry of attrition. He idly kicks the lurid prayer cushion in front of him, watching it bounce and spin. She will be here soon.

After a few minutes, he hears the hinges of the door clamour once again, and Aletheia walks in, her boot-clad footsteps ringing out on old stone. She is dressed in a long black coat, dark jeans, her hair wrapped inside a large woollen hat. She sits next to him on the pew, a wry smile on her face. One hand appears from inside her coat, and he clasps it briefly, before she tucks it back away. When they talk they do so in quiet voices, which echo faintly in the emptiness.

'It's good to see you, Al, it really is. How have you been?'

'I've not been home in four days. I'm staying in empty government flats that not many people know are empty. I've not seen my mum, which is driving me mad. I'll have to take a risk at some point just to check in. She'll be terrified without me.'

Jake nods sympathetically. 'What the hell is going on?'

She is looking forward towards the altar. Above it is a crucifix – Christ's body slender and twisted, the wood itself appearing to take on the frailty of his flesh, the bloodied wounds shrouded in the half-light – which swings gently in the wind whipping against the walls, and sneaking intruder-like through some of the cracks.

'Here's what it amounts to, I think, though I'm not sure I can really prove anything well enough to stand up in court. From the instant I've been investigating No Taboo I've received attention from their representatives. I got warned off, you remember, and pursued it more quietly, but then you got involved and since then we've all been watched to whatever extent. Why is that? Well, it must be because we're getting close to something. I think we can reasonably conclude that Laura's abduction was connected to the organization, and that one or both of your cold cases were the same. Laura was returned as a way of reducing the heat around any inquiries as, with her at home, nobody will be that interested in pursuing things. The man with the weird eyes then shows up in the house of a local billionaire—'

'And then again outside Livia's house.' Jake explains briefly what happened.

'Right, so he's clearly on the scene. We have a link between your man Martinson and No Taboo, which could be innocuous, but that hardly seems likely.'

'There's much more, Al.' He fills her in completely on his experience first at Purple Prose, then at the hospital morgue. She sits in silence. She has removed her hat, her stiff, taut hair falls just above her shoulders, flecks of grey like mica in marble. Jake nudges the prayer cushion from its hook, and it lands loudly, impact in the quiet.

Aletheia looks across at him. 'So you think someone has been killed at that house, perhaps as part of a murder mystery?'

'It would fit, wouldn't it? No Taboo gets people illicit thrills: experiences that you can't get in normal places. Like stolen children, or murder for fun.'

'That would make Charlotte the victim?'

'Not necessarily, but she would be my first guess, yes. I'm seeing if Watson can find out where the real body is. If not, we might have to go back to that house and dig around.'

'Who is "we" in this scenario?'

Jake gives a mirthless laugh. 'Good question, which people keep asking. You and me, and Martha, we're pretty committed. My friend Rose has helped so far. Livia is supportive to an extent but . . .' He leaves the thought incomplete.

'I know, she has a daughter to think of. Quite right too.' Aletheia is smoothing down the thick fabric of her trousers as she speaks, her fingernails a soft pink, the colour of her palms. 'OK, some more bits of information from me.' She exhales, eyes now staring blankly as she considers things. 'First, our friend Smits, the prison warden, was granted compassionate leave yesterday and has disappeared. His file says a close relation has died, but I can find no other record of that, so I think we have to assume the absence is suspicious. The more I looked at him, the dirtier he seemed, Jake. Anyway, and secondly, I've got details of his main security box.' She hands him a folded piece of paper, hands darting back to the warmth beneath her coat. 'You'll have to ask Martha how we get round things to open it. She was always better at that sort of stuff than me.' She smiles for the first time, brilliant white teeth in the gloom. 'Do you like her? She's a bit of an acquired taste.'

'Very much so. She's someone I think you can do business with.'

'She clearly thinks the same of you, which is quite the compliment, I can tell you. When she was in the business, she was notoriously picky about who she worked with. Not fond of fools at all.'

Another long pause. Jake shifts his chilled body to the side so he can look at Aletheia directly. 'Are you OK, Al? Have I dragged us into something we can't get out of?'

'I was in it already, remember. That's my job, and I've never given it up. You need to worry about yourself and your family of sorts. Do you have the stomach for this? Do they?'

'I guess I have to. And to keep them away from it as much as I can.'

'I'm afraid that's right. You can't just back out of this sort of game; we either find a way to win, or we have to

203

face some pretty awful consequences.' A car's engine mumbles in the far distance, which disturbs the trance-like nature of their conversation. Aletheia puts her hat on.

'I need to get out of here. I hid my car off the road behind some bushes but, let's be honest, a tall black woman is not exactly inconspicuous around these parts.'

Jake clasps both her hands, places his head near to hers. He can smell the lemony soap she always uses, a hint of peppermint on her breath. 'No doubt about that. You stay in touch. I'll take a look at what we can find out from this box of Smits's, and then let's meet again. There'll be a route out. We need to work out how to take some of these players off the board. We have to get at their power somehow, stop them as a threat.'

He can feel her hands grasp his. She gives him a delicate kiss on the forehead, like a benediction. 'You look after yourself too.' With that she walks swiftly out, the door juddering behind her, the church once again cold and silent as a tomb.

Chapter Thirty-Six

Wednesday, 12.45 p.m.

The walk back for Jake is slow and hard work, sometimes through unwieldy drifts, where snow has half-melted and then frozen again, thick crystals that cling to his boots and ankles, sometimes slipping on the ice that has coalesced on the paths.

He gets to Parvum, his leg muscles tingling, his face pinked with exertion. He stops off at the Nook, where Sarah gives him a mug of cocoa in the kitchen, and a slice of fruit cake. She has been baking, and the smells of warm spices and home-brewed spirits bathe his senses. She hands him a folded note, and goes off to deal with a customer while he opens it. It is from Watson.

Jake, I ran down the body from Purple Prose. It was an old gardener who died of lung failure. A long-term case. There was a mix-up at the mortuary, and some papers were misfiled

*right enough, but no evidence of any other
bodies I could see. No claim of stabbing at all.
Maybe the problem of dealing with conspiracies
is that we see them everywhere? Anyway,
nothing for me to go on, I'm afraid. Let's meet
in a couple of days – I'll leave a time with
Sarah soon – but in the meantime enjoy the
family instead. Gerald*

'So that's that.' Jake mouths the words to himself, but does not believe it. He lingers with Sarah, talking of nothing significant, his face attentive, his mind preoccupied with uncertainty and something approaching a shapeless fear.

Outside, as he walks home, he pauses to look back at the village. The sky has clouded over once more, but the light is still good. He remembers a painting he had seen in Paris with Faye once, on one of the cultural trips they had taken as they sought to maximize the benefits of their childlessness. Spend an expensive week in Paris or Rome in early summer, they exhorted themselves, because you couldn't do that if you had children. Turn the pain into a freedom to be cherished.

Anyway, he remembers the painting was called *The Magpie* by Manet or Monet. Monet, he thinks. He could be looking at the same scene right now. That day in the museum had been hot and stifling and they had enjoyed the cooling sight of the image: a rickety gate submerged in a snowy landscape, a solitary bird looking off to the distance, the wintry ground given bold tints of blue in the shade beneath the laden hedges, the backdrop of fields, pale and spectral, as if the ground were halfway to becoming sky. Instead of a magpie, he now can see a robin, a bold flash of red amid the pallor, plumply fussing between gate and fence, so light that it can perch atop the snow and leave no trace.

He knows he needs to contact Martha and plan some sort of attempt on the security box of Garland Smits. But what on earth can he tell Livia? He isn't sure whether saying nothing, and just doing it, has become the better option. But their relationship has always been open and frank, and he enjoys that, both of them no longer young, neither needing to dissemble their intentions or desires. Their togetherness was strong because they both seemed to want the same things: peace, quiet, shared solitude, comfort for Diana, the sensations of nature all around them. She does not, she cannot, want what he must now embrace: danger, conspiracy, threat to the family. Nor does he, of course, but his choices seem limited. The flitting robin offers no solace as it follows its inclinations hither and thither, a warble of satisfied urgency the undertone accompaniment.

Back home an hour later, he sends Martha an update message (signed Knox, the name of an obscure figure from the twenties who once wrote ten commandments for detective fiction), tends to the chickens, does some light weeding in the greenhouse. When he returns to the library, sipping a coffee, Martha has responded, in her typically abrasive, all upper-case fashion.

LEAVE DEPOSIT BOX PLAN TO ME. I'LL DELIVER INSTRUCTIONS AT NOOK BY NOON TOMORROW. YOU'LL HAVE TO DO LEGWORK. YES, PUN INTENDED. STILL WORKING ON YOUR PIEBALD CHARLIE: I

THINK HE IS 'CW', FORMERLY SOME SORT OF SPOOK, CONNECTIONS EVERYWHERE. WATSON WRONG ON AUTOPSY: DEFINITELY A MURDERED BODY SOMEWHERE. UPDATES TO FOLLOW. KNOX NOT A PROPER CRIME WRITER. LOVE, HIGHSMITH

Jake smiles. Martha sends texts like she is writing telegrams, as if she cannot take whatever drama is happening as seriously as her enemies would like. It is reassuring and charming, even as a defence mechanism. He looks outside; the last light is leaching away. The sun is half-set behind clouds, bathing the world in a muted magenta colour, soft pink being swallowed by grey. He takes a walk to stretch his aching legs. His exercise regime is healthful, he reckons, the constant thumping of heart and running of sweat, the way his muscles tauten and flex, the hardening of his body, the way it has become useful and purposeful. But it makes him feel his age too; each month sees him a little slower to recover, a little more lactic acid lingering when he sits for too long.

Past Chandler Lake, he looks up as normal towards Sherlock Beech, just visible in the growing gloaming. And, yes, there is a flicker of gaudy material, some sort of luminous yellow, like something torn from a cyclist in a city. He wonders why he is being summoned, but welcomes the feeling, and picks his feet up, heedless of the coming dark, as familiar with this route as the very passageways of Little Sky. The gap in a hedge, the track on the edge of the field, the dip then the rise before the road. Even in the depth of this freeze, where landmarks are obscured, variation obliterated by snowy conformity, he knows where he is going.

He approaches Livia's house. The lights are on, yellow pooling on white outside. The wind gusts from behind him, and her front door shudders, swinging a few inches. Why is it open? He increases speed, giving it a hard push and tumbling in, calling her name. There is a guttering flame in the fireplace, and little heat left in the living room. He shouts again. Nothing. Another gust slams the door shut. Other than that, silence.

Chapter Thirty-Seven

Wednesday, 4.50 p.m.

Jake tries to calm the pounding in his ears, hectic within his blood. He shouts again as he moves swiftly between rooms, stepping over familiar clutter that lies reproachfully all around him. The relics of a happy home, but is that still exactly what it is? He goes out the back where the snow lies crisp and untouched. Nobody has come that way. At the front, he pauses to look for tracks, but there has been quite a lot of traffic since the last snowfall, and it is hard to draw any conclusions. He calls Livia's name once more, his voice swallowed by the dark. He heads into Parvum itself, which has no street lights, just the lamps outside the houses that are some distance apart, buried away, protected by hedges. He finds himself moving from darkness into small clumps of pale light back into darkness once more. The Nook is closed and Jake remembers that Sarah had told him about shutting early to visit a nephew. There is nobody else about on such an unforgiving evening.

He wanders back to the house, his boots sometimes sliding on the ice, as panic makes him careless. The door is shut firmly now, perhaps by the wind, he thinks. He thumps against it with little hope.

It opens. Livia is standing there, high colour in her cheeks, her soft green eyes sparkling with exertion. Jake engulfs her in a hug, which makes her step back. He is inhaling the cherry scent of her hair, inarticulate.

She pushes him back gently, her voice soft. 'Jake, what on earth has got into you. Are you OK?'

His mouth is dry, but he can feel his body fill with a palpable tingle of relief. His words emerge staccato. 'The door was open. Nobody in. Thought something had happened to you.'

She brings him close once more. 'You're daft. Di and I went for what she calls a midnight walk. You know how she loves the snow at night.'

They go inside. Diana rushes forward and grabs his legs before rushing back to the kitchen once more. Jake manages a friendly pat of her head before she escapes.

'I saw the sign on Sherlock, as I was going for a wander myself. Did you need me?'

'I didn't need you, you big silly man, I wanted you. You know, wanted to see your hairy face, and your hard body. Like a girlfriend does.'

Relief has been replaced by joy. 'I can live with that.'

Livia gives him a squeeze and heads off to the kitchen herself, her movements sedate and regal as ever. She speaks over her shoulder. 'I'll tell that Diana off for not shutting the door, though. She promised me she had, the little terror. Come in for a proper warm, lovey, the stove is better than that fire right now, and I have some soup nearly ready.'

Later, after they put Diana to bed, they make love in front of the fire, which Jake has stoked to a pleasing, pelting roar. The flickering light and heat on their bodies, their shared hunger for sensation, Livia biting her hair as it falls in front of her face to stop moaning too loudly. They wrap a blanket around them, and lean against the old sofa. Cyprian the cat stalks in, and settles above them, her golden eyes filled with disdain at their horseplay. Livia pours some wine and settles against his chest. Then her body, so languid and sated before, stiffens.

'Jake, just why were you so worried? We've never locked that door, apart from the first few months after, you know, Mack's visit that night. Do you think we should be acting more carefully?'

Jake had wondered when she would draw this conclusion. 'I think we always need to be careful. Nothing's ended, Liv, really. We're still surrounded by a mystery, aren't we? In fact, it's getting more mysterious, not less.' He takes a deep breath, and swallows. He has to tell her everything, it would be a betrayal not to. Plus, she does need to look to her own safety as well, to be cautious and aware. He explains everything that has happened this week, since he left this house on Sunday. When he finishes, there is quiet. The wind rises and falls, the logs of the fire shift.

He looks across at Livia. The fire is reflected in her eyes, but there is anger there too, fury even. She inches away from him. 'When were you going to mention all of this, eh? Your little jaunt to the mortuary. A man we think might be the head of a fucking criminal conspiracy following you to my house. Diana's house. Your cosy churchy chat with Aletheia. That woman Martha, who

I've never heard of or met before, sending you messages, dragging you deeper into something, God knows what. Something that endangers me and Diana. After all we've said about that, after what happened last time.' She pushes at his arm, the blanket falling from her, exposing her nakedness before she drapes it around her once more. 'God, I can't even look at you.'

Jake is beseeching, tries to be soothing. He explains his view, reached only after painful consideration, that walking away is not an option, that the safest thing to do is find an ending, not rely on the hope of being simply left alone. Livia raises a hand, resolute, her face etched with despair.

'Do you really believe that, or think I will believe that? We both know that you're happy with this retirement, except when you want to be needed, to be active, to be the decisive detective again. It makes me feel so inadequate, you know.' Her voice drips with scorn. 'Well, you probably don't know do you? We're a part-time family to you, Jake, aren't we? Your ego'll allow that, but not much more. You still need the freedom to run off and be a problem-solver, knowing that we'll be here, all quiet and domesticated and grateful for your fucking return.'

Jake reaches for her, but she flinches. 'Liv, that isn't fair.' He feels anger starting to build inside him, a flicker becoming a flame. 'What do you want me to do? Pretend that none of this has happened? Let you go off to a house that could be run by murderers? Let them pick their time to come after you and me? I'm looking to get out of this in a way that can give us back our peace. I'm not going to just close my eyes and pretend that peace is here already. You may think we can do that. I don't have that luxury.'

Cyprian stretches, her claws scraping against the

fabric. She buries her head in her tail. Livia stands, reaching for her dressing gown. 'Just get out. I feel like you've been here, I don't know, under false pretences. Who are you, Jake? What is this we have? What sort of life do you want? Until we can know that, I don't want to see you. I don't want you near us. And you know . . .' She hands him the bundle of his clothes, adds a shove to his chest. 'You know, from all you've been saying, maybe being away from you is the safest place to be anyway.' With that, she marches to the bedroom, the door shuddering shut behind her.

Chapter Thirty-Eight

Friday, 11 p.m.

Jake lies in the sauna in a sweaty welter of self-recrimination and anger. The light is low and he is smouldering and brooding in the enclosed space, like an animal hunted back to its lair. The heat is singeing the hair in his nostrils as he breathes deeply.

He cannot take his mind from Livia. He feels he can justify his behaviour and his attitude, at one level, and is firm in his belief that there is no simple route away from the situation. If he could walk away to be with her, he tells himself, he surely would.

But he is also enough of a realist to weigh Livia's scornful words with due care. She is right, up to a point. He knows he does like things both ways. He does crave the domestic seclusion, the freedom, the rejection of professional obligation and the tyranny of timekeeping. At the same time he also likes the thrill of the chase, the challenge of solving a puzzle, the endorphin rush of being needed, that sense of ever striving to be a winner. He wouldn't have been a good police officer if he hadn't liked slaying the occasional dragon, protecting the world from a mortal threat.

He wipes some sweat from his stomach, flattening the dark hairs, flecked now with grey. He idly watches the muscles move beneath the skin as he shifts position. He is as narcissistic as the next person, maybe more so. He sighs, the noise joining the hiss of the coals and the shudder of the wind as it paws the window from the outside.

Maybe you either have to renounce the world or not, it is a binary thing; you can't be a little bit pregnant, as it were. The metaphor rises bitterly to his mind. But all of life – outside the most improbably monastic – surely means not renouncing some things, staying entangled to a certain extent. Even his love for Livia carries some obligations (Diana, for example), though they are most often joyfully assumed. Nothing in life is truly simple. He reaches down and cracks the door a fraction, where a bottle of vodka is half-buried in a snowdrift. The fresh air tickles his legs. He brings the bottle in and swigs lustily, before pushing it outside once more and closing the door. He feels sad and desperate and self-indulgent. There is a big difference between living in the normal world with Livia, of course, and choosing to get involved in a fight against a shadowy conspiracy of child abduction and murder. That was her point. And yet, once in, just how did he get out without causing further harm? She refused to see the strength of his argument, but it was there, unresolved, even at the bottom of the bottle.

Jake stands, light-headed, drunk, and overwhelmed. He pushes the door open, fully this time, allows the howling

216

wind to enter. He staggers forward, upending himself unromantically in the drift outside, the shock of the cold, ice on mithered skin. He pauses, his body responding to the change in temperature, his mind clearing. He sees the ridiculousness of it all, and laughs out loud, brash and startling in the silent black of the night. He despises drunks generally, people who can't control themselves, and yet look at him now, naked in a snowdrift, incapable and ridiculous.

Ten minutes later he is in front of the fire inside, wrapped in a blanket, still shivering. He is too drunk to make any proper decisions, and abandons himself to the muzzy sensations. After three uncomfortable hours he wakes, the fire dead, his naked body stiff, his mouth filled with acid, his mind with self-loathing. He has come to some sort of subconscious decision, he realizes, as he gingerly dresses and heads to bed. He will give Livia space, and press ahead in the meantime against No Taboo. There is simply no other way forward he can consider.

The sun has risen by the time he wakes once more, though you'd hardly know. It is imprisoned in thick grey clouds that cling jealously to each ray of light. Some more snow has fallen while he has been sleeping. Jake makes himself change and go for a penitential run, each initial step a calculated misery, until his body releases some of the poisons within. His plunge in the lake is a final act of catharsis and cleansing. He has a hearty meal of bacon and eggs, a pint of coffee, soundtracked by the hectic janglings of Liszt's *Mephisto Waltz*, and feels almost human again.

The phone is flashing when he finds it, pushed into the side of the sofa, as he tidies the mess of the library. Martha confirming that material has been sent to the Nook for noon. She has signed it 'Rendell' this time, which doesn't require much investigation. Jake checks the time, he can be at the shop on schedule if he leaves now.

When he gets there, Sarah is sweeping fresh snow from the front porch, her hands pink and swollen, clawing at the broom. She gives him a wink. 'The wanderer approaches. You look like you might have tied one on last night.'

Jake is sheepish. 'How can you tell from that distance? I'm showered and clean and sober, I promise.'

'Years, my old duck, of being around drinkers. There's no way of shifting it entirely when you've gone down far enough. Summat around the eyes, I reckon. They're redder than they have any business being.'

He holds his hands up in acceptance and surrender. She takes a file from a shelf by her side and hands it to him. 'You're making a habit of getting messages from suspicious fellers, I'll give you that. This lad sped up on a motorbike, kept his helmet on when he walked into the shop, said your name and marched straight out. Anything you want to tell me about?'

They have walked companionably inside, where an electric heater is fighting a losing battle against the chill. Jake doesn't want to draw Sarah into this at all (though he notes with a passing pang that he has already done just that; another act of selfishness as Livia would see it), so merely refers to an old case. He does concede that his involvement has angered Livia.

Sarah nods equably. 'Ah well, I've always said you've got to work out how you two can make your lives suit one another. But I've also reckoned there's enough regard there to make it happen. I'll not change my mind because of an argument.'

'Let's hope you're right.'

Sarah lets him sit down in the kitchen, and he quickly reads through the document. It is short, a bullet-pointed explanation of where Smits keeps his safety deposit box, and instructions of how to get at it. Jake marvels at Martha's clarity and precision, and the scale of her influence. Clearly, she has not taken her retirement seriously at all.

Chapter Thirty-Nine

Friday, 4.30 a.m.

Martha's plan calls for him to be in the city first thing, before the bank – a small private affair he has never heard of – opens properly. He is dressed in dark nondescript clothes as he waits near the river for Rose to give him a lift to the station. Thick black jeans, a midnight-blue hooded jumper, and an outer jacket, soft and moulded to his body. He has made one addition, inspired by something he has read in his Bernie Gunther book: stitching razor blades into his lapels, an old Berlin trick apparently, a defence against anyone grabbing you unawares. He felt slightly ridiculous as he did it, but also reasoned that all of his past experiences would suggest he is in a fight for his life.

Near to him his heron flaps its wings in the icy pre-dawn, the flashes of its belly white like distress flares, but it doesn't shift its ground. Jake stomps his feet on the frozen mud, hard as concrete beneath his thick boots.

Twin headlights move slowly towards him, the beams catching the early morning mist that floats past. Rose raises a minatory finger when Jake opens the door and sits down, bringing the chill in with him. 'It's too early to speak. No pleasantries. Yes, I am generous to be taking you to the station. Yes, it really is too much. Yes, I would like to be in bed with an immoral woman. No, I don't want to know what nefarious business you have in the city, unless you say you need me then maybe I'll help.'

'I knew you couldn't keep up that big grumpy bear thing for long. No, your role can be restricted to transport; if I need you to put yourself in danger I'll give proper warning.'

'Good enough for me.' Rose drives quickly and incautiously, the car moving fast over slippy roads hemmed-in by snow-clad hedges that seem to be ever close to falling in on them. His dance music is loud and disorienting, metronomic thuds and pulses to which Rose moves his head in dreamy fashion as he drives. Jake gets out at a station in time for the first train, and he finds himself in the city before most people are up.

He has Martha's directions for the bank, which is only a few minutes north of the station. The roads are sodden with grimy slush, once-virgin snow soiled with pollution, the vaguely whiter drifts pushed up hillock-high against the kerbs. The pavements have been gritted, salmon-coloured salt that he can feel beneath his boots. This part of the city does its business much later in the day, he realizes, so it is deserted at this time of the morning. It is prosperous, old money, Georgian history, buildings well-constructed in a marmoreal white, places which once served as embassies, or clubs, or private homes for the wealthy.

221

Now much of the money that flows around the area is foreign in its origin, from Russia and Saudi Arabia and China. Many of the buildings are unadorned, apart from discreet signs that offer little indication of what business is transacted, hidden within. All of the windows are thickly draped, little slivers of apricot light falling outward, but no possibility of anyone being observed inside.

This was the sort of place where No Taboo would flourish, Jake thinks. There is the hum of power here, of the sort of quiet power that actually has bite, has consequences, but passes unnoticed and unrestrained. The more obnoxious vulgarity of the super-rich is also there, but only in the cars parked outside, heedless of restrictions, big, loud-engined monsters, Aston Martins, Porsches, Humvees. In one, despite the hour, a driver sits patiently, no doubt with the heater purring, his face impassive as he awaits his orders to prowl the city once more.

On his journey, Jake pauses in front of various shops, an antiques store, a charmlessly flashy bar, a jeweller's, and looks around to make sure he is not being followed. He can see nobody paying him any attention, does not see the same face twice. The few people who are about are wrapped up against the cold, walking briskly towards the underground station or their offices. A bus hums by, electric-powered, no longer belching exhaust fumes as it once would. It is empty apart from a solitary old lady at the back.

The bank is in a small square of uniform white buildings, solid and unspectacular, quiet enough as dawn begins to break. It is a charming sight. It occurs to Jake how little he likes the modern practice of building with glass and concrete, which lacks style or beauty or even real permanence. Much of the city looks cheap and brittle, but this part still contains constructions to be reckoned with and enjoyed. Not that he is here for any enjoyment. His heart races as he walks to the door. It opens before he can knock, and he finds himself inside an atrium, with marbled floors, heavy furnishings, and a briskly burning fire. The door closes behind him.

'I have been asked to obtain a password from you.' The voice is heavily accented, and comes from a slender figure in a pressed black suit, with dark hair, and sharp eyes.

Jake is prepared. 'The password is Oblivion.'

There is a pause.

Jake continues. 'And I am instructed to remind you of the ambassador's security guard.' He has no idea what that means.

The man smiles wolfishly and directs him to a sofa. 'That's good enough.' He raises a hand. 'There's no need for names.' His voice is staccato, businesslike, as if he does not want to delay Jake's presence any more than necessary. 'There are no cameras in here, at the wish of our clients. Nor are there any in the viewing room.' He reaches down. 'Please put these on.' He hands Jake a long overcoat, a trilby hat, and some sunglasses.

'There are cameras in the corridor. Keep your head down and walk quickly to the second door on your left. Here is a key. It will get you into a room, which will be empty apart from the safety deposit box. Do what you have to do, and then come out the way you came in. You have thirty minutes, no longer, or the door will lock. I will not be here when you return. Leave the hat and coat on the sofa and depart immediately. It is worth more than my life for you to be caught.'

This is the arrangement that Martha had made, and he agrees immediately. Soon he is inside a vault-like room, sound-proofed and heated, with a small table on which there rests a large stainless-steel box. He discards the disguise and slips off his hooded top. He can feel the film of sweat on his forehead and across his body, it must be twenty-five degrees warmer here than outside. The box opens with a click, Jake lays its contents out on the table.

There is cash, fifty-pound notes wrapped tight in rubber bands. More than five thousand pounds' worth, he calculates quickly. There are some pornographic images, lithe young women astride middle-aged men, clearly taken secretly from a camera overhead. Some of the girls look of age, some do not. There are slender boys there too, all their faces lacking expression, their eyes pools of unstated hurt. He wants to stop looking, his stomach roiling, but he keeps going until something stops him. There. He pauses, as if kicked in the chest. A young boy, naked, terrified, a large, sweaty body pressed next to his, in gleeful possession. He can still remember his face from years before: James, just eight, robbed from his parents, never found or freed. It had always nagged at him, what might have been James's fate, and now he knows what he always feared is true. He tastes bile in his mouth, and puts the photographs down.

There are account books, the first page of which contains the various bank details of Garland Smits. Jake looks at the regular payments he has received, all sourced through a variety of foreign banks. He has cleared more than a hundred thousand in the last two years. Beneath them is a notebook where Smits has kept an account of work he has undertaken, described in terse phrases. Jake flicks through at random. He sees references to meetings with CW, which are regular and are normally followed with specific jobs, just given as an abbreviation like 'Kid' or 'Knife' or 'Coke' and some sort of reference number. A couple mention WJ, which Jake wonders about. He pulls out the phone and snaps photos of the pages, pinging them across to Martha as he goes.

Time is running out, he does not want to be trapped here. He recalls the date of the Nathan White murder, the homeless man who died with two different violent cuts, whose death was linked to the soldier. He looks through the books, and there is the entry: 'White, knife, extra action.' He weighs up his options, and slips the book into his pocket. He thinks again and takes the money too, his anger at James's fate clouding his thoughts.

He leaves the room with a minute to spare, discards his disguise in the drawing room as directed, and is out of the door into the press of fresh, enlivening air. The sun has risen, sullen and reluctant, while he has been inside, and the morning is obstinately grey. Jake's eyes dart all around as he walks back to the station, his mind racing. At one point he crosses another square, and posts the packs of money into a bin for dog mess, one by one until his hands are empty.

Chapter Forty

Friday, 4.20 p.m.

'That was, if you don't mind me saying, fucking dumb.'

Jake has been texting Martha since he got home (he signing himself as D. Hammett, she as Robert Galbraith), before she decided to call him on Signal. This is her opening gambit.

Jake lights a small joint he has ready-rolled, sucking in the thick and heady smoke. He feels oddly deflated and fatalistic. He shrugs as he exhales.

'It was. But I don't suppose he goes and counts his money every day, and there was no way I could leave it there for him.'

Martha leans forward. Her eyes are glimmering bright, as if she were fevered. She is wearing shorts and a vest, despite the season, her tattooed skin bulging as she grips the arms of the chair. 'Are you feeling vengeful, Jakey? Maybe there's something to work with there.'

Another shrug. 'Actually, I feel overwhelmed with it all.

Just look at it, all this conspiracy stuff, all this – I don't know – evil that's gone on without fear of punishment, and what can I really do about it? You could get your security buddies to break open that box and arrest Smits, I suppose.'

Martha is drinking an outsized mug of coffee loudly. 'I've thought of that. But I don't even know whether someone in my old outfit is in the No Taboo conspiracy or not. I trust some of them, but not the whole apparatus. Not from what I've seen. And your friend Watson is not senior enough to bust open something like this. No, we need another plan.'

Jake nods in helpless agreement. 'Right, what do we think we know, what does it all boil down to? That's what I would always do in a cold case. Try to pare it back to essentials. Run through what we think – between you, Aletheia and me – we've actually got here.'

'Let me start by saying it's nice to be the sober and practical one for a change. OK. Most of this comes from you, but I have other sources, and so does Aletheia. Let's start with your early cases. The homeless guy Nathan White for a starter.

'He's in prison, a weak and tired and friendless man, pretty chewed up by the system. Our friend Garland Smits is a big figure there; he uses his job as a prison warden to scout for targets to use on behalf of No Taboo. Not with any specific job in mind, just as assets who can be exploited. Smits spots White, and then it's easy to provoke an outburst of petty rage from him that has him sent to solitary.' She finishes her coffee and puts the mug down, belching softly. 'When he has his claws on him, Smits bullies him, intimidates him, makes him a snitch in prison when he returns to general population, and then has him to command – for depressingly small amounts of money – when he gets out.

'One day, some client of No Taboo must have requested the experience of committing a killing, close-up, and visceral. They needed a target, a victim, and Smits knew immediately that they had White, who they thought was a worthless man, at their command.'

Jake sips some water. 'But it didn't go smoothly.'

'As we know, the difference between the idea and the action is often very considerable, especially when we are talking about the messy business of murder. I can imagine our amateur killer, nerving himself with booze, finally got the stones to strike White once with a blade. A blow to the gut, painful and damaging, but perhaps not enough to end it. And then panic overtook our brave assailant and he fled the scene, no doubt questioning his manhood as he went.

'Smits has, of course, foreseen such a contingency, and has a back-up to finish the job. The note in his book said "extra action" didn't it? So this other chap Sergeant Jones was there, a man on the hook with the relevant experience in close-quarter combat. He finished the job. That's why there were two different wounds, from two different blades.'

'But he left some DNA at the scene, which was triggered when he was later arrested for rape,' Jake says.

Martha finishes the thought. 'And when that happened, he became a risk to their operation that could not be tolerated, so he was disposed of. A tidy suicide. Your cold case was completed: you had a victim and a killer, neatly tied up. And, actually, it had the benefit of being true: the one had killed the other. Then Jones was dead, and couldn't testify to any conspiracy.'

Jake thinks for a moment. 'So Smits is our man here.'

'Yes and no. He works for "CW", who is this bloke Charlie with the funny eyes. He is, from what I can tell, the main boss of No Taboo, probably helped by others. He's the man, or one of them.'

'Does that include Martinson?'

'We have to think yes, right? Charlie was at his house, he's a rich and powerful figure with a questionable reputation. I'm sure he's part of the mix.'

'And that party at his house I went to?'

'I've looked into that. It looks like a gathering of clients. The super-rich, brittle folk in search of excitement: that boringly adventurous couple of swingers, the Lambs, Fenella Jewell, a monied princess in search of adventure, the doctor, all of them. I think they were there for a real-life murder mystery.'

'So why invite me?'

'To mess with you, to play a game. Plus, I think they wanted to know what you know. They knew you'd been involved in the past, that Aletheia was quietly investigating the existence of No Taboo, that your chum Watson had come to you. They needed to flush you out. I reckon they gave wifey – sorry, Livia – the vet job to get you. And then they could have compromised you with the murder, or maybe come after you directly. You left before it could start, and they didn't want to risk a big confrontation by making you stay.'

Jake puffs his cheeks. 'Liv won't like that at all.'

'That's love for you. Meanwhile, there are the separate abduction cases of James in the past, and Laura in the present. A snapshot of the child sex business that Smits is involved in for No Taboo.'

'So why let Laura go?'

'Because they wanted to lower the temperature. You are a bit formidable, you know, for all your hippy airs, and they quickly found out that you and Al were something of a threat. They wanted to finish checking you out without their operation being compromised. Instead of you damaging it, they let it go, no harm done.'

'It makes sense, kind of. What do we do now?'

'I want to run things past Aletheia, to see if this all checks out. Then I think we need to dig around Purple Prose. There's been a murder there, we reckon, which has been covered up. You've got the damaged dress, and saw the unedited file. Maybe that's our road to exposing them all.'

'That could be tricky with no corpse, and a police view that nothing happened.'

'We need such incontrovertible proof that your chum Watson will have to act without taking a risk, and my security friends can get involved too. To blow the conspiracy, we have to prove beyond doubt that there is one. Otherwise, it's the theory of a legless woman and a hairy burnout. We're fairly easy to dismiss still.'

She is right on that, Jake realizes. 'And walking away is still not an option?' He is thinking of Livia, the idea of her apart from him making him wince.

'Jakey, I don't think you would walk away even if you could, however much you love her. You've seen too much. You know what happened to little James. That's going to eat at you. Plus, I think they'll be coming for you too. You're too much of a threat now, even if they somehow believe you've been convinced to leave them alone, even if they think Livia or whoever has made you see sense. Look, I know this is awful, but we have to keep going. Leave me to speak to Aletheia, and then we'll come up with a plan.'

Jake nods. 'Fair enough. And, by the way, are we really allowing Robert Galbraith into the canon already?'

'Detective novelist isn't he, or rather she? Look I fucking love Harry Potter, which helped me through some pretty dark times in hospital, so yes, J.K. Rowling's alter ego counts. Stay in touch.' She hangs up with a sparkle in her eye.

Chapter Forty-One

Saturday, 9.30 a.m.

Jake didn't sleep much. He made sure Little Sky was locked up tight, and lay on his sofa in the library letting his mind wander. That is one problem with solitude; your own company isn't always the healthiest, but it's all the company you have. You brood, anxiety rising and falling like a tide, but never departing entirely, that palpable nag in your stomach that does not leave you in peace. Sleep comes and goes, elusive.

He is up early to exercise; then, freshly showered and wrapped up, he heads to Parvum over the pale land, the snowfall now firmly crystallized into crunchy ice. The lake is partially frozen, plates of glass on the surface, thin and fragile, which disintegrate into the black of the deeper water. The reeds on the edge are motionless, held in place, the life that normally leaps and falls around them utterly silenced.

Jake knocks on Livia's door, still uncertain of what he

will say. She opens immediately, and is clearly on the way out to work. She looks tired, her green eyes cloudy like pondwater, her skin taut and sallow.

They both try to speak at once. Jake presses on, an unplanned burble of thoughts. 'Liv, I wanted to tell you that I know I can be arrogant and unthinking. I know you think I'm captured by my ego. And I want you to see that I see it, I'm not completely innocent, God, I realize that.' His mouth is dry, his voice cracked. 'But I'm not off on a Boy's Own adventure here either. If I could get out of it, I would, but I think I can't. Can you see that, can you forgive me?'

Livia is trying to remain aloof, but he can feel the turmoil emanating from within her like a wave. 'Jake, I know you. I think you mean that. I really do. But, even then, I'm not sure where me and my family are on your list of priorities. I don't want us to be the flutter of human connection that you get when you want it, to be ignored when you want your freedom. Do you see that?'

Jake presses himself forward, feels the throb of her heart against his chest. Her warmth amid the thievish chill. She pushes back, not without some affection. 'Can we talk inside?' he says.

'I've got to go out on a job, and then my rounds. I'm not sure I'm ready for a big reunion, however much I'd like one.'

'I'm not asking for that, Liv. And actually I agree – for the moment – I'm not safe to be around. I know I've dragged you into something. Again. I know you hate me for it, and I don't blame you.'

She whispers almost to herself. 'I don't hate you. I just feel you don't value our thing as much as I do.' She draws herself up. She is strong and beautiful, he thinks, her body taut with resolute power. 'Look, you go off and do what you need to do. Then we'll look at what we have. Just take care, please. I'm taking Diana away for the rest of the weekend anyway. We're leaving this lunchtime.'

He is relieved about that. 'That makes sense. Let's see where we are then. And, Liv, I know I have no right to say this, but I think you shouldn't go back to Purple Prose.'

'I actually sent them my resignation yesterday. Whatever else, the place gave me the creeps. I got a call from Josiah accepting it, creepier still. That bit's over at least.'

He runs his hand up against her arm, feels each fold of fabric. She turns and locks the door, and heads off to her car. He watches her wistfully, she is silhouetted against the pale sun, a dark drawing in the soft light. He turns away, and walks up the street, going nowhere. Before he has moved two yards, she is behind him, turning and grasping him towards her in a fierce hug. She whispers in his ear, 'I love you, I'm angry and hurt, but I love you. You be safe, and do what you do to get free, get us all free. I'll be waiting.' He hugs her back, feels the sinews of her arms, the soft bulge of her breasts, the flatness of her thighs against his. There is something ineffable between them, he can still sense it, and he cherishes it like a flame. Then she walks back to her car and is gone.

He goes to sit by the church a few hundred yards up the road. The wind has stilled, and the temperature has risen slightly. A slant of sunlight strikes the bench in the churchyard, lingering on the various scuffs and scratches. The overhanging yew has protected it from the snow, so it is mostly dry. Jake muses with his chin on his chest and sightless eyes. A shadow falls across his legs. It is Watson.

'One of the villagers saw you come moping up here. All well?'

'It's been better. I'm getting closer and closer to the idea of what No Taboo might or might not be, at the same time as Livia wants me to be as far away as possible, and all your official channels are getting silted up.'

Watson places an avuncular hand on his knee. 'Do you want to share your unofficial information?'

'As it involves breaking and entering, probably not.'

Watson stretches his long legs out before him. He always looks like he is cramped, except when in repose like this, as if he is a piece of cloth to be unfurled. 'Jake, I was the one who got you into this. I tried to shame you and appeal to your sense of duty. And now I'm telling you this. Let it go. Stop chasing this insubstantial thing, it's like trying to grip the mist all around you, if you'll let a tired man descend to a poeticism for once. Whatever you're up to, whoever you're up to it with, let it go. You don't need to be ferreting around in morgues, or banks, or country mansions. Get yourself back to your family, who need you.'

'And hope that one day I'm not suddenly hit by a car out of nowhere?'

Watson pats him once more. 'We make enemies in this job. Always have and always will. You've got to make peace with that. It doesn't mean you have to win every fight. You can't sometimes, and you can't now. Go find that lovely vet of yours. Enjoy this wintry brilliance we have.' He dabs at some snow that has fallen on his shoulders. 'You know, I've never appreciated just what a sight this church is. Look at how the stone seems to surge to the sky. Imagine seeing it when it was first built: this big bold blot on the horizon, the only man-made thing in sight, dwarfing all and sundry.' He looks back across to Jake, his kindly face furrowed in concern. 'Listen to an old soldier when he tells you that some battles are unwinnable.'

A bird trills in the tree above, and another answers, their songs interwoven for a few seconds. Jake taps Watson's hand. 'I understand the advice, chief, and I'll think on it.'

Watson stands up, legs retracting like a ladder. 'Do more than that, my lad, for everyone's sake.' He nods goodbye, and walks back to the road, his whistle a tuneless variant of the birds above.

Chapter Forty-Two

Saturday, 11.45 a.m.

Jake is walking towards the Nook, heading home, when a tall man emerges from it ahead of him, wide as the door. He is wearing his coat open, his hands pushed down deep in the pockets. His face breaks into a leer when he sees Jake, and he increases his pace slightly, his gait bow-legged and loose. Jake recognizes him immediately, as you do when it is somebody you have robbed recently. Garland Smits.

They are on a collision course, Jake sees, with the man opposite looking unlikely to give way. Jake steels himself, stiffens his shoulder. Smits is a few pounds heavier, but the weight hangs a little loose from him. He is out of shape, a bit breathy even as he walks, an athlete only in memory, now gone to seed. He has the sort of cruel softness you get in bullies: big enough to intimidate, but without any core of actual strength. Smits's victims in the prison system could never truly fight back. Well, he is not in prison now.

Their bodies connect by a drystone wall, clammy with cold on its jumbled front face, its top cushioned with snow. Smits grunts as he falls into it. He had misjudged Jake's frame, which is wiry, but has the latent power of someone who exercises it every day, and whose muscles are not showy but useful, honed to make his body tough and efficient, not for display. Jake's momentum has taken him past, and as he turns he sees the doughy face contorted with rage, those lizard eyes narrowed. Jake puts a hand out, as if in regret, but instead uses it to hold Smits down against the wall. 'Excuse me, I didn't see you there.' He keeps his voice measured, the tone neutral. 'That must have hurt a little bit.' He doesn't move his hand or release the pressure, pushing Smits's back hard against the rock.

Smits lurches to his feet, bearish, and steps from him, brushing snow from his jacket. He is clearly trying to recompose himself. When he speaks, his voice is oddly, dangerously quiet, a snarl more than a roar. 'I know you. You're that hippy detective who likes to meddle in things. That's a dangerous game to play, especially out here in the wilds.' There is a hint of the veldt in his voice, a South African lilt at the end of his words.

'You seem a bit familiar too. Something about a prison guard who's a thug on the side. Is that right?'

Smits pads forward while Jake is speaking, and, without appearing to move quickly, hits him once, hard, near the right kidney. Jake doesn't see the blow coming. It spears him to the ground, a high note of pain arcing inward, leaving him breathless on the floor, retching.

Smits leans down, his voice no louder than before. 'You've no idea what a thug I am, boy. That little move is one of my specials. I get all sorts of tough guys in my jail, as you'll know, full of spunk and swagger. They all curl up like babies in the end, I promise you.' He stands back, as if satisfied.

Jake sucks cold air in, holds his left hand up, palm outward, almost in submission, using his other to propel himself swiftly up so he is standing only two feet from Smits. He leans forward, twisting his hips, and with a mild smile on his face, springs his own hook from nowhere, a punch he has been practising, quick and vicious, which lands about where Smits's liver would be. Smits falls back into the wall, confused.

Jake shakes out his hand, which stings, and allows Smits to square up to him. 'You like to punch people who don't hit back. That doesn't go very far when it comes to impressing me.'

Smits's face is now close to Jake's. The sourish smell of his breath, the individual bristles on his oily skin. Their eyes lock in mutual contempt. Suddenly from behind them comes the honk of a car horn. They turn and there's the luxurious black car Jake had seen outside Livia's. Charlie is standing outside it, clad in a long tailored overcoat, hands in black gloves. He waves one peremptorily.

Smits gives Jake a shove, but starts off towards the car. 'The boss wants you right away. Walkies, is it?' Jake says.

Smits turns, the arrogance back in his expression, the flush of the exertion high in his cheeks. 'We'll have another chance to finish this. Let's hope nobody else gets hurt in the meantime, know what I mean?' He lopes off and slides directly into the car's back seat. Its wheels spin, the engine growls, and it is gone.

Jake leans against the wall, hard stone chill against his back, seeping through his coat. His kidney hurts. He can feel the cruelty of the punch, wielded by someone who knows all about weak spots, places where the pain is cruel and ebbs only slowly. He feels bile rise in his throat and spits feebly to the ground. This is not a man to underestimate.

There is nothing much else to do but limp towards home, his mind occupied, his soul troubled, the ache when he thinks of Livia almost as real as the one in his side. He scarcely notices the regular landmarks of his journey, his feet bringing him heedless along accustomed paths, invisible tracks stomped into the ground and bordered by hedgerows, sharp holly leaves glossy in the light, blood-red pinpricks of berries. A small grey bird with a black head flits and warbles, a song of angry rolling syllables.

As he reaches the approach to Chandler Lake, the sun flares from behind a cloud, pouring light upon him. It wakes him from his trance and he looks across the valley towards his house. The water shimmers and shudders, the ground is barren and colourless. Soon the clouds reform, and dimness returns. A bird of prey is circling above the roof, black speck against the ashen sky. It hits him as a sort of portent, and reminds him to concentrate on the idea of potential danger. He speeds his walk. To his left, he can hear the distant noises of his chickens, which sound faintly agitated, rather than the benevolent cluckings and fussings that normally greet him. Something feels a little wrong. He comes off the path, and crosses the corner of a field so the hedge camouflages him slightly. There are no visible tracks in the snow ahead of him, but that doesn't mean the area is empty. The easier point of access to the property comes down to the back of the house, from Poirot Point.

He crouches at the point where the hedge turns away from the house and stops offering him cover. His hands are tingling with the cold. The bird is still there, a buzzard from the look of it, a white splash halfway along both wings, which beat languidly, making it swoop and rise, always coming back on itself. Its cries pierce the air, sharp and unsettling as a baby's screams.

There is no movement on the ground. Jake's feet are getting cold, his joints stiff. He rises slowly, and then approaches the house. The doors and windows seem locked tight, but there is a shape on the floor of the courtyard, lying against the glistening cobbles. He gets closer. He sees human hair frozen against the ground, stiff like the ice-gripped sedges near the wood. He sees a long neck, black with what must be blood. He sees no body attached to it at all.

Chapter Forty-Three

Saturday, 1.45 p.m.

The head has clearly been dropped to the floor and left. There is a faint mark in the snow where it has rolled, a pinkish smear along an indentation perhaps a foot long. The sacking it must have come in has been thrown against the wall, where it still nestles. Jake touches it gently. It is stiff, frozen folds preserving its discarded shape. It has been here for a while, a few hours at least.

The buzzard has ceased its shrieks, and now soars away in search of other carrion. The bloodied head must have been tantalizing for it, even so close to human habitation. Quiet descends once more, oppressive.

Before he can investigate further, he knows he must check he is alone. He tries the handle of the door and it is locked. Moving carefully, his flank pressed against the wall of the house, he makes a cautious circuit, trying windows and the other door. No sign of entry or disturbance. There is a ghostly track coming down from Poirot

242

Point, but no more than that. He thinks the wind must have blurred the footprints. Another indication that time has passed since his visitor. He follows the trail up the ridge for a few minutes, but it is soon lost in the drift. There may have been more snowfall too, which obscures things further. He can't tell anything about the people who came here, even how many there were.

He moves back to the house, his boots sliding on the slope. The whiteness of the landscape looks free from clues, a blank slate. He slides the key into the lock and goes through the back door. The intimidating silence of emptiness in the corridors. In the kitchen, his stove is still puttering away, giving warmth and reassurance. Nothing seems out of place. Jake passes quickly into the library, where he retrieves his gun from the secret cupboard. He checks it is loaded and heads back outside.

Nothing has changed; his footprints a scuffed parade on the ground. He has grabbed some leather gloves from the side in the kitchen, and slips them on, steeling himself as he looms over the head. It has slipped, so the face is mostly pressed against the ground, half-buried in the snow. He turns it over, it is heavy and inhuman with cold, a block of fleshy ice. The mouth is tight shut, the eyes half-closed, but he can tell straight away who it is. The young woman from Purple Prose, Charlotte.

Jake has seen enough corpses, enough maimed and dissected body parts, in his life not to be shocked, but the sheer wastefulness, the unfairness, the pain and horror strikes him. He hadn't known Charlotte well, but had liked her honesty and bravura. She had been someone full of undoubted life, a forceful figure in any room. And now she was ruined, stone-cold, unresponsive, a shell of flesh and nothing more.

243

He licks his lips, which have gone dry, brings his guard back up, the automatic mechanism that had protected him when he was a policeman and never went away. He looks for details. The cut at the base of the neck is jagged, the ends stiff, the spine sheared all the way through. The individual movements of the knife are visible, which makes him think it was done slowly, post-mortem. It wasn't something a weakling could have done. He looks around him, suddenly helpless, but nothing more than the familiar sights of home greet him. His workshop shut up tight, his outdoor shower glinting, the sentinel birch tree that overhangs a corner of his house, its bare branches like black bones.

Still nothing seems out of place, apart from the severed head on the cobbles of his courtyard. He goes to the sacking and opens it. There is congealed blood at the bottom, purple in the wintry light, but nothing else. He places it over the head, where it juts ridiculously, too firm to act as a proper covering.

Inside, he goes to the library and grabs his phone. There is a message from Martha.

HAVE IDENTIFIED CORPSE, BUT LOST TRACK OF WHERE IT HAS GONE. CALL, CONNELLY

Their jolly detective sign-offs feel obscene in the circumstances. He clicks on the app, and the video call gets through. Martha is at her desk, brow furrowed.

She senses trouble immediately. 'Jake, I have bad news, but so do you by the look of it.'

His throat is parched, and when he speaks, his breath puffs out, a visible cloud. The fire must have gone out

244

hours ago, and the room is unpleasantly cold. 'Someone left me a head outside. It's Charlotte, from Martinson's house.'

Martha nods. 'I knew she was the body. There was a reference to a young woman in the computer system, in a ghost file that has been taken out of normal circulation. And all her details matched those of Charlotte. I'd been digging around the whole of that country house party, and already had quite a lot on her. It looks like she was stabbed twice, two knives, like our friend Nathan White. The head coming off was after the event; must have been done to shock you.

'It all has the feel of a clean-up operation. They think they've got away with all of this, and I reckon they're making their move to come for you, Jake, they need to tidy things up, bring any risk to an end. This is a warning, or, worse, just a taunt. And there's another problem too.' She gulps, her armour of irony and bemusement lowered, her face a picture of her real thoughts for once. 'Aletheia's gone missing. I think they've taken her.'

Chapter Forty-Four

Saturday, 2.30 p.m.

'How do you know they've got her?'

'We have a system of check-ins, and she's missed the last couple. And then I hacked into the CCTV outside her flat and saw two men force her into a car. Very professional. No commotion. Looks like they injected her with something, she suddenly went limp. I followed the car registration on public cameras as far as I could, and it went along roads heading in your general direction. I reckon she must be in Purple Prose. God, I hate the name of that fucking house.'

Jake makes a faint motion of acknowledgement, the fear rolling inside him. His mind, though, pretty much as soon as he saw Charlotte's sightless face, has been thinking of Livia. Martha is no fool. 'Are you worried they're coming after your missus?'

He finds an old glass of water on the side, and gulps it down. 'Of course I am. She resigned the other day, which they won't like, and if, as you reckon, they're bringing this to some sort of end, why wouldn't they? The only thing is she was heading off with Di, away from here. They might be too late. Oh God, I need to find her.' The image of Livia's face rises up like a sickness in his imagination, blood drained and lifeless, her beautiful skin scarred by a blade.

'Jake, listen to me.' Martha has raised her voice. 'I thought this would be the first thing you worried about. From what I can see, not that there's much CCTV around your benighted neck of the woods, she's fine. I put a trace on her car, and got a glimpse of her heading up towards the coast. She's driving, there's a wriggly little creature in the front seat next to her – which is illegal, by the way, if her daughter is only eight. So, she's the lucky one. They won't have the time to come for her right away, or next. You're still deep in the shit, our good friend Aletheia is in mortal danger, and for all my contacts and computer wizardry, I'm a seriously disabled woman who can't exactly lead a cavalry charge.'

It is the first time, he thinks, she has admitted to any weakness. Her bluff and bluster was one of the reassuring things about her. He nods thoughtfully. Livia's departure fills him with temporary relief. He puts Martha on hold with a raised hand, and tries telephoning her. Rings out.

He clicks back across to Martha. 'So what's the plan?'

'I was hoping you might have one, actually. What are you willing to do now?'

Jake's mind is racing, the pulse a thudding drum in his ears. 'I need to go to Purple Prose. Smits is there, no doubt. And that Charlie character. There needs to be some sort of ending.'

'How will you get there?'

'I'll contact Watson. He must be able to help now, especially as we have a corpse, or a piece of one, but I won't wait for him. Rose can get me there and wait for me.'

'Your chum Rose, the minor criminal? Has he ever done anything like this before?'

'No, but nor have I. And he is involved now anyway, so I'll ask him. What can you do your end?'

Martha is pushing a pencil into one of her tight spikes of hair, face crumpled in thought. 'What I've already been doing. That Charlie character has a background in military intelligence, from the little I can pick up about him. I can't get the authorities involved, because he's definitely got establishment cover, which will probably include spies as well as cops. Are you tooled up?'

Jake shakes his head at the ridiculousness of the question. 'I have a gun, and I'll bring it. But I'm not going to win any shoot-outs against a crack team. I'll go in tonight, see if I can find Aletheia, see what's going on, and then call Watson. At some point, we'll need to risk the conspiracy. I'm not going to shoot everybody there.'

'OK, roger all that. Use Rose. I actually think his criminal past helps us; they won't have associated him with any law enforcement. Find Aletheia, and try to get her out if you can do it safely. I'll work on Charlie's background some more and start seeing what case I can build. Smits's security box, by the way, has now been removed from that bank and is sitting in a secure place. You made me realize that we need to start building the evidence, and there's not much point sneaking around anymore.'

'Let's speak before I go in, but it will be tonight.'

'Aye, aye. Keep calm, we'll find a way through.' A jerk of a hand, and her face disappears. The room, cold and unconsoling, feels even more silent than before.

Jake stands in silence while his mind restlessly rolls. He then steels himself to do something about the head cast off in the courtyard outside. He grabs an empty cardboard box from the basement, then approaches it slowly, his stomach faintly aflutter. When he gets up close, though, it feels oddly impersonal, a block of shaped ice, nothing suggestive of the playful flicker of existence that formerly animated it. He places it with gloved hands into the box, and carries it to his workshop. With no heating there, it will be as cold as in a freezer; the box is unlikely to interfere with the forensics to any great extent. Evidence preserved for when they make their move, whatever that move might be.

Chapter Forty-Five

Saturday, 6 p.m.

Jake has dressed as warm as he can, in funereal hues, including a thick woollen hat that barely covers his long brown hair. He has a bag packed with the phone, a bottle of water and his shotgun, an old but carefully maintained legacy from his uncle. He puts some spare ammunition in his pockets, along with a trail mix of his own devising, nuts and dried fruit and shards of dark chocolate. He wants to keep his energy up as he moves.

Night has fallen, the wind is up and cruel, as he walks across to Parvum, almost invisible in the sightless black. Still no reply from Livia, but she wouldn't be expecting a call from him, so the absence is no more than a troublesome buzz at the back of his mind for now. At the Nook, Sarah ushers him inside with barely a comment. She seems to be able to tell from his expression that serious matters are underway. As he speaks, she holds up her hand to his lips, the scrubbed-smooth flesh smelling faintly of the clementines she has been hauling.

'No, don't tell me. No good can come from me knowing. You use the phone, or the cellar, or whatever, and God look after you, that's all.'

He goes quickly to her phone, but can't raise Watson, who is not at home or the office. That worries him a little too. He messages Martha, who promises to try to make later contact with him once they are on their way. Rose is more amenable, and agrees to meet him immediately. He bursts through the door, full of insouciant energy, ten minutes later. Together they sit in the cellar, private, surrounded by barrels of sweet, autumnal cider. Sarah has left two mugs of cocoa, which steam dramatically.

Jake has been filling him in on everything. He appears unconcerned, relaxed and limber on his upturned apple crate. He has rolled a small cigarette while Jake speaks, and lights it. He inhales deeply, then expels a lusty puff of smoke.

'I'll drive you there, but I think you need me to help break in, surely. I'm far less upstanding than you. Plus, we've done it before.' They had independently snuck into the house of the rapist Jake had apprehended, and pooled their resources while they were there. It was one of the foundations of their friendship.

'And how did that end up exactly? You half dead, and me at gunpoint. It wasn't exactly a military operation.'

'Well, the military ain't coming, we know that much. So we enthusiastic amateurs will have to manage. Do you have a plan?'

'I know the layout, so I think I can get in and snoop

around. There are two things I want to find. Aletheia, first and foremost. Second, whatever evidence there is about No Taboo.'

'So no full-frontal assault?'

'No. The exterior perimeter is patrolled, so we'll need to get past them, but then within it's a big old pile with staff, maybe a few guests. We should be able to move around if we're careful enough.'

Rose stubs out his cigarette inside an old cigar tin, kept in the cellar for the purpose. 'Glad you're saying "we", my friend. Because you'll need me to get in, no question. I'm a poacher, among my many talents. I've been in and out of more country estates than you've had illegal venison dinners. I can't guarantee further than that, but I can be useful. Are they expecting us?'

'They might be expecting something, but they won't know we're definitely coming, I'm fairly sure of that.'

Jake still has the plan of the property from his first visit, and they look it over together, trying to find a point of entry. Jake casts his eyes up at the clock, which has been poised serenely above them, marking the time slipping away.

'Package for Dorothy Sayers!.' A messenger is shouting from outside the shop. Sarah gingerly carries it down the stairs, her face a mask of ironic disdain. She drops a large box on the old barrel they have hewn into a rough sort of table, and shakes her head as she climbs up out of the cellar.

Jake can't help but smile when he opens it. A note flutters to the ground, on which there is a short, untidy scrawl, all in capitals, naturally:

SOME GOODIES FOR YOUR ADVENTURE. PLUS,
A LIST OF WHO I THINK IS AT THE HOUSE.
LOVE, SPILLANE

Rose looks over his shoulder as he reads. 'Who is this Spillane, and why is he calling you Dorothy and shouting at you?'

'It's a private joke, and it's from the woman I told you about, Martha.'

Together they unload the box. There is a file with some loose papers inside. A sturdy pair of bolt-cutters. A pair of night-vision binoculars. A tightly rolled rope ladder. And, beneath some heavy-duty gardener's gloves, a handgun and ammunition. Rose lifts it out; it is a Beretta 9mm, sleek black, with an incongruous walnut grip.

He whistles between his teeth. 'This is a pretty useful gun. I like this Spillane chap already.'

Jake checks the clock once more. It is not quite nine o'clock. They probably should wait until at least midnight before making their attempt. He flicks through the file, while Rose unloads and examines the gun, a childlike delight on his face at the lethal engineering.

The file has a detailed schematic of Purple Prose, a map of the surrounding area, plus a printout of the guard pattern. God knows how she managed to get that, Jake thinks. There is also a guest list: Martinson and his wife Adele, Fenella Jewell, Dr Hamed, and a figure who is never named directly, who Martha thinks must be Charlie. She has also scrawled the name of Garland Smits, and a note beneath:

INTERESTING THAT A COUPLE OF THE HOUSE
GUESTS ARE STILL THERE. TRY TO FIND THE
ORIGINAL PLAN FOR THE MURDER MYSTERY,
IT MIGHT LEAD US TO CHARLOTTE'S KILLER.

He folds it up and frowns. The phone buzzes. A message
from Livia: All safe here, please take care. I love you. Not
effusive, but something, a worry to be postponed for a
few hours at least.

Chapter Forty-Six

Jake and Rose argue in the car about the plan, and especially Rose's involvement in it. Jake wants to limit the risk to his friend, and has suggested he helps with the break-in of the perimeter but no more. Rose is stubbornly laconic in return, pointing out that the opportunity for this sort of adventure is too interesting to pass up.

They are now a mile off from the edges of the property according to Martha's map. Rose douses his headlights and pulls the car up to a verge. They stand in the bitter air. The moon is shrouded, the merest hint only, wrapped in heavy swaddles of cloud. Stray snowflakes drift unseen past their faces. The silence is complete. Jake has his bag strapped to his back. In it is the Beretta, the binoculars, the wire cutters, the rope ladder and the phone. Rose is happily toting the shotgun, resting atop his shoulder like a guardsman, while his other hand holds a torch. They still have not resolved their difficulties.

Rose points the torch at Jake's chest to avoid blinding him. Jake gives him a wry grin, and reaches into his bag. 'We need to agree now. I'm going no further unless you say you'll get me in, but keep more or less on the perimeter. I need you to keep a watch on things, call Watson if anything happens.'

'How will I know that something has happened unless I'm with you?'

'I think if they catch me, you'll hear it. There's no breeze, and I don't think their response would be subtle or quiet. It doesn't need to be out here. We're really in the middle of nowhere.'

'Just how you like it.'

Rose agrees to wait in the chapel by the lake, which is close but not part of the main building, the best compromise Jake is going to get. Rose kills the torch, and together they climb the nearest stile. Their initial journey is over two sprawling fields, which will take them up to the imposing fencing that surrounds the whole of Purple Prose. They pause while their eyes strain to adjust to the forbidding dark. They can see the glow of the house in the distance, but little else, apart from that strange illumination that comes from thick snow on deep winter's nights, a sort of pale iridescence that softens the black but does not overcome it.

They walk, each enrobed in their own thoughts. Jake can hear the murmurous shifting and shuffling of livestock. Rose flashes the torch, and sheep eyes glint back, the faces passive and inert. They both look no further than a yard ahead, planting their boots carefully, hearing the icy crunch. The second field is completely empty, a barren swathe of subdued whiteness.

Rose is now a scarcely visible ghost to his left. He slows his pace, and walks next to Jake. He whispers something, and Jake strains to hear it.

'Whose woods these are I think I know.
His house is in the village though;
He will not see my stopping here
To watch his woods fill up with snow.'

'What on earth are you mumbling about?'

'It's a poem. I saw it on a Sherlock Holmes TV show once. You're not the only literary man in the world. It's about being in the snow at night. And get this, the bloke that wrote it was even called Frost. I thought it was fitting.'

It was, Jake supposes. And it gives him something to think about as they trudge onwards. As they approach the fence, Jake takes out the binoculars and switches them on. Immediately the black becomes grey, textures etched on the lens. He can see the branches of trees, the individual bushes beneath, the shape and warp of the land about. He spins around, a panoramic view of the night. In the distance, he can make out a fox, padding away from him, its body a paled blur. It pauses and turns to face him, eyes bright and knowing. Jake feels confident that the range on these things will be good enough for his purposes. He points his sights at Rose, who is aware he is now visible, and is making an obscene gesture at him.

They stand together, in brief and silent communion, beneath the looming bulk of the fence. It is fifteen feet high, with bushes and the occasional tree growing against it. Rose takes over now, whispering curt instructions. He grabs the binoculars and hangs them around his neck before approaching the fence. He is muttering, half to Jake and half to himself. 'The grounds are too big for light sensors, but there's one camera to worry about.' He looks back at Jake. 'The snow's going to be our friend here. Once we've disabled the main camera, we can just topple over the fence and be lost immediately to sight. We're alongside the lowest paddock of the property, so they won't waste money on patrolling properly down here. Give me a leg up, will you?'

Jake hoists Rose into the lower branches of an old ash tree, bared and hardened by winter. He makes astonishingly little noise and is soon swallowed by the dark. Jake knows that he is going to inch close to the fence at a considerable height, reach over and smear the surface snow onto the lens of the camera. It will look like an accident to anyone carefully monitoring, which itself is probably unlikely. Jake hears a sigh of satisfaction, then the gentle slap of the ladder against the fence. Rose makes the agreed noise of an owl hooting. Unnecessary really, as he could have just whispered for Jake to get climbing, but style is important to him. The ascent is not easy for Jake, the ladder swings as he kicks against the fence sheathed with slippery ice, and he jars his elbow on the unseen surface. When he gets to the top, he senses Rose astride the narrow surface. He has carefully snipped a patch of barbed wire clear with the bolt-cutters. Rose hauls him up and the ladder after him. He lowers it to the other side, and hoots again, before slithering down.

Jake's whisper is short. 'Stop fucking hooting at me.'

He hears a wry chuckle, and feels a tug on the rope. Going down is even worse than going up, he has taken off his gloves for better grip, and can feel the pull against his skin as he grips a little desperately. He collapses to the ground inelegantly, his black clothes smeared with white.

They are just behind a planted section of thick bushes, and Rose risks clicking the torch on. The snow hasn't stopped and dancing flakes are trapped in the light, miniature gleams and flurries. He rolls up the ladder and tucks it within one of the bushes in case they need to come out the same way later on.

Rose points in the direction of the house, which becomes visible as they peer cautiously from within the bushes. It is uplit, but far in the distance. Another, milder splodge of light is the chapel, which adjoins the lake, something dark and enveloping Jake can sense but not see. He takes the binoculars back from Rose and surveys the scene. Nothing moves but the scarcest shifts of the branches of the skeletal trees. Nothing seems alive but them.

Once they break this cover, they are committed, he thinks. He feels a moment of paralysis, which he swallows immediately. He wishes he wasn't here, but, as he is, there is nothing to be done but go on. What was that quote from Aletheia? 'I see your broken eggs, now where's that omelette of yours.' Time to try and make an omelette. He snorts quietly.

Rose pats his arm. 'What are you giggling about?'

'Eggs. Never mind.' With that, Jake places one foot in front of another, and begins the trek across the virgin snow towards the chapel. If he is going to do this, he might as well get on with it.

Chapter Forty-Seven

Saturday, 11.45 p.m.

They take stock once they reach the chapel, as agreed, sitting on the cold hard stone with their backs to the wall, facing away from the main house. They are in the pool of shadow between two lamps that illuminate the windows and spire, and provide enough light to see one another properly. Jake stretches his neck and looks upwards, notices some of the statues set into the ledge above the entrance have had their faces scratched out, probably hundreds of years ago: that protest bit of Protestantism, he thinks, as the establishment turned on idolators and questioned the legitimacy of their faith.

Rose gives him a prod, his white teeth gleam as he speaks.

'OK, stop admiring the architecture. When you go, I'll break into the chapel, stay out of sight, wait for you to come back. You've seen the plan of the house, what's your thinking?'

'There are some ground-floor rooms in the east wing that have bars on them. Martha thinks they are the most likely spot for Aletheia. If not, there's also the basement of the tower. I'm going to see where I can get in and take it from there. I also want to find Martinson's office, if I can, see if there is any documentary evidence of No Taboo.'

The clock chimes above them, a brittle, metallic sound that scarce disturbs the night. A crow, hidden in the black, answers with a laconic croak. Rose takes the bag from Jake, hands him the Beretta and the phone, and gives him a brief hug. 'Good luck. It's twelve now. If you get nothing by three, come away, and we'll live to fight another day.'

Jake nods, and stands slowly. He had forgotten the cold temporarily, but can now feel it inside his aching limbs. He heads towards the lake, shaking the acid from his leg muscles, making his move just as the snow pauses, and a thick cloud shifts. The moon, gibbous and obscenely large and bright in the muted sky, falls on the water, its beams fracturing into glimmers on the partially rippling surface. The patch of water in front of him has frozen over and has collected a spattering of obdurate snow. He pauses, imagining the depth of cold in the water, cold as death itself, before the cloud shifts back once more and gloom descends.

From the fresh darkness a hand falls on his shoulder, half spinning him around. His stomach lurches, his hands rise instinctively to his face, he crouches ready to defend himself. A throaty chuckle greets him.

'You forgot the night vision. Might come in useful.' With that, Rose hangs the binoculars over Jake's neck, and lopes away. Jake waits for his heart to settle, before making for the house. There is a tree – a beech, he thinks

– that stands just in front of the wing that faces the lake. He leans against it and looks around for movement through the binoculars. Nothing stirs ahead of him. To his right, he can just about make out the stables, faint heat outlines of the horses within, shifting their heads, restless soft snorting, the warmth of their bodies surrounding them like a mist.

The guards, he knows, will begin their second perimeter walk of the night in about thirty minutes. He needs to be inside by then. He makes his own circuit of the building, cautiously picking his way across flower beds and patios and pathways. The main entrance is shut up tight, and he can see the atrium is empty, guttered fires and dimmed lights. He has gone past the east wing, and is now heading to its mirror opposite. This looks more inhabited. He crouches behind an ugly statue – its chiselled nakedness a mild distraction – and looks through the binoculars once more. The two lit windows glow suddenly in his eyes like circles of fire, but nothing seems to move. Then the door of a first-floor balcony suddenly opens, and a figure emerges, haloed by the same fiery blossoming.

It is Martinson in a dressing gown, smouldering cigar in hand, which he tosses casually on to the snow. Instant hiss. He belches loudly and sucks in lungfuls of cold air.

'You're so vulgar, Sam.' A disdainful voice emerges from within. Adele, Jake thinks. 'Come in and wait for Charlie. We may have to move quickly, he says.'

Martinson grips the balustrade and surveys what must be the blank landscape in front of him. 'Of course, my dear. I'd hate to disappoint Charlie, after all.'

The door closes, and Jake exhales. He moves forward to the ground-floor windows beneath Martinson's balcony.

Through the bars he sees nothing but empty rooms, furniture mostly shrouded and clearly unused. He edges further past, peering around a corner. Two security guards stand motionless in front of a door, clad all in black, muffled in hats and gloves, their collars pulled around to obscure most of their faces. Suddenly, they stiffen and Jake fears he has betrayed his presence. Then he realizes they have been contacted on their radio headsets. After a few seconds, they whisper some sort of assent into their concealed microphones, look at one another, and double around to the front of the building. From behind him, Jake can hear short shouts and can sense movement, but when he raises his binoculars he gets nothing.

Perhaps Rose has been discovered, perhaps their entry point has. But he cannot affect that or let it slow him down. The safest place is now inside, undetected. The door is unguarded and he walks boldly across and gives it a push. It opens silently upon another dimly lit atrium. Jake checks for watchers, and finds none. Dragging up some nerves, he pads in and closes the door behind him.

Chapter Forty-Eight

Sunday, 12.35 a.m.

He clenches and unclenches his hands, breathing in and out, a trick Livia had taught him to help relax. He lets the tingle dissipate as his breathing slows, feels the full weight of his whole body in an instant, the force of gravity driving his feet into the ground. A sense of solidity, the heft of calm.

Then he looks around him, superimposing his surroundings onto the schematic in his mind. He thinks a flight of stairs will take him to the office area, which is on the other side of the wing to Martinson's bedroom. He moves from one atrium, hard lacquered wooden floors beneath inert chandeliers, through a corridor to another. This one has the ghost of a fire, some glowing coals puffing a sad trail of smoke toward the chimney, a visual sense of the lateness of the hour. In the corner is a carpeted stair, well-worn with use, the track of heavy steps over a long period of time. The light bulbs are dim and discreet, like the late-night lobby of an expensive hotel. There is nobody around.

He climbs and is soon in another corridor, dominated by two doors, thick and imposing, set beneath plinths that suggest security. This whole area is more extravagantly lit, the carpet plush and well-cleaned. There's a rich executive feel to it. The first door opens immediately. It is a boardroom: big mahogany table, plush red chairs, blank screens on opposing walls. The shutters are closed on the two main windows and only a gauzy hint of the outdoor lamps enters the space. It feels unused, dormant.

He returns to the corridor. A clock somewhere ticks loudly. The next door is locked, something sturdy and new, unbreakable. Jake pauses, then heads back into the boardroom. To the side of the bureau against the wall is a door that connects to the adjoining room. It seems to be seldom used, and the lock is flimsier. Jake takes the gun from his waistband. He grabs the barrel, raises it, and slams the handle against the lock. A splintering noise, painfully loud, and then quiet once more. He replaces the gun in his waistband and pushes the door gently open. They don't use this boardroom much, he thinks, so he hopes nobody would notice the damage any time soon.

Inside is the most luxuriously furnished room he has seen in the house. Thick maroon carpets, an antique writing desk with an ergonomic leather chair behind it. It is warm, but the fire is being allowed to die, orange embers pulsing with each gust of wind. Bookcases with ersatz leather-bound volumes surround two big television screens on opposing walls. They are on, silently playing news channels from the US and the UK, immaculate presenters with blemish-free skin and dead eyes, as lurid blurts of breaking news scroll insistently beneath them. The stories mean almost nothing to Jake.

There is music playing from a radio somewhere. Soft, delicate music: Bach, he thinks, the Cello Suite he has played so often at Little Sky, plangent strings to watch the sun set with, rich and languorous and reassuring. He wishes he was back home now.

He shakes his head to clear the thought, and approaches the desk. There are papers on it, which he flicks through, then puts back as he found them. Nothing to see there. They are business presentations about opportunities in cryptocurrency, a summary of a successful takeover of some Chinese mining assets, and an investigation into the volatility of the American real estate market. There is a sturdy appointments book also on the desk, and he puts it down onto the chair to examine later.

As he does so, his eyes are drawn to the bookcase. The top three shelves are all old company reports and legal documents, which have been carefully bound to look like antique library volumes. They clearly haven't been moved in years. The lowest shelf seems the same, but he notices that the last two books are newer, they look glossy in the light, and they have not been aligned correctly with the others. Jake takes the nearest. It has no title on the spine, but inside it has one, which feels like some sort of wry joke: *A Curious Affair at Purple Prose*.

He flicks to the next page, excitedly. It is clearly the original plan for a murder mystery event, no doubt the one held in the last week. Jake squats to the floor and reads. The guest list from their last visit is written clearly. The narrative on the next page declares an intent for

Charlotte to be the victim, stabbed and then hidden beneath the bedclothes in her room.

It also records that Fenella Jewell had paid a considerable amount of money to do this. Jake wonders whether she had actually gone through with it. He reads on. He and Livia were supposed to be part of the game, he as the detective, but that had clearly been derailed by their early departure. Thank God for Livia's instincts, he thinks.

There is a note at the end, which refers to the 'clean-up operation': any 'hostile subjects' allowed to make their escape, and then being picked off as they fled. Bodies to be disposed in normal fashion. It was clear they were relying on local police support to handle any fallout: *CW to manage*, it said in a scrawl.

There is confidence here, Jake sees. The confidence of a body that feels beyond or beside the law, something that pursues its goals safe in the knowledge that little can truly trouble it. And yet they had been troubled, surely. The threatening behaviour, the taking of Aletheia, the obscene delivery of the head to his house, the way they had sought to hold him so close to them, as a potential threat: it all bespoke a certain nervousness, an uncertainty. Smits had not looked like an efficient stormtrooper on manoeuvres yesterday, but a thug acting outside instructions, bluff and prowling and spoiling for action. For all this wealth and power, there was human frailty. Jake feels better for that.

He goes back to the appointments book on the chair, and flicks through it. He wishes he had brought Smits's notebook with him for the purpose of comparison. This one gives brief references to business appointments that don't mean anything to Jake. He sees that in the last couple of weeks there have been three meetings with

Charlie, and someone called WJ. That was an initial in Smits's book too. Charlie was CW, so this must be someone else. There was a hurried note at the bottom of the entry, which looked like it had been doodled on, saying *15k? to WJ?* It had then been underlined a few times.

Jake returns the book to its original place, and sits back on the main chair.

Idly he runs his thumb beneath the level of the desk, and finds a button. He presses it, and, after a faint whirring sound, a small platform rises up in the corner. It is a communications console, shaped like an imperfect star, which, from what he can tell, is basically a speakerphone that can work on its own or when connected to one of the screens.

Jake weighs up the risk, and decides to call Watson, whom he had not been able to raise since they decided to come here. He taps in his mobile number, one of the three or four he can remember without effort. Not having a phone himself means that numbers still exist as memorable realities in his brain, something to latch upon and recall when needed, not just unnoticed digits beneath names on a screen.

It rings loudly, three or four times. And then a familiar, gruff voice.

'Yes, what is it now?'

'You're a hard man to get a hold of, chief.'

A long pause. 'Jake is that you? What's going on, where are you calling from?'

Jake pauses to weigh up what to say. 'I'm in Purple Prose, Martinson's main office. Quite a lot has happened. Somebody left me a present of a woman's head – Charlotte, who I last met here. She was murdered, whatever cover-up you've come across, there's no doubt about that. And my colleague Aletheia has gone missing, you know the one we both dragged into this at the start. I'm not backing off from it. I can't.'

Watson gives a grunt. 'You're a determined man, Jake, I've always known that. What do you need from me?'

'I just wanted to let you know I'm here. Be ready to come with the cavalry if I call again. But only the cavalry you can trust, if you know what I mean. Who knows where this all goes to?'

'How much do you know?'

'I can't talk now, for obvious reasons. But I can connect the prison guard Smits to No Taboo, and I can put Martinson and a colleague of his called Charlie at the top of it. If I can get Aletheia out now, I will. And then we must meet. There's a friend of mine I want to introduce to you too, who's been helping on this.'

There is a pause. 'Jake, I'm here to help you too, but you have just told a serving police officer that you're currently involved in a break-and-enter.'

Jake laughs briefly. 'You're welcome to come and arrest me, chief, but I think that would be messy.'

Watson appears to see the sense of that. 'OK, but I'll get mobilized and wait for your next call. Keep your head down, and get out when you can.'

'Roger that.'

Jake presses a button and ends the call. He is frozen in thought, brow furrowed, heart lurching as he contemplates possibilities, none of them attractive or optimistic. He rips the relevant sheets from the appointment book and puts them on top of the murder mystery plan. He needs to collect whatever evidence there is. He goes to the bookcase and pulls down one of the bound company reports. He puts the loose paper inside, and thuds it shut, finds a loose wire from what looks like a phone charger beneath the desk, and winds it around the book to keep it closed. He moves to the window and pushes the sash open. Cold air billows in. He pokes his head out cautiously, and hears nothing. Whatever disturbance there had been with the guards has ended. He drops the heavy book onto the snow-soft bank below, where it nestles, partially obscured. It would be unlucky indeed if somebody found it tonight.

All this has taken time, and the large mahogany clock at the end of the room is inexorable in its reminder. He pauses to hear its steady beat, and hears something beyond it. Two voices, one stentorian, some distance away. Moving quickly, Jake heads for the door back into the boardroom, closing it deftly shut behind him at just the second that the handle of the main door into the office turns. He stands in the gloom, body tensed, as Charlie and Martinson walk into the office together. Frozen to the spot, he can hear every word of their conversation.

Chapter Forty-Nine

Sunday, 1.30 a.m.

They settle comfortably on the available chairs. Jake can imagine Martinson swinging luxuriously back on his, stub of cigar in one hand. Charlie, from what he has hitherto seen, is more controlled, more tense, like an animal poised in stillness, only betraying the danger inside with the sudden twitch of an irrepressible tail.

'We need to move her tonight, the spy lady, what's she called? Campbell? Some black woman's first name.' This is Martinson, in best boardroom intonation.

'We don't need to move the delightful Aletheia at all. If the police, or any other interested service, were coming, we'd hear about it in plenty of time from our friends. She needs to go nowhere in the meantime. You must learn to keep calm, Sam. Not everything in life happens just because you shout loudly for it to. I can imagine that's how your wretched newspapers operated, but this all takes calm and finesse.' His voice is more gentle, syrupy even.

'What about our unofficial investigator, the hippy cop? He'd show up unannounced, I reckon.'

'We'd know if he was on the move. Plus that half-caste vet of his has definitely left the neighbourhood, so he's probably followed her.'

'I'd follow her, certainly. If they'd have stayed any longer, I'd have smacked her bottom for her.'

'Sam, my dear, don't make me tell the formidable Adele about you. No, Smits wants to have a chat with our captured spy, and needs it to happen somewhere quiet where, how shall we say, the mess can be contained. She's in the best place, beneath that monstrosity of a tower for now. God, I hate historical buildings. They're so boringly solid, don't you think?'

Martinson doesn't answer immediately. Jake imagines the cigar twirling. 'OK, but in the morning I want her gone. This whole thing has got too complicated, and I hate complexity. We should have cancelled the murder mystery and just dealt with Jackson quietly. Job done. You always want to do everything at once.'

There is steel in Charlie's voice, hard and brittle. 'I want to do everything profitably and quietly, Sam. We needed to know what that detective knew, and what investigations into No Taboo he'd left behind him. From him we got confirmation of the spy Aletheia. Poor Charlotte was doomed anyway, and she was just a little whore, so nobody is going to miss her. I agree we didn't need to be throwing her head around the countryside, but Smits does have his sadistic quirks, and we all agreed we wanted the detective unbalanced until we come for him. So everything is under control, as you would prefer it. Let's close things off in the next twenty-four hours: we'll drop the spy's body, shuffle Jackson off the mortal coil, and be clear. You can then do what you like with his widow, provided Adele lets you get away with it.'

'You mustn't tempt me. Not when I know your job is delivering the undeliverable. No, I see your point, as I always do. I'll try and keep calm for tonight – let me get the brandy.'

Jake's muscles have been tensed for the last five minutes, and he stretches quietly. He knows he needs to go after Aletheia, but strains to hear a little more. There is a clinking of glasses, a resettling of positions.

'One other thing.' This is Charlie, voice so soft Jake has to strain to hear it. 'Someone has been helping Jackson, someone with some contacts and imagination. It may be that Campbell woman, but she's been under careful surveillance. It's something Smits will no doubt squeeze out of her, I'm sure, but that is one complexity I want ironed out.'

There is a knock at the door, and the hinges creak as it opens. A female voice, brassy over the smoky confidences of two plotting males. 'Josiah has shut the house up and is going to bed. I'm going to follow him, and I think you two bad boys should as well.'

'My dear Adele.' This is Charlie, unctuous. 'Have a final snifter with us, and then we can all call it a day. I'm sure tomorrow will be full of surprises.'

'Just a small glass. I need to keep a clear head around this one, even after all these years.' She pulls a chair from near the inner door to the boardroom, and Jake steps back at the proximity of the noise. Time to go, he thinks, while the exit is clear.

He pads out, shutting the door silently, and walks down

the stairs at the opposite end of the corridor. He pulls out the gun from his waistband, and checks it is loaded. He knows where to go now, and knows that, whatever happens, it will not happen quietly.

Chapter Fifty

Sunday, 2.00 a.m.

He has come back around to the front of the property. Moonlight floods into the entrance hall. The fire opposite the door has burned down to angry coals and the air is cool. Outside he sees the snow settled upon the land, a few inches thick, making the individual uniform in the night. An owl hoots twice. Nothing moves.

The old tower is at the juncture of the central house with the west wing. He had read that it was an original feature of the first manor building, and dates back to the fifteenth century. It has warped with age, and forms the only sight in the whole property that is not rigidly symmetrical. Imperfect, flinching reality preserved in stone. The tower's base is accessed through a low door, another original, the oak scarred and chipped. Through that is another large hall, with ceiling beams, and thick slabs of paving, a dash of moonlight falling through a lonely window onto the centre of the floor. Winding stairs go up and down. Mild light is suffused from below and Jake hears the faint sound of movement.

He wishes he had Rose with him, or Watson, or Livia, but realizes that so little in the last week has been as he would like it to be. If he is going to start wishing for something, better to wish not to be involved in the first place. To be back at Little Sky with Livia. Diana in bed, the two of them drinking red wine in the library, their skin tingling from the sauna and lake, the lazy languor that comes after exertion. The pleasure of peace. Instead he is on his own in a strange old building in the middle of the night, and there it is.

The stairs downwards are sandstone, he thinks, smooth and pale, softened by the tread of unseen generations, with freckles of quartz glinting in the darkness. He places his feet carefully once more, controlling his breathing, the stairs curving before him in downward search of the elusive light.

Three steps down, then four, no sound now at all. To his right there is the overhang of the spiral staircase, casting a pool of black shadow beneath. He passes it, to the fifth and sixth step. The next sensation he feels is the barrel of a gun, pressed hard against the nerve at the top of his neck.

He can tell from the sour scent it is Smits, his bulky body pressed close against his. That sibilant voice in his ear. 'Keep walking, scout. I had a feeling we'd bump into each other again.'

They take a few more steps, Jake shuffling, his mind racing, hackles raised. As the staircase begins to come out of its spiral, the space opens up a little, and there is a panel built into the opposing wall, varnished wood that looks black in the gloom. It has a door-like opening about two feet high.

Smits pushes the gun harder into his neck. A spasm of pain. With his other hand, he is probing Jake's pockets, first grabbing the gun and the binoculars, dropping them with a clatter on the ancient stone. Then, on the other side, Jake feels his hands gripping the phone.

'Well, well, what's this? They told me you were some sort of Amish bastard, who never touched technology. I have to say, Jake, I'm disappointed in you. I admire a man with principles, I always have. They're such fun to break in the end. Still, you won't be needing this anymore.' He drops it with a sharp crack, and it skitters across the ground. Smits gives Jake a shove. 'Take a look inside.'

Jake peers in the opening. A narrow passageway, the ceiling low like in a mine, at the end of which – maybe ten feet away – there is another open panel. Behind that there seems to be a small cell, lit by a lonely, flickering candle.

'I'd like to spend some time with you, one-on-one, finish that little wrangle we had. But I've got to speak first to your lovely black friend. Make sure she doesn't hold out anything from me.'

Jake's mouth is dry, and he can feel the gall rise within him. A lethargy suffuses through him. He twists the skin on his thigh to wake himself up, feel the pinch of actuality. He tries edging his body around, so he can get closer towards facing Smits, give himself the chance of snatching the gun. But Smits is too wary.

'No, no. You can either crawl into that hole, and get to the cell. Or I can shoot you in the spine and push you in. You have three seconds to decide. One.'

Jake crouches down, inhaling deeply. No choice for now. Every person has a silent fear, a funk, a visceral reaction they try to tamp down and ignore in ordinary life. Jake has always been terrified of close confinement, the nightmare of being trapped immobile without hope or agency. And yet he compels himself to crawl forward into this dark space, his final momentum aided by a push from Smits's boot. The floor is smooth and cold and hard on his knees. Even hunched like this, the tips of his vertebra are brushing the ceiling. Only ten feet to go. He looks up, the candle dancing before him.

He hears the guttural blurt of a cruel laugh. All of a sudden, the light dies. The door behind him closes. The one ahead swings shut. He hears a lock. Then silence, and blackness, and narrowness, and fear rising within him like a sickness.

Chapter Fifty-One

Sunday, 2.35 a.m.

The first ten minutes of his confinement pass in a flap of panic. He squirms forward, and scrabbles at the end door, but it is firm, unheeding, no handle to cling to. As smooth and impenetrable as a rock face. He cannot turn around. There is acid in his throat. His breaths are short, and a film of sweat envelops his body. He can feel it trickling again into the small of his back, and a chill sweeps across him as the moisture meets the cold air.

He pushes himself backward, crawling in unsteady reverse, knees chafed by stone, until his feet are resting on the door he first entered. Looking over his shoulder, he can see no band of light around it. He is sealed in. He rolls over onto his back, raises his legs, and kicks downwards. His boots clunk and thud, shocks of painful contact go back through his thighs. But there is no give, no shudder, no source of hope. He shouts, the noise is loud in his ears, but it feels entombed in the stone, nothing escaping. Entombed. A tomb.

He is now sweating furiously, his clothes damp, the cold immediately seeping deep within him. He realizes that he has to calm down, slow his movements, retain some heat and semblance of self-control.

He reckons he is stuck in a priest hole, or at least the entrance to one. The house was the right age, and he had seen those Catholic adornments to the chapel, as well as their ostentatious removal. He wonders if the first house had been the property of a family who'd clung on to the old faith in successful secret, or had been discovered and punished, someone stuck in this very place dragged out without mercy, disembowelled on some lonely scaffold, the land handed over to a time-serving loyalist.

The thought is hardly a pleasing one, but Jake takes comfort in trying to place himself in the context of history. He still has rationality on his side; he is using his brain, not surrendering to total mindlessness. He buttons up his jacket and wraps his arms around his chest. Reason is still with him, like a blanket. There are still puzzles to be solved, answers to be found. Starting with one to this question: how did he end up trapped so easily?

Smits had not been surprised to see him, had been waiting in apparent ambush. Jake had hardly known himself that he was heading across to this part of the house until a few moments before, so how could Smits have predicted his movements? Jake thinks back through what he had done, the conversation between Charlie and Martinson, and before that the sudden dispersal of the guards. It was not impossible that Rose had been taken, and told all he knew. But that wasn't much. The plan had been largely Jake's and Martha's. Martha. He had told her everything, followed her advice, let her lead in formulating the plan, which did mention the tower as a possible holding place for Aletheia. Could she have been compromised? He shivers noisily. There is no chance that Martha is connected to No Taboo. Except there is, of course. The problem with conspiracies is that, if you believe they exist, you have to believe they could reach anywhere, corrupt anything. His mind flashes through his conversations with her, and his every instinct cries loudly against the idea she has been turned. Aletheia had vouched for her, and that must mean something. And yet.

And what now for Aletheia? He imagines Smits entering the room, her in the corner bound and immobile, the sadism writ large upon his sallow face. The questions, the cruel and bloody prompts to answer. Jake chokes down the acid once more, kicks out, feels nothing but unheeding rock.

Impotence stings him. And, however many times he argues to himself that he is not going to be left here slowly to go mad and die of dehydration, the sense of looming oblivion still persists. They need to know what he knows, they're not going to just let him rot. But why not? They have Aletheia, they need him out of the way, this could be the malign and final act of retribution towards him.

Moments pass, heavy. He is blinded by the black. He is desperately cold. A sob emerges, and he chokes it back. He will not give way. Hold the hope alive like an ember. He tries to keep his movement slow and deliberate, and traces the contours of the ceiling and walls of the tunnel with his numb fingers, the feel of cold stone worked by unseen hands. But there is no secret switch, no auxiliary tunnel, no story-book way out. The tomb is just as it appears to be.

The activity has warmed him faintly, and he rolls once more onto his back, and rests his feet on the panel again. He has never before been in a place so divorced from the light: it is a blackness that never diminishes however accustomed your eyes strive to become. It is like being consciously unconscious. He slows his breathing some more. After a few minutes, he struggles to tell if he is awake or asleep. And then he no longer cares.

He has no idea how many hours pass. His eyes open to nothingness again. Panic grips him immediately like the freezing air. He is stuck, confined, helpless. He tries to stamp his feet against the door, but his legs have stopped working properly. His boots shuffle ineffectually. Gradually the blood begins to flow and the blows get firmer, louder. But nothing happens. He screams, once, twice, three times, his throat raw. The echoing loudness an affront to hope. A wail of humiliation. He wants to move, to stand, to see light, but he can't. His heart races again, throbbing in his ears. He retches, tastes iron in his mouth.

He realizes he is in real trouble here unless he gets a grip on himself. He tries to marshal his mind, think thoughts that take him outside of himself and his plight. He is in a situation that he cannot change, and that, he thinks, is unusual for him. He has spent all his time recently in a place with a view, where he can walk out and immediately be enveloped in expanse, go just exactly where he pleases, become lost. And at no point in his life has he really experienced true restriction before. There has always been a way out. Except a plane, he supposes. You are stuck in the air for the whole length of the flight, aren't you, whether you panic or not. Strange that more people didn't panic in mid-air. He'd never seen it happen on all the planes he'd been on. Maybe twenty or thirty in his life, as many as that. Though people who'd be that scared probably avoid flying altogether. That probably explains it.

Prisoners in solitary must feel like this as well. However much they cry out, complain, throw themselves against the padded walls, the unforgiving apparatus that surrounds them doesn't care. You're on your own, get used to it, suck it up, serve the time. Madness beckons, but that's on you. In that situation, you'd do anything for relief, for a sense of normality.

It makes him think of the old cases that brought him here: the dead soldier Daniel Jones, James the abducted child. Smits, who was there when a man hanged himself in solitary, when another got sucked into No Taboo. Did he think about his role in causing misery? Hardly likely. Took the money, denied his conscience, went home and breathed free air.

So how do you kill yourself in solitary, if you don't have a guard to help you, or make you? They are careful about what they let you have as a prisoner, Jake knows that. No sheets to twist into nooses, no blades, no glass to grind down and eat. Maybe you could break a toothbrush in half, sharp shard, and nerve yourself before plunging it into your wrist. Open the vein before anybody notices, hope life seeps out quickly enough to do the job.

His mind races on. What about him, what if he is left here, what is his way out? He can't just lie here and slowly dwindle. He could bang his head on the ceiling, but doubts he has the strength to end it all that way. And if it went wrong, he'd be stuck in this dark tomb with a bloody, damaged skull, still liable to cling on until thirst or insanity took him. A terrible option. Jake thinks of other people in history who have been walled in, imprisoned in darkness with nothing. It must have happened to thousands over time, maybe tens of thousands since the beginning of civilization. All disbelieving that it could happen to them, all suffering anyway. That was the thing: however awful a fate you can imagine, it has almost certainly been real to someone in the past, a savage event at the end of their life. How did they all die? Slowly getting weaker, their mouths dry and aching, their bodies consuming themselves, desiccating, despairing. Or plunging their skulls against the wall, cracking the bone open like an egg. What happened to them after their panic was exhausted, did dim acceptance take over? Can you ever truly accept a death like that? Did they die screaming, or sobbing, or in quiet horror?

Perhaps he'd run out of oxygen, try to suck in a breath, and be greeted with nothing but an empty retch. Silent asphyxiation. He thinks that would be bad, but not prolonged at least. There is no sign of airlessness yet. There must be some crack somewhere letting the air in. Maybe he should try and find it. Despair and lassitude holds him. No hurry, he supposes. He doesn't want to complete a painstaking examination in the blackness and be left with no options. Then he remembers with a short cry of triumph: he has his razor blades still fixed into the lapels of his jacket. His hands move in the dark, fingering the edges. They would work as a final option: maybe you'd have to cut down on your left wrist, bubbling the blood out, and then immediately, before you weaken, a savage horizontal cut to your throat. Double your chances of the fatal stroke. Just grit your teeth and say goodbye.

Could he really do that? He somehow doubts it. Sorrow throbs up again. His thoughts have become inimical to his well-being, slipping into unwelcome areas, making the situation worse, not better. He needs to control them once more. Life with no options, no openness, no joy, should remind him by contrast of all he has found at Little Sky. If he slows his breathing, and focuses his thinking, he can summon up the sights and smells of his own land, the refuge he has discovered there: the breeze across the lake, the summer evening scent of baked grass, herby and warm, the crackling chill of autumn and winter; the glorious quiet, not absolute and unnerving like this, but textured quiet, rich with life and opportunity, enhanced by the hissing of the branches, the warbling of the birds, the scuttles and scurries of unseen life in the hedgerows; and all of those colours, the blue of the lake, turquoise, in fact, in summer, and that abundance of green, a sea of green, overflowing and overwhelming, hues that wash over you. He can sense it all for a second. It calms him. His eyes droop once more.

Chapter Fifty-Two

Sunday, 5.35 a.m.

At some point later, he wakes again. Despair overwhelms him. Then, the door beneath his feet wobbles for a fraction of a second, and light pours in. He feels his legs being grabbed, and his body being drawn, half-gently, towards the brightness. He can't do much in response, he is totally stiff, his joints locked into place. As bendy as a one-day-old corpse.

Hands hurry him out. The soft-lit gloom blinds him momentarily. He falls against the wooden panelling, his body a traitor to his mind's desires. Gritting his teeth, he holds his hands up to his face to protect himself, forestall the unseen blow. His whole being shudders, still gripped by cold and the after-effects of complete and unredeeming despondency. The light, such as it is, feels unreal.

There is a strong grip on his shoulders. He feels revulsion, but can do nothing. Then he looks upwards and sees Rose's face, normally a picture of sardonic unconcern,

286

now creased with unfamiliar worry. Behind him, almost as tall, looking fierce, is Aletheia.

Jake is stammering, shivering. 'What's happened? Where did you come from?'

Aletheia is looking up and down the stairwell. 'Come on, there's a storeroom one floor down. We need to get you warm and functioning. And quick.' Leaning against Rose's bony shoulder, Jake staggers down the steps, each movement an agony, but each letting the blood pump and flow, restoring some sensation. The feel of being alive.

They usher him through a door into a room which is lit by two small lamps. There are some crates stacked randomly about the whole space, and Rose arranges three of them in front of an incongruous electric fire, which is plugged into an extension cable that snakes off into the darkness. Jake stands over it, lets the hot air hit him, luxuriating, his eyes tight shut.

'Be careful you don't get too close,' cautions Rose. 'I can already smell the singed fabric. You're still too numb to feel it, but trust me, take a step back. You're out, you're alive, you'll be OK.'

Jake shares the sentiments profoundly, starts to get a grip on himself, but only by walking his mind back from the precipice. Stray thoughts of his confinement threaten to return panic inside him. Aletheia leans forward and strokes his arm, like you would a frightened animal.

He gives her a bitter smile. 'I thought I was supposed to be rescuing you.'

'You did, indirectly. Your friend Rose here was searching for you, and he heard Smits shouting at me. Thankfully, Rose didn't stop when he saw I was the prisoner not you.'

Rose stands, eyes alive with pleasure. 'Nope, I gave him

the old golf swing with the shotgun. Hint of a slice perhaps, but good enough to put him down, and Al and I could get acquainted.'

Al already, thinks Jake, happy that two people he can really trust are with him. Then returns to the point. 'I thought you were supposed to be in the chapel?'

'Let's just be glad I've never followed an instruction I didn't want to in my life. No, I was watching the house, not that far from you. And then I saw the guards disappear.'

Jake has stopped shivering, and is stretching each muscle, working out the kinks in turn. 'I hoped that they hadn't caught you.'

'No, it was definitely a planned move, which unsettled me. I was tucked away out of their sight, though, and you snuck in. And then I kept by the windows and watched some of your progress. It was lucky I saw you go into that tower. It took me a while to break in myself, and then I must have walked straight past that ratty hole you were in.'

'From what I can tell, they knew you were coming.' Aletheia's voice is quiet. 'I think the guards wanted to open the place up to let you in.'

'But how?'

'We need to work that out. But not now. Not here. As far as everyone is concerned, you've been caught, and Smits is torturing the truth out of me.' Her expression is flinty. 'I reckon by six, the place will be crawling with guards, and Charlie and Martinson will want their report.'

Jake nods. 'Tell me what happened with Smits.'

Aletheia is stretching her legs out, tightly encased in black denim, her eyes not still. It is amazing to witness her like this, a woman who Jake had only ever really seen behind a desk, relentless in her pursuit of information. Impressive, of course, but still sedentary. Here he could sense her concealed strength, something coiled within her.

'I'm lucky he was so confident you were locked up out of the way. He took his time, talking a lot, trying to get me to speak. I know I'm just a Searcher, an office girl, but I did get hostile capture training you know.' A wan smile. 'So I encouraged him to speak, without saying much. I was still wobbly from all the drugs they gave me. Anyway, he was just starting to get frustrated, he slapped my face a bit, hit me in the kidney.' Jake winces in sympathy. He can remember that one. 'And he was moving in for more, when this reprobate arrived, and put him to sleep.'

'Where is he now?'

'Still out. Rose checked him a few minutes ago. We've been frantically up and down this wretched tower, and were going to have to get out. Dawn is about an hour away at best. So we were standing together moaning, then I recalled my history – Tudor priest holes and secret passages and that – and started pressing panels, and luckily enough, one opened and your sorry backside emerged.' Her face is tender despite the brusqueness of her words.

Jake stands, with some effort. 'All right, I think I can move without endangering anyone. Let's take one last look at Smits. We don't want him waking up while we're getting out of here, do we?'

Rose looks sceptical. 'I don't like the look in your eyes, Jake. You're not going to off him, are you? I don't mind my cheap shot, but I don't see you as the bullet-in-the-neck type.'

Jake, whose rage against Smits is burning deep within,

a hot coal of hatred, can indeed imagine something like that, but he has tamped his emotions down, and is now broadly in control of them. Vengeance a mere formless thing, to be cherished but not acted upon. 'No, we just need to close that end off before we leave. Show us the way.'

Aletheia goes first, looking up and down the stair before guiding them downward. There is a thick wooden door, which must have been there when the tower was first built. It is brown-black and ridged, and stained with age. She eases it open. Inside is a room with no windows, a dungeon of cold sheer walls, and not much light. Sprawled on the floor in the middle is Smits, a thin trail of blood smeared across the stone emerging from the back of his head.

Jake looks across to Rose. 'Is he dead?'

'He wasn't last time I checked.'

Rose approaches the body, the shotgun still in his hand. He crouches and presses his hand on Smits's neck, searching for a pulse. Then he stiffens suddenly, as Smits's meaty hand rises up from nowhere, gripping his throat, twisting and throwing him head first down onto the floor where he lies crumpled like a discarded suit. The gun falls into a corner, useless for the moment. With a primeval roar, Smits is on his feet, jaw clenched so the bone shows white through his pale skin. Aletheia is in his bearish range, and he picks her up like a rag, dashing her against the wall. Jake has never seen such power close up, it throbs and surges outwards towards him.

Smits is somehow fast still, despite his condition, on his toes, swinging a punch that came all the way from the soles of his feet. Jake ducks it, hears the whoosh of air above his head, and steps away from the short hook that follows, then darts forward, just slipping a spiteful third jab thrown fast without apparent effort. Smits knows how to fight, no question.

He has, though, allowed Jake to come close; in fact, it is a deliberate plan that Smits has somehow clung to within the foment of pained rage inside him. He wants Jake in range. With a savage smile on his face, Smits reaches out, confident in his size and strength.

Both of his hands shoot out like piston rods to grab Jake, fingers sliding beneath the lapels of his jacket and gripping hard. The exact place where the razor blades have been carefully stitched. Smits yelps, looks down at his hands, ribbons of blood appearing everywhere. The fourth finger of his left hand is almost hanging off, the bone visible, the end a jagged mess. Jake takes the opportunity now to step up to him, turning his strength to a weakness, content to be briefly within the circle of his arms. Smits looks up, face aghast, anger animating every feature. But before he can move further, Jake strikes forward with his head, allowing his distaste and frustration, his fear of dark places, to feed the movement, feeling the disintegration of the cartilage in Smits's nose when the headbutt lands. Smits falls to the floor, more blood to paint the old ground, and Jake kicks him hard in the head, snapping his neck back. No movement.

Jake turns first to Aletheia. She is dazed, but slowly shaking free from it, favouring a bump on her head where it connected with the unforgiving wall. She motions limply towards Rose, who hasn't moved. Jake leans forward. His pulse is thready but there. His hands explore the bumps and ridges of Rose's skull, but there seems to be no obvious break or indentation.

'I think he'll be OK.' He laughs as he sees Aletheia's pained expression. 'That went well – so glad we came down.'

'At least we got him front on. It would have been worse with him behind us on the stairs, I guess. We need to get out of here. The house will be waking up soon.' She walks forward and puts one hand on Smits's chest, the other on his neck. She shakes her head. 'Which is more than I can say for him, Jake. You put him down for good.'

Jake feels a flicker of interest in the information, but no remorse. Not yet, at least. He is no killer, has never – to his knowledge – taken a life, only fired his weapon once, with cause, during his police career. But lines had been crossed a long while ago with this one.

Aletheia's hand is on his arm again. 'It was him or us, my friend. Plus I reckon the first shot from Rose weakened him a bit, though you couldn't tell from his attack. I was paralysed back there.' She shakes her head. 'I'm glad you got to rescue us in the end.'

'Just returning the favour.' Jake looks around the room, and sees his phone, binoculars and gun. He stuffs them in his pockets. Rose is starting to stir, thankfully. Together Jake and Aletheia heave him to his feet and half drag him out through the door and up the steps.

Outside, dawn has not broken, but it is there, a heavy hint, a looming presence somewhere in the dark sky. Snow is falling more quickly, flurry upon flurry, picked up and jounced by the wind. Good. Jake thinks they'll need some cover to get out. They crouch in the lee of the house, looking across a courtyard. No windows are lit, but that won't last. Jake shifts Rose across to lean against Aletheia, and squeezes her arm. He needs to get the evidence he threw from the window, so he moves quickly around the border of the house until he is outside the office, where the lights have remained on, a helpful indication to his reeling brain.

He scrabbles in the snow, his fingers encountering rough stones and tangled bits of bush that have been concealed overnight. But the book is there, and he hefts it into his hands. By the time he is back, Rose is looking a little more limber, Aletheia – from what he can tell by the halo of the outdoor light a few yards away – a little more relieved.

Rose grimaces. 'I can walk, I promise. Man, that ape moved fast.' He pauses. 'I'm glad you put him down. What's the plan?'

'Escape would be nice. Then we get back to Little Sky and have to come up with something. War has been declared tonight, if it wasn't already. You think our way out has been discovered?'

'Doubtful. Even if they knew we were coming. I reckon the fence line goes round about five miles. It would be impossible to check it all. Plus, they didn't think we were coming out again, did they?'

Aletheia has stood, brushing snow from her coat. 'Enough chat, I think. Time to go. Stay close. This filthy weather makes it hard to see anything at all. I take it we head for that church thing?'

The chapel, still heroically lit, stands lost in a sea of snow, but is something to aim for as they run forth. They soon lose contact with one another but Jake keeps his legs driving, half-sprinting and stumbling, his eyes blinded, as black night starts to bleed to grey all around them. After the chapel, where they stop no longer than they need to catch their breath, Rose leads the way tentatively, torch

293

on, a bouncing, feeble ribbon of light that guides them until they are up against the fence. The ladder is there, and they heave themselves over, unagile and near-frozen.

Jake can't remember much about the cold plod back to the car, except his constant glances behind, and his stumbles upon the iron-hard ground. The weather saves them, he thinks. Nobody is traceable in this cascading, swirling mess, where white conceals as much as black, and the breaking of day is no relief.

They fall into Rose's car, which has blended into the bone-coloured landscape, its shape just a ghostly suggestion by the side of the road. He drives carefully on empty roads, before bumping them along fields, slippery and uniform as sheets of ice, tracing the route as the crow flies back to the haven of Little Sky.

Chapter Fifty-Three

Sunday, 10.45 a.m.

The wind has blown itself out, the sun now a lurid glare
bounced back from a tumbling sea of white that stretches
beyond the horizon, and Jake is making breakfast. He had
crashed out for three hours on their return, while Rose
sat swaddled on a bench outside, watching the light pour
in, looking for any dangerous movement in the silent
landscape. Rose was now asleep in a guest bedroom, one
along from where Aletheia lay, far gone herself, her system
still working out the drugs that had been poured into it
in the last couple of days.

As soon as he was up, Jake had called Livia. She
answered, in a flurry of accusation and remorse, self-
reproach and uncertainty. He explained all that had
happened, and how they were scheduling a council of war
for the approaching day. An end was coming, they all felt
it. She was silent for a second, and gave her grudging
approval. She promised she would keep herself and Diana

safe, change cottages, visit friends further out, stay on the move for a couple more days.

Martha was next, and he eventually woke her up after several attempts. She had kept vigil overnight, waiting for news, and had fallen asleep at her desk at about the same time as they had been scaling the fence to freedom. They spoke for half an hour, trading information, and agreed to talk again when everybody was up and functioning.

After that, Jake had kept watch. But the pallid flatness of the snowed-in land proved to be the best possible security system, any movement leapt out immediately, especially through the binoculars. When he padded a few hundred yards to the north he could see the furtive explorations of the chickens, who soon hopped and fussed back inside their sheds after the shock of landing belly-deep in the snow. A deer, lost and disoriented, trod gently on the corner of Bosch field, and then departed, nosing at the barren ground. Nothing else stirred.

And Jake had felt hungry, had not – he realized – eaten much in the past twenty-four hours or more. So he wrapped up warm, and scurried across to one of his greenhouses, picking clean three of the big tomato plants. He threw in a handful of chillies as well, and got back to the kitchen quickly, eyes dancing in all directions as he went.

A giant pot of coffee is bubbling, joining the smoke from the stove in a symphony of homely scent. He has a record playing softly too, a cello sonata from Chopin, which rises and falls, meandering and melancholic. He is not comfortable exactly, but he feels at peace somehow, the sense that the enemy is in front of him, and resolution is near.

He takes his largest pan and starts stewing the tomatoes, with onions and chopped chilli and garlic, adding in some tomato sauce he had made the previous summer. A splash of cider vinegar and salt and pepper. It smells hearty. In a separate pan he cooks some flatbreads he had stretched and rolled himself, each action soothing and loosening his own complaining muscles. Finally, he makes indentations in the bubbling sauce with a big spoon, and cracks eggs – six of them – into each space. Ten minutes later, all is done.

He puts the pans in the warming oven, and goes outside once more. Everything is still. When he returns, he sees that the scent of food and drink has woken his companions: Rose in his boxer shorts, wrapped in a heavy blanket, skinny legs protruding, his shins smooth and hairless like planes of balsa wood; Aletheia, back in her jeans, with a big maroon jumper of Livia's she must have found in a cupboard.

'This smells delicious, Jake, but I'm worried you've been cooking when you should have been keeping watch.'

'I did a bit of both. But let's move outside now: there's a table beneath the overhang that's clear of the snow.' He had lit the firepit next to it, too, so there is now the beginning of some artificial warmth. Rose grumbles and yawns, but follows them outside.

They eat silently, hungrily, wiping up sauce and eggs with bread, and then they sit, sated, faces flushed by the chill air, staring outwards. Jake is clutching his coffee mug protectively to him for warmth.

'So, what now? War is declared, then. As simple as that.'

Aletheia holds up her hand, her palms pink against the snow. 'Before all that, I just want to say I appreciate you both coming for me. Especially Rose, who I had no claim on. But I was in deep deep trouble there, and I didn't think I was getting out.' Her voice thins, her chest rises, as she gulps back the retrieved terror. 'Anyway, I won't forget that.'

Jake and Rose look awkwardly into the middle distance. Rose slurps his coffee loudly. 'I think it all evens out in the end,' says Jake quickly. 'You saved me from the priest hole, so let's call it a draw.' Rose gives a wholehearted nod to this. He puts down his coffee and rolls a cigarette, which he lights using a log he has lifted carefully from the firepit.

Aletheia continues briskly on. 'But we do need to look forward, you're right. So what do we know, and what can we prove? We have evidence of a man called Charlie, who has infiltrated the high echelons of the intelligence service, running a criminal company that specializes in sex crime and murder. We can connect him to Smits, a disgraced prison officer, and Martinson, a notable billionaire. We have the evidence from Smits's safety deposit box, plus what you took from Purple Prose, Jake, plus material that Martha and I have gathered.'

'Plus a head, currently frozen about a hundred yards from here, and a document planning the murder of its owner.'

Rose lets his cigarette end fall into the snow with a hiss. 'That sounds lovely. Why not turn them all in? You're still a copper of sorts.'

Jake has thought about this. 'The problem is, we don't have a lock on who Charlie is, or how far up any conspiracy goes, so we can't feel confident in who we report to.'

Aletheia winces in agreement. 'That's sadly true.'

'We can probably bring in Watson at some point, but he'll need freedom to act and report, and we can't hand him that mystery.' Jake slaps his hands against his knees. 'There's another thing we have to address. How did they know we were coming to Purple Prose. Al?'

'I have a theory on that, actually. Rose drove you to the mortuary, didn't he? They probably lifted his details from CCTV and have been tracking him since then, maybe his phone, but more likely his car. I'd be prepared to bet there's a device on it.'

'Why didn't you tell us last night?'

'Because we were coming back here anyway, and they could have guessed as much. This is the most obvious place to check, so they've gained very little by the knowledge.'

This does make sense to Jake, who is quietly working on a theory of his own as well. 'Why don't I check? One of us needs to do a sweep of the area anyway. I'll go search the car, you two go about making sure we're as protected as we can be in the short-term. And you can do the washing up as well.'

He stands, thrusting his hands into his deep cardigan pockets. He had shucked off his clothes from the night before, sour and reeking from sweat, congealed blood on the lapels of his jacket, and was now dressed in jeans, a thick shirt and swampingly large top Livia had bought for him, chocolate-coloured and comforting.

'There's one other thing, Al.' His tone is cautious, and he makes himself look her in the eye. 'Can we be one hundred per cent confident that Martha hasn't been compromised? She's been the lead in much of this.'

299

Aletheia shifts her weight on the hard bench. 'I don't blame you for asking, and the thought had occurred to me. All I can say is that I've trusted her with my life, and we wouldn't have got anywhere near this far without her. She could be playing a long game, giving us rope, getting us to reveal what we have, and then turning on us. But I don't think so. The question is, can you trust her?'

Jake thinks back to their conversations, the way they have found common ground, all her hard-won experience, her charming cynicism and bitterness. 'Let me ask her. See what she says.'

Rose laughs ironically. 'The old "are you a traitor?" approach. I'm sure she'll roll right over.'

'Fine, I'll do what I have been doing, keep a close eye on everything she says, everything she gives us. My answer as of now is I can trust her, I feel that in my gut. But I've been wrong before. We've all been wrong before. Let's move, and we'll regroup with her later.'

Rose and Aletheia take the crockery inside. Jake puts the binoculars around his neck, the Beretta in his waistband, buttons up his cardigan, and heads out into the still of the wilderness beyond.

Chapter Fifty-Four

It is a long slog back up to the car, and Jake moves with slow and deliberate caution. He stands at the crest of Poirot Point, filling his lungs with cleansing breaths, and looks back down into the valley, so often a reassuring patchwork of pastels, comforting hues of browns and reds, yellows and greens. Now all white, lit fantastically by the unfiltered sun. A pair of birds are soaring and swooping, too far in the distance to be identifiable, the blue behind them an ever-deepening pool.

He speeds up as he moves across the fields at the edge of his property. The car is about a mile away, and he can see it gleaming in the distance. He can identify their earlier tracks coming down towards Little Sky, frozen in place like fossils, but nothing else. The car itself looks just how they left it, no evidence of further visits imprinted in the snow. He spends five minutes circling, looking beneath it.

After an examination of the interior, he pops the bonnet

and there, just as Aletheia predicted, is a small device that has no place being on a car engine. He has seen this type of tracker before, and picks it up carefully in his gloved hand. It is high-end, he thinks, military grade, or certainly the sort of hardware that tends to be in the hands of state intelligence services. He puts it back; they can keep it or throw it, depending on what plan they adopt.

His return to the house is not direct. He loops behind Agatha Wood, dark and compact despite its snowy cloak, looking for signs of surveillance. He knows every inch of this ground, even carpeted in white as it is, so he feels he holds an advantage against any unknown assailant. He sees no sign of another's presence. He keeps going, almost as far as the river, glinting like a necklace, bejewelled by the beams of the sun, before doubling back again, along the incline up to his own land.

Finally, something catches his eye. Movement at last, up on the ridge which lengthens and stretches down towards Morse Field. Someone heading towards his house, unquestionably. His palms clench, heart starts to race. Jogging lightly, he moves himself around to an adjoining field, keeping a hedgerow, dense with knotted branches, thick with concealing snow, between him and the figure. That enables him to move forwards in parallel without risk of discovery, provided he stays quiet. A pair of sparrows, prim and neat, fly up startled from the other side of the hedge, a sign of the other's presence. Jake has drawn level, and slows his pace, his breath a heavy cloud before him.

There are two beech trees that have grown close in the top corner of his field, and he knows there is a gap between them just big enough for him to squeeze through. He quickens his step once more, and gets to them, scraping, ungainly, his body into the space they have allowed. His gun presses obtrusively into his back. He wonders how quickly he can pull it, or if he will need to.

The figure is coming up towards him. He can't see around the trees, but can hear the very faint panted gasps of an advance up the incline, occasionally obscured by the louder crunch of footsteps. He has seen no evidence of anybody else in the area, and it would be hard for there to be someone trailing in support who would not have been immediately visible at the beginning. So it is one-on-one, and him at least with the element of surprise. Good odds.

The crunching gets louder, in a couple of seconds whoever it is will be level, and stumble across Jake's place of concealment. He has to decide what to do. Steeling himself, he waits until the shadow – which is small and indeterminate, the sun is high – appears on the patch of ground before him. Then he leaps, throwing his whole body against the unseen opponent, forcing them to the ground, Jake clinging to stay on top, arm raised, ready to strike.

And then, flooding realization. The body is soft, the face is familiar, though distorted with a faint moue of annoyance, green eyes alive and sparkling, the long black hair fallen free from a woollen hat. A wonderful sight in the snow.

'Livia,' Jake breathes.

'What's left of her. God you're heavy when you spring from nowhere.' She leans forward and kisses him, lingering a second, before stroking the side of his beard. 'Nice to be home, lovey, nice to be home.'

Chapter Fifty-Five

Sunday, 3 p.m.

The council of war is in session. From the second she arrived, Livia has fitted seamlessly into the mood of the place, is semi-proprietorial in fact. This is a little bit her house, this is partially her fight, and she wanted to be there at the end. She had said to Jake, as they walked up past the misty lake, arms interlocked, a sense of joyful surprise running through him, that she realized she could not simply make him choose between two impossibilities: a normal life with her, or an isolated life without her. Reality was messy, all compromises were, and she saw he had a responsibility to help investigate, to bring this to a conclusion, and she felt similar herself. For better or for worse, they had become embroiled in something bigger than them, more dangerous than they would have wanted. And escape was impossible. She saw that now. That was why she had reluctantly entrusted Diana into Joanna's care, with a warning; and that was why she wanted to bring things to a head sooner rather than later.

With each step, Jake had clutched her more tightly, with more gratitude. Then he had explained in detail everything they had learned over the last few days, so that when she got to the door she felt part of something, was able to greet Rose with familiar enthusiasm, and Aletheia with genuine affection and concern. Jake then fed her with some cold venison, some leftover tomato sauce, freshly warmed bread, and a big mug of creamy coffee, while Rose stood guard by the lake. At three, they all trooped to the library, sat at a table littered happily with books, on which two loaded guns now sat, black and spidery, while Jake locked the doors all around them and called Martha.

She is small on the screen, her spiky hair bright, and she makes her presence felt. She greets Livia jauntily, does the same with Rose as well. 'So the crack team is gathered. I'm sure the enemy will be terrified.'

'Let's start there,' says Jake, after a short pause to let the sarcasm sink in. 'Who are we facing?'

Martha's voice is clear and controlled, brisk in its articulation of the facts. 'We are facing, I think we now know, No Taboo, a well-connected criminal conspiracy that makes a profit from servicing high-end clients with whatever they desire. They are run by Charlie, initials CW, a shadowy figure who comes out of military intelligence. I haven't got a final identity yet, but it looks like he was a sort of unofficial quartermaster for spy agencies, working in country to get operatives whatever they needed, sometimes on the books, sometimes off. He then moved this talent into the private sector. His funding has come from

305

Sam Martinson, the billionaire who probably began by seeking to use a service like No Taboo, and ended up bankrolling it. From the books I have seen it looks like it runs at a pretty high level of profit.'

'I was wondering about that.' This is Aletheia, brow furrowed. 'The money we have seen circulating is good, but not outrageous. Martinson has made eight-figure profits in legitimate businesses, and has assets worth nine figures. This still would be small beer.'

Rose leans forward. 'But think of what No Taboo gives him. A line into all the rich folk who use it, the chance to partner with them, use their expertise, get protection from them. Plus a sense of power. He holds their reputations in his hands. Plus again, No Taboo seems to come with police cover or intelligence cover, so he's getting freedom to do what he wants. You can imagine someone like Martinson getting up for that.'

Livia nods. 'That certainly fits in with what I've seen of him, and his wife. They love the power. The money is an added benefit.'

Jake looks back towards Martha. 'Where does Smits come in to all this?'

'Ah, the late Smits. RIP. Jake, you did some stout work when you put that slab of South African shit out of business. He was an important contact in the prison system, getting them access to expendable criminals. They used them as victims, or mules, or muscle. Outside of that, Smits was something of an enforcer as well. I think someone like Charlie will instinctively like men from institutions, because that's his background. Josiah, who works with Martinson, looks like he comes from the military too, probably was brought in by Charlie. Thanks to Jake's larceny, we have a lot of paper evidence of the workings of No Taboo. And we have direct evidence of a murder for fun – poor Charlotte Sampson – that was commissioned by them.'

'I wish we could have helped her. Dammit, Jake, we knew something was off with her.' Livia drums her fingers on the table in frustration. Jake agrees. He feels he let Charlotte down, sacrificed her, when they left Purple Prose that afternoon.

Martha continues, sipping a large glass of what looks like red wine. 'Charlotte may have her revenge in the end. Her death is one of our best bits of evidence against No Taboo.'

'Who killed her?' asks Jake.

'The final blow was undoubtedly struck by Smits. He was paid to do it, as he was with your old chum Nathan White. His accounts show that. I think Fenella Jewell is our likely culprit – she made a big payment to an account connected to No Taboo a week ago. My reading is that she tried to do the job, and then Smits finished her off. I reckon, if we come out of this alive and on top, we grab La Jewell, roll her, and get her to testify. She isn't an actual murderer, so might want to do a deal.'

Jake stands, restless. He pokes the fire, watches the sparks dance, nimble and random. The room is warm and comfortable. He sits back down.

'That's the real question,' he says. 'How do we get out ahead now? Martha, Aletheia, you're the closest thing to professionals, what do you think?'

'You cheeky so-and-so. I'm still a full professional. Martha was always a bit on the fringes of professionalism.' Aletheia gives her a warm smile, and Martha raises her glass in a mock toast. Aletheia continues: 'I think we all agree, we need to get Charlie and Martinson out of Purple Prose. We need to offer them something they have to have, get them out of their place of security and power.'

'I'm sure that's right. But what's our endgame?' This is Jake getting down, he feels, to the heart of it. 'What do we actually want at this point?' He'd once read a line in a novel by John Buchan that made him sit up, fumble for a pen and underline it: 'you can have success in this life, if you don't get victory.' He worries that he isn't – they aren't – in a position to go crusading against a secretive organization and destroy it. He can feel their comparative weakness, his family's vulnerability, pulsing within him, a feeble heartbeat. Victory might be impossible, but some form of success is not.

Martha snorts when he makes that argument. 'Firstly, you and I need to have words about John dreary Buchan at some point. Second, I think we have to play to get them off the board, and that means victory of sorts. But that won't be easy, I concede that.'

'I think whatever our final position is,' says Aletheia quietly, 'the trade is the same, right? We offer to meet them at a neutral place, swap our knowledge in return for their cooperation. They close No Taboo, get out of the game, or everything we have goes to authorities they haven't managed to corrupt yet. We show them what we have, and make clear we have the ability to use it.'

'Do we, though?' This is Rose, his face rapt, utterly engaged in the detail of it all. This is the most serious Jake has ever seen him.

Martha takes up command of the conversation once more. 'I think so. We prepare a dossier of all the evidence, show our hand, as Al says, and then we threaten to send it to newspapers, broadcasters, senior MPs, police figures we know from Watson upwards, Al's bosses. Spread it far and wide and indiscriminate. We'll bump into some who are already in the conspiracy, sure, but that level of coverage will be devastating to them. They can't beat everyone. They refuse to do a deal, we send it. They try to take us out, it's sent automatically.'

There is quiet. The light is already starting to dim outside, as wintry evening steals a march on the piercing beauty of the day. Jake switches on a lamp, reaches for Livia's hand and rests it in his, dark and slender against his lumpen flesh. He clears his throat.

'That's the basic plan, then. I email the dossier to them, and arrange a meeting. We confront them, and we try to end it. What are our obvious problems, Al?'

'First, security. I think here is too isolated. They could decide to overwhelm us by force. We need somewhere that's secure and private, but would be too hard to openly assault without comment. Second, they could still call our bluff, and try to wipe us out. So we can't all be in the room. Third, we need to know what we're willing to do here. What if they pull a gun, what if they refuse to play ball, what if they bring a hostage, are we really willing to do the ultimate and take them off the board?'

Martha's voice is laconic. 'Happily, we know that. Jake has already rubbed out one of them. Whoever is there, they must be willing to go as far as that. We can worry about the clean-up later. Al, you can help with that?'

Aletheia nods. They all contemplate the enormity of the situation, the extent of the stakes. Jake realizes he had tacitly accepted all of it some time ago. They were where they were, and there was no point grousing about it.

Livia punctures the pause. 'I think we should do the meet at my house. It's quiet, in a tiny village, but there are people who would notice a full-frontal attack. Parvum is the middle of nowhere, thank God, but it's not absolutely deserted.'

Jake squeezes her hand gently. 'Liv, are you sure you want this at your door?'

Her smile is assured, her eyes wide. 'It already is, we all know we're past the point of no return.'

Jake summarizes the position. 'So, we propose a meeting. Al wires Liv's place for sight and sound. She and I go in, Rose and Livia conceal themselves nearby, Martha stays as our remote eyes and ears, willing to hold the dossier over them if they don't play ball. I tell Watson that we're up to something, may need his support, but keep him on the edge for now. And we try to do the deal. We're clear that our best result is these men.' His mind roils with disgust as images of James and others spring involuntarily into his consciousness. 'These appalling men agree to close down No Taboo, in return for which we let them go. And then they walk, and we go back to our lives. Can we live with that?'

There are nods around the table. Martha adds a coda: 'Whatever else happens, though, we do what we have to do – if it gets messy, we have to be willing to go as far as they would. No hesitation, no regret.'

It sounds simple even put like that, but it is a plan nonetheless. They sit in quiet contemplation as the shadows stretch around them. Rose starts to polish the shotgun. Little more needs to be said at this point.

Chapter Fifty-Six

Sunday, 11 p.m.

Jake stands by the lake, alone, a long silhouette against the broad, pale moon suspended in the sky above him. It is still cold, but he can smell a thaw coming in the thickening air, a murmur of life that may be little more than his imagination. His hands are stuffed in the central pocket of his hooded top. To his right, thirty yards away, stands the heron, a welcome and heartening presence, stilted legs emerging like scaffolding from the reeds. It flaps off, languorous wings grey in the half-light, when Livia walks up behind him.

She is shivering and puts her arms around his ribs, leaning into him for warmth. He looks down at her upturned face and smiles.

'I thought you were going to bed.'

'Too wired. I'm just a country vet, remember. This is the first time I've been involved in a hodgepodge taskforce to fight an evil conspiracy.'

'Strangely enough, same here. I do like being part of a hodgepodge at least.' They are silent for a moment.

She sighs. 'Is there any actual chance of us pulling this off?'

Jake is not at all sure, but does not want to worry her at this point. 'They're businessmen. We've just made the cost of doing business very high. They're already super-rich, the smart thing is to go off and enjoy their money, limit their risk, avoid the hassle.'

'I just don't really believe amoral powerful people ever would walk away from something like this. It's not in character.'

This is an excellent and undeniable point, Jake thinks. He squeezes her back. 'No point in worrying about it now.'

Jake had sent the message, enclosing the dossier that Martha had provided, to Martinson just as dusk had fallen. She had also sent it off to some secret accounts too, with automated instructions to forward it on to a large mailing list if she did not countermand the order. Martinson had responded curtly, acknowledging receipt, then more punchily an hour later. The upshot was that he and Charlie were coming to Parvum at six tomorrow morning, to meet Jake and Aletheia. No weapons, no support teams, though neither side was likely to abide by that.

Livia shivers once more. 'This is all too cold for me, even with your hot body to hold on to. I'll see you inside. I'm up at three to keep watch anyway. Don't freeze your-self out here.'

Jake watches her go, her slender, dark form absorbed by the night. He knows that Aletheia is on watch some-where to his left, just behind and above the house, which

312

gives the best view of the land surrounding Little Sky. She has the night-vision binoculars, and is mummified against the cold with all the clothes that she can find. Each of the team will take their turn on surveillance before they gather at four o'clock in the kitchen.

The phone beeps, a sharp noise in the gauzy quiet. A final message from Martha.

ALL IN PLACE FOR TOMORROW. MAY GO OFFLINE AT POINTS, BUT DON'T WORRY. HAVE NEWS OF CHARLIE BUT THAT CAN WAIT. LOVE

Jake's stomach contracts. No detective novelist sign-off. Is that an oversight? Or has something happened? He responds immediately.

Let's speak at 4 to check in. Keen to hear about Charlie. Take care, Stout

He hopes she gets the note of concern implicit in his use of her favourite author. He waits for a response, shifting his weight from leg to leg, eyes half on the lake, half on the phone. Wretched technology, even more wretched for bringing with it the fear that something has miscarried. No return message comes. He tries calling on Signal. No response. Perhaps she is getting some sleep before the big day. But it is a very worried Jake that walks back to the house twenty minutes later, feet sliding on the treacherous cobbles, hard like iron for at least one more day.

Chapter Fifty-Seven

Monday, 5.15 a.m.

No hint of false dawn as Jake approaches Livia's house, the warm orange light of its outdoor lamp ablaze like a beacon. Aletheia had gone ahead to check the place, and put cameras and microphones into the living room. A package, from Martha, full of technological surprises, had arrived at the cottage just after four that morning.

Of Martha herself nothing further had been heard. They all agreed that they had no choice but to press ahead, but Jake's thoughts were aflutter with worry for her, distracting and unbalancing him. Everyone else looked strained, pale from stress and lack of sleep.

At 4.50, Rose and Livia had dropped him off by the church, before taking Rose's car up to the nearest service station. The idea was that they would drop the tracker onto the back of a long-distance lorry, before returning 'dark', in Aletheia's parlance, to observe the cottage from outside.

Anyone following the trace would have a lengthy wait, and a surprise, at least.

The light was a sign that all was well inside, and Jake knocks softly on the front door. Aletheia welcomes him in. He is amazed at how businesslike she is, controlled as a purring engine. She had been a deskbound Searcher when he worked with her, a quiet figure of intellect and authority, but soft somehow, comfortable as a cardigan. This new Aletheia is bolder, more physical. It reassures him.

'We're good to go. Room is wired, and the footage sent to a special server for recording purposes, and onto Martha, if she's there to pick it up. Don't worry, Jake, no plans ever survive first contact with the enemy. Think of it that ours just got to that point even quicker.' She touches his arm. 'Plus, she may have got overwhelmed with the strain, and the booze, and the weed, and whatever else she puts in her body, and flaked on us.'

He doesn't believe that, and Aletheia probably doesn't either, but he can't do much about it now. He is wearing the razor-bordered jacket over a T-shirt and jeans, the Beretta tucked into an inside pocket. Cyprian the cat has come up to him as he talks, tail arched in the air, leaning against his shins with a faint mew of acknowledgement or restless complaint. He picks her up, presses his face into the soft warmth of her head, then shoos her into the kitchen, closes the door.

'Coffee?'

'I'm so buzzed already I think it might send me over the edge.' Her first acknowledgement of stress or weakness, he thinks.

The grandfather clock, scarcely visible in the pools of

darkness in the corners of the room, is gravely intoning the hour when the door knock comes. Jake opens it carefully. Martinson and Charlie are standing outside, clad in thick coats, breath ballooning in front of them. They push past him briskly and enter the house. Jake looks around, and sees the dark shape of a car at the turning of the road, Josiah's face at the wheel. Rose and Livia must be somewhere in the gloom too, unseen for now.

Jake closes the door and turns back into the room. Martinson and Charlie are already sprawled on the sofa, their faces a mixture of anger and arrogance, but a hint of bluster perhaps there too. This cannot be as straightforward as they would have hoped. Aletheia is leaning against the wall, arms folded, uncowed.

Martinson opens the discussion. 'So, detective, you've definitely got our attention. What's the deal to be discussed?'

Jake sits down at the table, runs his fingers over the scarified lines, the dents of childish exuberance etched into the old wood. He thinks of Diana, and Livia. 'You both know, or you wouldn't be here. Let's drop the act, guys. We can cause you all sorts of bother, link you to multiple crimes, and no doubt find some people still in the police and security establishment who'd be willing to bring you down. You've had a good run, you've made your club a success, but you've reached the end of the road. We just want you to recognize that.'

Charlie frowns, his thick black eyebrows meeting like kissing caterpillars. 'I think you downplay what we do, Jake. You don't give me enough credit, actually. As you imply in your little dossier of smears and suspicions, I got into the business of making money twenty years ago. I had

316

been involved in logistics for certain, more secretive branches of the armed forces, and got used to getting things both from official sources and let's say the darker corners of military life. Then I left the service of the state, traumatized no doubt by the pain and suffering I had witnessed, and decided to employ those skills in the private sector.'

'Are you sure you're not trying to avoid admitting you're a pimp?'

He can see the whites of Charlie's knuckles, as he squeezes the wooden arm of the sofa. 'There you go again, full of bravado. And yet there's nothing in human history more honest than a pimp, actually. I'm a high priest of supply and demand, no more, no less. You want something, I get it, provided you can pay for it. No taboo.'

'Even if that means snatching a child, or exploiting one of your old comrades in the army.'

'You're such a police officer, Jake. Remembering past cases, investigative failures. You mustn't confuse morality with business; it's a dangerous and naïve mistake. I've managed to become indispensable to a whole series of people, as you can see, by not judging them, and helping them get what they want. I can walk into almost any government department or security service in the country and know I can find an ally or two. I have powerful billionaires who owe me a favour whenever I ask. You really should be more impressed: keeping No Taboo effectively secret is a work of art, it really is.'

Aletheia's voice is loud from across the room. 'I'm sure that's right, Charlie, but only as far as it goes. If you were really that confident, you wouldn't be here. You'd have sent some folks in to shut us up and risk the consequences.'

Charlie turns to her, runs his fingers through his hair,

317

thick and black as a bear's pelt. 'Ah, Miss – it is regrettably still a Miss, I believe – Campbell. I told Sam you were too dangerous to be left free for long. I'm afraid he has a colonialist's disdain for people of your colour, so didn't really believe me. But you're right, as far as it goes. I do think a deal needs to be done. We just need to work out guarantees on both sides. I would hate for things to get messy. Jake has a new family for example, a daughter of sorts just a few miles away in the home of a journalist friend of her mother. One call from me, and . . .' He luxuriates in the pause. 'Well, as I said, messiness.'

Jake leans forward, his muscles screaming with tension, the gun a tempting weight against his heart.

Charlie raises a hand. 'Calm, detective. As I said, a deal needs to be done, we all have needs to be addressed. We don't need messiness, do we, Sam?'

Martinson has been chewing a dead cigar all this time, alternating his glowering stares between Jake and Aletheia. He is projecting an aura of calm authority, but Jake can see the raging tension within. He's like a piece of Gothic architecture threatening to burst free of the bonds of stone and wood. When he speaks, it is through a tightly clenched jaw. 'Enough of this foreplay. I was all for blowing this place up and daring the consequences. Publish and be damned, and all that. But Charlie here has convinced me to be reasonable, so what's on the table? I've done more deals than anybody in the room, anybody in the country, more or less.' He gestures grandly towards the window.

Jake follows his arm, and sees a shadow pass, a quick flit but discernible, someone there. He looks back to Aletheia, but she is keeping her eyes on Charlie.

He speaks, playing for time, folding his arms to be near

318

the handle of his gun. 'Is No Taboo just a money-making venture to you?'

Charlie's chest swells, he feels confident on this one.

'I'm not here to defend my lack of ethics, Jake, or even to acknowledge the existence of ethics. We live in a world of power and money and pleasure. What did Hemingway say? "What is moral is what feels good after." That has always been the basis for No Taboo. A recognition that, if you're rich enough or great enough in spirit, if you're ambitious for excellence, well then ordinary, miserable, footling rules should never apply to you. You can shrug them off like an overcoat. You can dare to be different.' His odd eyes sparkle as he speaks, and Jake can see how he has managed to make his way in the shadowy world of the rich and domineering.

'True power, detective, is not to strut on the world's stage or bring a banking system or a nation to its knees. True power is not showy or obvious. It's not flashy, written about in newspapers or on websites. No, true power is simply to live without fear of consequences. And that is a dream, an idea, that people will pay a fortune for.

'No Taboo, as you now know, was created for that very purpose. You want to know why Charlotte, that poor fragile female, had to die. Because it didn't matter if she did or didn't. People like Fenella Jewell, the life of empty privilege slowly sending her into a spiral of self-destructive boredom – what does she crave? Sexual deviation from the norm? Fine, easily done. The whiff of mortality close up to her? I heard, you know, she once sat in the back of a car sipping champagne, while it knocked to the ground two cyclists on a back road somewhere. One of them died, I believe, based on her capriciousness.

'She wanted to be close to death, and paid a price for it. As it turned out, as it so often turns out, she didn't quite have the guts when it came to the blood, the messy reality. So our recently lamented South African friend did the rest. You know all this, and there is no more reason behind it than that.' He strokes his arm gently as he speaks, purring like a cat before a fire.

A sharp retort against the door breaks into the false feeling of calm woven by his voice.

'Police, I'm coming in.'

It swings open, and in walks Watson, his face – so often genial, amused at the world – a mask instead of grave calm. He is dressed all in black. After he enters, he pauses, and then leans back out through the doorway, picking up a heavy weight from the ground. He staggers slightly, and Jake thinks of the ribs he has hurt in that car accident, the cast on his wrist. Then he notices what is in Watson's arms: a woman with short hair, handcuffs, and a furious expression on her face.

Chapter Fifty-Eight

Monday, 6.20 a.m.

There is what seems to be a stunned silence. Jake and
Aletheia share a glance of consternation. Martinson clamps
down on his cigar and does nothing. Charlie opens his
arms, and begins to stand. 'A policeman. This does seem
an odd development. And yet not a planned one, I see.'

Watson hoicks Martha into the room, bears her
awkwardly for a second and then drops her on the edge
of the sofa. She pushes herself back against the cushion,
eyes blazing, chest still raised and proud. Watson looks
brusquely at Charlie. 'Sit down, you, and say nothing.' He
gives Jake a wintry grin. 'I'm sorry to crash the party. I
know you wanted me clean from all of this. But I've been
pursuing my own line of inquiry, whatever else you might
have been doing this last couple of days. And look who
I found at one end of a thread that linked all the way
back to No Taboo. This one here, a pretty good spy when
you think about how much she got you all into.'

Martha's body is seething with frustration. 'Jake, Al, this is all rubbish. I know Watson is your friend, but he's making a huge mistake. I'm not with them, I'm with you. He's misunderstood my undercover work, that's all.'

Watson pulls out from his pocket a handgun, and rests it on the shelf of the bookcase by which he is standing. 'Jake, I think we have all the main players now in one room. The question is what we do with them.' He puts his hand next to the gun, his fingers twitching.

Aletheia has moved forward, is standing alongside Martha's chair, her hands reaching to touch her, as if to make her presence real.

Watson looks across to Jake. 'We could end this here. I'm not saying we arrest them all and prosecute, but we have three people who are our enemies, and I have a gun, I'm sure you have a gun, we have control of the room. We're in the powerful position here, the question is do we take advantage of it.'

He picks up his gun, and raises it slowly, pointing towards the sofa, his arm steady, tight clamp of his fingers, bone-white. The end of the gun sweeps slowly across Martinson, Charlie and Martha.

'Maybe we start with Martha here first. She's the traitor, after all.'

His grip tightens. Jake lets his jacket fall open, his right hand instantly gripping the walnut stock of the Beretta. Charlie and Martinson have not moved, appear spooked by Watson's words and actions. When Jake pulls the gun, he lets it rake across the sofa too, pausing on each figure. But then he points it directly at Watson himself, and moves no further.

'Steady there, chief. I think we need to avoid getting ahead of ourselves here. You're right, there is a spy. But it's not Martha. It is, I'm so sorry to say, you.' Aletheia tries to speak, but he waves her silent. Watson has not moved.

'So let me be clear. Make no move against her, or this gun goes off.'

Watson grimaces. 'Jake, what are you doing? You can't be serious about me. Don't let her distract you – she'll have cooked something up with those two.'

'Enough.' Jake, who never raises his voice, is loud and imperious. 'Enough. I've worked it all out, I'm afraid. Someone has been keeping a check on us, and it could have been Martha, I suppose. And I wish it wasn't you. But it is. You started this all, if you remember. Came to me to see what I knew about No Taboo. You wanted to know how far Aletheia had got with my old cases.

'You were careful, I'll give you that. The time you got run down by that car – perfect to keep your cover. The way you let Laura be given up, handily getting a text at the same time I was there.

'My guard dropped. But then some things began to bother me. When I saw you the other day, you warned me off, probably genuinely. You didn't want me any further involved. I'd like to think that was friendship talking. Maybe I'm naïve.' Still nothing comes back to him in return. Martha is stretching her arms out, face thoughtful.

'But when you were warning me, you said something like "you don't need to be ferreting around in morgues, or banks, or country mansions". That bank reference was odd. I *had* been in a bank, after Smits's safety deposit box, but we hadn't told you about that. I think your masters had worked it out after they followed Rose's car to the station.'

323

Watson's face is hard to read. His arm remains stiff, the gun pointed either at Aletheia or Charlie, impossible to tell. 'Go on, Jake, this is interesting.'

'And then when we broke into Purple Prose. You hadn't been taking my calls. But when I called on Martinson's phone, you answered immediately. As if you knew the number, and had already been speaking to him. You weren't surprised to get the call, you were surprised it was me. Minutes later, I overhear a chat between these two chaps, which sends me direct to the old tower where Smits was waiting for me. Yes, they had tracked Rose's car, but how could they have known I was coming there and then? They didn't, until I told you I was in the office. You were part of the set-up.'

Watson's voice is quiet. 'Jake, if you make another move with that weapon, I fire, and then we see who makes it out of here. It's a game none of us want to get into.'

Jake grips the gun yet more tightly and holds it in position. He feels tired and disappointed and grubby. 'We're still in the business of walking away, Watson. I have to say, I thought you'd stay out until the end, not come in like this, or with Martha. But I'm telling you now.' His voice is cold, sad, but resolute. 'I'm telling you now, you can still walk away, just put the gun down, unlock Martha, and let's get this done.'

Watson's face is rueful. 'You were a brilliant detective, Jake. I always said it was a waste that you were out here in Parvum, in that big old Little Sky, that you were too young and gifted to retire. You might have worked me out, you might have worked out No Taboo, but you've still got your leverage wrong.' He leans back, toggles the outside lamp off using a light switch by the door. 'And we're not quite all here, are we?'

324

There is crunching outside, and Rose is pushed in, staggering and unwilling, Josiah at his back with Rose's shotgun. Watson looks over his shoulder. 'And the divine Livia?'

Josiah shrugs, Jake's heart leaps. 'She wasn't there. This one says he dropped her off to see her kid after they ditched the tracker device.'

'A minor point. We can deal with her later.' Watson swings the gun around until it is facing Jake's chest. 'We have plenty to settle here first.'

Chapter Fifty-Nine

Monday, 6.45 a.m.

The room is growing perceptibly brighter, as the darkness is peeled from the sky in layers. There is a sort of purplish light falling through the window into the room. Everything looks and feels unreal to Jake.

Watson's face is impassive. 'Put the gun down, Jake. If you move, I shoot. Then Josiah here shoots Rose, then Aletheia. If you keep calm, we can still talk, as you say. You're still bargaining for your lives, and Livia's and Diana's, after all.'

Jake looks across to Aletheia, who nods faintly. They were never here for a shoot-out, the risk now no longer seems worth it. He lays the gun down on the floor, where it clunks mournfully against the old wood. Josiah pushes Rose into an armchair, moves to stand next to the sofa, eyes watchful, gun resting easily in his hands.

Watson puts his own gun back on the bookshelf, and glances around the room. 'Whoever could have guessed we would have ended up here?' He raises his hands in mute apology. 'I know, no need to become all doe-eyed about it.'

Jake's response is a flinty shrug. Watson continues to hold the floor.

'I suppose I do owe you an explanation, Jake. I have been, and am, foremost a police officer, paid too little, demanded of too much, struggling to do my best to fight crime in my own humble way. At the same time, I took money from Charles here, to help him, let's say, minimize the chance of rare and specific crimes being uncovered. But not many, and hardly at all since I left the city to work in this neck of the woods. On most things, I would have been on the same side as you, just as we were on the same side two years ago.'

Jake cannot help but ask, though he knows the answer. 'But not with Laura's abduction?'

'No, that was an example of me being dragged in, somewhat against my will. I was rather pleased when it was judged good business to let her go. I liked to see her happy face; I shared that moment of joy with you. But I knew my job. You see Charles over there was always the mastermind, always the schemer. He didn't need me much, but when he did, I was there.'

Charlie has relaxed once more. 'Come, Junior, don't pretend you didn't like the money I threw your way, or the excitement of the conspiracy.'

Quiet settles in the room. Martha leans back, face open with malicious glee. 'And for fuck's sake, Jake. WJ, CW. Charlie, the ex-quartermaster, works with someone with one similar initial, not a big part of the scam, but one who got recent payment. Gerald Watson, Junior. Charlie Watson, the senior figure. Look at the resemblance – brothers, then, I guess.'

Charlie moves forward, as if a spell has been broken by the naming. Nobody denies anything. Jake's arm shifts slightly in his direction.

Watson's face is grave. He seems not to have heard Martha's outburst, his eyes, a little watery now, fixed upon Charlie. 'I never valued the conspiracy side, no I didn't. I won't pretend to be moral in this setting, but I won't pretend to be a big player either. I did what I did for money, and perhaps out of some family loyalty, but no more.'

There is tension here, Jake feels, an imbalance of power. Watson is becoming smaller as each second passes, the initiative slipping over to Charlie himself. He now stands, gesturing at Jake.

'Let's get down to business. You have a dossier on us that this young woman.' He points at Martha, who scowls. 'This young woman has fail-safed. We need you to unpick the fail-safe.'

'That's not the deal. The deal is that you walk away, and the fail-safe is never needed.' This is Jake, trying to put more certainty into his voice than he feels.

Charlie dismisses him with a casual wave of the hand. 'Jake, Jake. Look at the situation. You have lost control. There are two men with guns in this room, one of whom is a policeman. If you don't cooperate, someone gets shot. We might start with this man, Rose, but then we go on. And then we go find your little nuclear family too.'

Watson's body stiffens as his brother speaks, but he says and does nothing. Rose looks daggers around the room, but keeps his thoughts to himself.

Charlie continues: 'Junior, pick up your gun and point it at Miss Campbell here. Josiah, you keep pointing it at Rose.' His voice is modest, calm, as if he were arranging

328

the placement of guests at a dinner party. 'Martha, it's perfectly simple: undo the fail-safes, retrieve the document, electronically, or we start shooting people.'

She is looking strangely at Jake, then over his shoulder, before another glance back to him. Her expression is – briefly – warm and amused. Then her eyes flash back to Charlie, entirely uncowed. 'You'll have to free up my hands, and give me a laptop. I can't do much in these cuffs.'

Charlie nods at Watson, who throws him a key. He hands it to Martinson, who has been contributing little, clearly wishing he was elsewhere. 'Unlock her, Sam. I can't see what damage she can do.' Martinson fiddles about, clumsily removing the handcuffs, brusquely shoving her this way and that.

Martha is staring at him with contempt as he does so. 'Has it occurred to you that someone who had her legs shot from under her while serving her country is not going to get spooked by some shouty, vulgar mogul like yourself, or your little spy friend here? Or that someone who can no longer walk or dance or look normal to strangers really gives two shits about the prospect of death? Cowards like you don't understand bravery, but look around. Am I trembling? Is Jake or Rose or Aletheia? None of us want to be here, but none of us are intimidated by you. I just want you to know that.'

Martinson had been walking away, but turns back, his body twisting into the slap that catches her full across the face, spinning her around so she is almost facing the back of the sofa. He looks savagely towards Charlie. 'We need to teach these folk some basic respect.'

'All in good time, Sam.' He motions to Watson, who retrieves Martha's laptop where he had left it just outside the door. She is rubbing her cheek, a dribble of blood running unheeded down her chin. 'Is that really all you have? I've been hit harder than that before.' She takes the computer and starts typing away.

Jake realizes she is playing for time. He turns behind him, casually looks out of the window. The road outside is as empty as you would expect on an early morning in Parvum. The white snow is faintly begrimed, beginning its inevitable retreat into muddy slush. A change is coming. There is a breeze shifting the naked branches of two trees he can see in the near distance, one of which has a T-shirt flapping somewhat forlornly and incongruously. It is the one Livia was wearing earlier, he is sure. A sign showing she is there, outside, alive, but what else did it mean? And had Martha seen it?

Charlie is now standing over her, hand on her neck pushing downwards, a leer of disdain splayed across his features. 'Now I'm sure you can move more quickly than that. Josiah, why don't you encourage her concentration?'

He pads forward, raising the gun, bludgeoning it down onto the back of Rose's neck, sending him sprawling from the chair onto the floor. Jake moves instinctively, and Watson turns to point the gun on him, shaking his head regretfully. Meanwhile Josiah covers Aletheia with his gun, no expression on his face.

Charlie puts his head near to Martha's. 'The next time I ask, he gets a bullet in the leg. You know how that feels, I guess. Then in the back of the head. Do you understand? Show me that those files are back.'

Martha looks up again, and winces. 'Give me two minutes, and you'll see them on the screen. No need to hurt anyone.'

Charlie paces to and fro behind her, while she continues

to type. Then halts. 'You have thirty seconds before your little band gets another cripple as a member.'

'Hold off, something should be coming any second now.' She looks back to Jake and gives him a wink. She leans back against the sofa, taps a key, breathes in. And then mayhem ensues.

A high-pitched siren hammers into their ears, disorientatingly loud, emerging from the computer. At the same time, a car – revved loudly, a thunderous rumble that comes from nowhere – screeches along the road and crashes into the window, caving it in, sending brick dust and wood shards everywhere. The vehicle's front end is poking through the rubble, crumpled like a discarded Coke can, the metal twisted and sharp.

Jake is first to react, as he was expecting something, if not quite this. He barrels into Watson, knocking him to the ground, before launching himself against Josiah. They grapple for a frozen instant. Josiah clings to his gun and half grabs Jake by the lapels with his free hand, cutting his fingers on the razors, before letting them go with a shriek. He is not disabled though, and swings the barrel of the gun hard and fast, with lethal intent, a blow which Jake just manages to duck.

He lets the momentum take him low and forward into Josiah's body, left fist driving into his stomach, then right hand grabbing the barrel of his gun and forcing it upward. No shot is fired, and Jake's weight is back on his left leg, so he hooks again, this time to Josiah's head, and again, smearing his nose across his face, then again, caving something solid like a cheekbone. Josiah falls to the ground, limp as a rag.

Meanwhile, the tableau around him has shattered completely. Martha has thrown away the laptop to a corner of the room where it rests, splayed open, emitting its hideous wail. Aletheia, herself paralyzed initially, has reached forward and grabbed Charlie by the collar, flinging him back into the wall as he tried to force his weight towards her. He is now a shambles on the floor, semi-conscious.

Martinson meanwhile has been cowed entirely by the din. All of a sudden he starts to make for the door, but Aletheia trips him and sends him sprawling. She picks up Jake's gun, and stands above him, foot on his neck, motionless.

And then the noise just stops, all that pressure in their ears, the bleeding force of the high pitch absent, leaving a ringing echo only.

Jake looks back and Watson is getting to his feet, reaching for his gun on the bookcase. He takes it, and points it directly at Jake.

Jake holds his arms up, begins advancing towards him. 'Chief, you're no killer. Come on, you're not going to shoot me. You're not like these people.'

Watson's face is a mess of uncertainty. The gun wobbles but stays on target. Then, absurdly, the front door swings open and Livia walks in, brandishing a piece of wood like a sword. Watson wildly turns to her, and then back to Jake, by which point Jake is in reach, grabs at the gun. A moment of tension, then anti-climax. Watson offers little resistance, and Jake – almost tenderly – removes the weapon, and pushes him gently into a nearby chair.

He looks at Livia with relief, and joy, and love. She is smiling and shaking, laughing at the ridiculous sight: her own snatched weapon, her house half-destroyed, bodies strewn across the floor, blood and dust in the air. But something else is between them: the thrill of success, and even perhaps victory too.

Epilogue

The winter was long and hard, especially compared to recent years, but it is now late April, a time of blossom and softness and plenty. The land around Little Sky – scarred and subdued by the snows and ice and rain – has recovered as it always does. A carnival of green everywhere, shades as numerous as leaves on a tree. The lake is dark and cool. The horizon stretches out endless into the ozone blue. After all, the seasons always turn, the darkness gets driven almost from memory.

Jake, Livia and Diana are walking to Agatha Wood, where Jake has promised the little girl a surprise. He had completed the treehouse earlier in the week, and was anxious for her to see it. It was on two levels across the two trees, planks sanded and varnished to a smooth chocolate, a ladder built into one trunk. He had panicked a little about the safety of the zip wire, doubting his own engineering abilities, so had paid for a bemused expert to come up from the city to check his work. It was fine. The effect of the whole structure was magical, when you stood beneath it, the leaves hissing in the breeze, the stencil of sunlight on the mulchy ground, the sense of a haven constructed within the living wood. He just hoped she liked it.

Diana had been little affected by the drama of a few months earlier. She had enjoyed the excitement of hearing that her house had been damaged by a car, that she would be getting a newly improved living room, and that they would be staying at Little Sky during the rebuild. The adventure of early rising to go to school from there, tramping across soggy ground in the half-light, cold and giggling, broad fields all around, so Jake or Livia could drive her each day. Her mum had hardly spoken to her about what had happened, except to say that she and Jake had been involved in an adventure, and had returned triumphant. Livia still sometimes held her longer in her arms than was comfortable or necessary, perhaps, kept watch over her as she played with a more searching and eager eye. But her life had soon fallen once more into its familiar and happy rhythm.

For Livia herself that had been harder, and for Jake too, but happily not impossible. Her cottage could be repaired, even if the shock to their world had been profound. And there was something essentially strengthening about the conclusion of it all when they paused to consider it. At a moment of grave peril, they had come together, their priorities united: not Jake out alone pursuing a benevolent crusade while Livia fussed and worried, but the two of them, both accepting the risk and the responsibility, taking a gamble and bringing it off.

Things had moved fast from the second Watson had surrendered his weapon. Josiah lay unconscious, and Jake moved to make him immobile, tying his thumbs behind his back with a strip of cloth. Meanwhile, Aletheia covered Charlie and Martinson with the gun, and then Jake bound them in similar fashion. He left Watson to one side, listless and broken, though Aletheia never let her gun or guard down when it came to him. Livia tended to Rose, who had suffered yet another blow in pursuit of justice, but was soon back on his feet, sad to have missed the sudden ending.

Jake had returned the laptop to Martha, who gleefully waved it at their prisoners. She conferred with Aletheia, and they sent messages to their most trusted contacts, together with an image of the room and a copy of the dossier. Within three hours, the road outside was filled with dark, official-looking cars, a police van, diversion signs keeping the area quiet and contained.

In that time, Charlie and Martinson refused to speak. You could see the fiery anger in their eyes, but also their frantic inner plotting. Jake and Livia left them to it, under Rose and Aletheia's mistrustful gaze. The two men's swollen sense of power had dissolved, they were enfeebled despite themselves. Instead of bearing witness to the humili-ation, Jake and Livia stood, content, by the window, as the sun rose in the sky, watching the icicles melt from the eaves above.

'How did you know to send the car in?' asked Jake.

'We had put a fail-safe to the fail-safe, you know. It was a Plan B we kept in reserve from you and Aletheia. Martha didn't know she was going to be taken, but worried she might be, so she insisted that we work something up. She could have sprung the alarm remotely if she had needed to. As it turned out, she was stuck in the room and Charlie handed the computer right to her.

Anyway, when we saw Josiah outside, Rose and I agreed to split up, so I was tucked away in the Nook, out of sight, keeping Sarah baffled while he kept watch. After he was taken, I came back. The plan was – if things were desperate – Martha would find some way to create a distraction. I put the T-shirt in the tree to show I was ready. Rose told me how to tie the brick to the accelerator. I don't know how he knows such things, I really don't.'

Jake laughed. The combination of naivety and pluck was remarkable, and had saved the day. They held each other tight, while the cavalry started to arrive. Soon they were shaking hands with a grave woman in her late fifties, short hair greying at the temples, with a hard but amused face. She clearly knew both Aletheia and Martha, and must have been a significant figure in some branch of intelligence. She gave no name, nor asked many questions. A sly wink alone indicated she was grateful for their work.

In the hours and days that followed, the consequences for the organization of No Taboo were immediate and dramatic. Much was kept out of the public eye, given how parts of the security services had been compromised by Charlie's activities over the years. But careful observers of the British establishment had much to chew over. The sudden retirement of two high court judges, one MP choosing to spend more time with his reluctant family, unexplained resignations in the police and military, a suicide in the minor branches of the aristocracy. In the city, without ever any adequate explanation, several private banks were raided, lights burning in the windows for many long evenings, as quiet men and women pored over records and files. A couple of fairly substantial companies ceased to exist, their assets brusquely disposed of.

336

The investigations into Gerald Watson, Sam Martinson and Charlie Watson have been fast-tracked and tightly supervised by the most senior figures in two police forces. The dossier put together by Martha, plus the recordings made in the cottage itself, was explosive, especially about the latter two. Further evidence was discovered in the rooms and grounds of Purple Prose, and the rest of Charlotte's body that had been removed from its misfiled place in the hospital, along with the head from Jake's workshop. Josiah and Adele had also been arrested, kept apart from employer and husband.

The two men immediately hired expensive lawyers, and sought to use every bit of leverage and influence they possessed, but it is now clear that they cannot escape justice. A plea bargain beckons, to be inevitably followed by incarceration somewhere high security and unpleasant. The British establishment is slow to rouse, but resentful of being made a fool of.

Watson's corrupt acts over the years were clearly traceable through payments to his bank account, which in turn connected to cases he had failed adequately to solve. But he had also proved willing to confess in the broadest terms, as an act of penitence, and in return for a shorter sentence. As he was taken to the van that morning, he paused to hold both Jake and Livia's hands. There was remorse in his eyes, a silent plea. They allowed him his moment, but privately bewailed their misplaced trust in him. They are fairly sure they will never see nor speak to him again.

The career of Garland Smits was unpicked, and cases involving him re-opened and settled. A story was circulated, including in an article written by Joanna – perhaps in return for her silence on other issues – that Jake was being used as an independent consultant to rid the police and prison services of improper behaviour. His public reputation, what of it there was, has been further burnished.

Fenella Jewell is currently on remand, with no bail, on charges of conspiracy to murder two cyclists, and the attempted murder of Charlotte Sampson. She has taken to the structure of prison with the aplomb of someone who grew up in boarding schools. She has expensive lawyers, and much of the evidence is circumstantial, so Jake holds out little hope for her eventual conviction. Her business interests have collapsed in the meantime, even as salacious attention upon her personal life has increased exponentially. A career on Instagram seems likely.

Jake impulsively hugs Livia as they pause in front of the lake. The sun is turning the surface into shattered glass. The water sparkles and sways. Diana is eating an ice lolly made from early raspberries from the greenhouse. Her lips and tongue are stained purplish-red with fruit.

There is little noise other than the breeze, punctuated by the quibbling sounds of a bird buried somewhere in the hedgerow, a chiff-chaff according to Diana's book of woodland wildlife. The twin notes of its song like a question that gets an immediate answer. The air is clean, something to inhale like a drug.

Livia turns to Jake. 'Have you heard from Martha?'

'She's messaged two or three times. I think she's torn between writing a new book, and getting back involved in the security business. Aletheia has recommended she becomes an analyst again. She's certainly good at it.'

'Do you like being in touch with her and Al?'

'It's nice to hear from them, but they're both busy now,

so it's not much of a big deal. I think Al's career is about to go supernova actually, after all this.'

Livia puts her head against his chest, feels the steady rumble of his heart. 'It's just I wonder whether we've let the world come too close to us without really wanting it to. You got involved with Watson, I got ambitious with the Martinson place, and look where it led us. I like the idea of us being cut off again.'

Jake smiles. 'I've been worrying for months, you know, that all this isolation was going to come between us. I thought you and Di would need to get closer to the world, not further from it, in the end. I thought you might find me – and this place – a drag.' He makes a wide sweep with his hand.

She pulls his face down to her level. His beard is wild and luxuriant as ever, the hairs already turning copper in the sun. 'You're no genius, are you? I love the freedom we have here, I love the chance to get away. We'll let Di have enough of the world so she can have a shot at a normal life, but I want our home here at Little Sky to be a haven away from it. We've made it work over the past few weeks and we've loved it.'

'So you don't want me all of a sudden to get the internet, is that what you're saying?'

She reaches into both of his pockets, her chin jutting against his collarbone, a lightly lascivious brush of wrist against his groin. 'Not only that, I want to get rid of this one connection we already have to it, too.'

She pulls out the special phone Aletheia had given him. He'd taken to carrying it around with him, because in the immediate aftermath of the arrests he had been regularly summoned by the authorities. And then he'd kept hold of it, checking it occasionally. A normal, modern habit he had previously shaken off.

Livia holds the device in her hand, the bright light making it shine. 'What do you think? Shall we commit to losing ourselves together whenever we can?' Her face is tilted to the light, a flit of shadow plays across her brown throat. 'Maybe we can build our nest even more strongly here. It's a good place for a child, maybe it would be even better for . . .' She pauses, magnificently. 'For children, Jake.'

She bites her lip. He is entranced as ever, strokes the soft expanse of her neck. 'I have made a giant treehouse after all,' he says eventually. 'It seems wastefully big for just one child. Are you sure you're serious?'

She nods, eyes wide, the colour of the turf beneath their feet. A sense of future and family makes him dizzy. Then he takes the phone from her hand, leans back, and sails it into the water where it disappears with an anti-climactic plop. Their friendly heron, who had been negligently perched on a nearby rock, flaps lazily away, as if inconvenienced.

'Can we go and see the surprise?' This is Diana, lolly gone, looking for adventure. Jake sends her on ahead and hears her playful scream of joy when she sees the house looming out of the treeline.

It can't last, he thinks, the fight against the modern world, against normal life. But, in the meantime, he has absolutely no doubt that it will be a fight worth having.

Playlist

I have gathered together all the music Jake listens to over the course of the book, so you can do the same while you read. (If you want to, of course. I love reading and writing to a background of music, but not everybody does).

Pavane for a Dead Princess by Maurice Ravel
Ave Maria S. 558 by Franz Liszt
Carnival of the Animals by Camille Saint-Saens
Guitar Concerto in D Major by Antonio Vivaldi
Adagio for Strings by Samuel Barber
Symphony Number 5 by Gustav Mahler
"O mio babbino caro" from Giannia Schicchi by Puccini
The Spruce, Op. 75 by Jean Sibelius
Appalachian Spring by Aaron Copeland
New World Symphony by Antonin Dvorak
Piano Concerto in A Minor by Edvard Grieg
Mephisto Waltz by Franz Liszt
Cello Suite No. 1 in G Major by Johann Sebastian Bach
Cello Sonata in G Minor, Op. 65 by Frederic Chopin

Acknowledgements

The first thing to acknowledge is the sheer pleasure I have taken in continuing the story of Jake and Livia and Little Sky. You can imagine me, if you like, on a commuter train or sitting on my bed, music playing in my headphones, relishing every moment of the day I got to spend writing this book. It is a joy and a privilege doing crime fiction, and then being able to meet readers who love the genre as much as I do.

This book nearly had a different shape entirely. I wrote the first draft as a country house mystery, before my editors read it and suggested it was better set more broadly in the environs of Parvum. When they gently put that to me, I did what all writers do: harrumphed. I then did what all writers should do: listen to folk who know what they are talking about. The team at HarperCollins is a wonder to work with. That starts with Kathryn Cheshire and Angel Belsey, who had the delicate task of helping me improve my original thoughts. Then there is the crime fiction badass Julia Wisdom, who's overseen more great detective novels than anyone I can imagine, the wonderful Kimberley Young, all the way up to the big boss Charlie Redmayne, who happily loves his wife almost as much as I do mine. The publicity team have to listen to me talk about myself, and they always seem to hate it marginally less than I do: Liz Dawson has been such a kind and supportive figure (and reader), as has Maud Davies, who along with Olivia French initiated me into the mysteries of Instagram.

Cathryn Summerhayes has been with me from the beginning of my writing career, and I know would run through a wall – leaving a silhouette like a cartoon character – for me, and all of her authors, and you can't ask more than that from an agent.

I'm lucky that I have some people in my life who read early drafts of the book, and I'm grateful to each of them. Needy authors demand support, and I get it from my mother-in-law Jeanette and from others including Xand Van Tulleken and Steve Kennedy.

My parents also read everything early on, and with the kindness and encouragement that has characterised everything they have done for me for more than forty years. They are my great champions: when a bookshop in Loughborough was slow to stock the first Little Sky, I had to stop my mum from staging a sit-in in protest.

Everything else begins and ends with my own family. My eldest two, Teddy and Nelly, are old enough to read the novels now, and it is such a thrill when that happens, even if they moan about the sex in them (which I think is pretty tasteful and discreet, actually). And my little one Phoebe is still at the stage when all she does is clamber over me, demanding that I spend every second with her. And that does my heart good every day.

Obviously, the last name in this list is the most important. I write firstly so my wife, Nadine, has something to read every night in the bath. None of this would exist without her. She even drew the map at the front, clever thing that she is. But her main role is being the source of inspiration, consolation and toe-tingling joy in my life. I feel grateful every day that we met, had a torrid office-based affair, and decided to spend the rest of our lives together.